PRIMAL

D.A. SERRA

ISBN: 1-47819-803-6
ISBN-13: 978-1-47819-803-1

PRIMAL

The most dangerous place on earth is between a mother and her child. . . .

CHAPTER ONE

- - - - - - - - - - - -

SAMUEL SLIPS THE KNIFE TO Rex.

Wilkins rocks forward onto his toes, to get a clear look at Ben, who sits in reverence with his head dropped forward, exposing the pale smooth nape of his vulnerable neck. The air is rank with odor from damp armpits, oily hair, and decaying gums. It's the smell of rot. When Wilkins has guard duty on Sunday mornings, he watches Ben Burne, because it makes him feel hopeful here among the human scrap meat. He is drawn to the devotion on Ben's face, and so he doesn't notice the jagged-edged homemade blade as it is passed from one inmate's hand to the next, underneath the lip of the stainless steel pew.

Rex hands the knife to Heto.

This ascetic chapel with a plastic altar is populated every Sunday by lifers who, if given the chance, would slash God's throat. They attend services as an alternative to sitting in their cells. Wilkins thinks about how no one wants to be here, no one except Ben. Ben is enraptured. He communes with the hanging wooden crucifix lost in a personal reverie: Hail Mary full of grace the Lord is with thee. The lime paint of the prison's cinder block wall doesn't tint Ben's face in the same ghoulish way it colors the skin of the other inmates. Wilkins wonders if this is a

1

sign. Yes, he thinks it is. Yes, God is trying to tell him something. He has cast the glory of His forgiveness on Ben Burne.

Ben nods his head in prayer. He has lost a lot of hair for only fifty-three years old; the penitentiary food and harsh soap are hard on the body. Ben has managed to stay muscular by lifting weights in his cell and using the window bars for chin-ups. He raises his face. Real tears swim in his eyes as he swells with piety.

Ben, with his reputation, is a celebrity here; as long as Ben is around with his superior air and his attention grabbing ways, well, it pisses off some of the others who feel just as deserving, just as tough. And they are just as tough -- they just aren't as smart. In any room, in every room, Ben is the puppet master.

Heto passes the knife to Leon.

Leon is an obelisk of a man: tall, thick, and sitting directly behind Ben. A grisly anticipation ripples through the room, knowing glances are exchanged and eyes light up, giddy with expectation. Wilkins tilts his head, sensing a palpable shift in the room. His eyes narrow; where is it coming from? He scans the pews up and down. He peers underneath at the shoes solidly on the floor. What is it? He can't place it. At the altar, the chaplain prays fervently for each of these men's souls. He feels some solace in knowing that at least he has saved one man. He has saved the soul of Ben Burne.

The inmates in Leon's row shudder eagerly. Leon likes holding everyone's attention this way. They are waiting for his move. He tenses first. Then, his jaw drops slightly open. Saliva moistens his mouth and a drop of spit forms on his canine tooth. Right next to him, the skinny hollow-eyed inmate giggles in a small sharp burst—the sound of caged madness. Leon's fingers clench around the knife. Ready. He springs up! The chaplain looks. Leon's knife hand juts up and then powers down toward Ben's bare neck. Miraculously, Ben's hand jerks up and grabs the blade. It sinks deep into his palm. He makes no sign of pain. He closes his fist around it and the two men stand in a struggle of power and will. The room erupts. They are animals sprung loose—clawing and fighting.

Wilkins battles through the melee to get to Ben and Leon who are locked eye-to-eye and motionless as blood gushes from Ben's closed fist. Wilkins is almost there when an inmate jumps him from behind reaching for his weapon. With eyes in the back of his head, Ben uses his other hand to karate chop the inmate, breaking his neck and sending him to the floor without even a scream. Wilkins regains himself, grateful to Ben, who has not taken his eyes off Leon. Wilkins pulls his gun out and shoots four rounds into the ceiling. The fighting stops at the sound of the gunshots. Other guards burst in. Wilkins moves in next to Leon where he and Ben are frozen in inert combat with the blade closed into Ben's fist. Wilkins levels his weapon at Leon's head.

Ben scolds, "Leon, this is a place of worship."

Flooded with adrenaline, Wilkins rests his weapon on Leon's temple and adds, "And I hope you've been praying."

Ben turns his eyes calmly to Wilkins, "Not in God's house."

A tremulous silence, they all wait for Wilkins' decision: life or death. He has the choice. He could pull the trigger and no one would care. One less animal to feed and cage. Society might shake its head, but it would be grateful to be rid of him. At this moment, with the muzzle of the gun at Leon's temple, and with everyone waiting, the choice is his. He could take this life. He wants to take this worthless life. The muscles in his face give a little. His blood calms. Two other guards sense it and step forward grabbing Leon. They slam him to the cement floor breaking his jaw and his nose. They pull his arms behind his back and cuff him. Other guards have taken charge of the rioting rabble and order is harshly restored. Ben opens his hand. Wilkins carefully pulls the embedded knife from Ben's palm.

"I'll take you to the infirmary," Wilkins says.

Ben nods, turns to leave with him, but then stops and asks the chaplain, "Father, are you all right?"

The shaken chaplain nods. He drops to his knees and says a prayer for Ben's soul. Wilkins leads Ben out of the chapel and down the hall toward the infirmary.

Wilkins is amazed at Ben's ability to withstand the pain and asks, "How did you do that?"

"God did that—saved us both—you and me. But evidently he has turned his attention to other things because it hurts like a motherfucker now." These two men almost smile at each other. How strange, Wilkins thinks, to see the budding of humanity in a man with this kind of history. What was it that turned Ben Burne?

CHAPTER TWO

HARBOR HILLS ELEMENTARY SCHOOL BLENDS in with the serene suburban neighborhood: sweet two-story homes of white, yellow, and blue, stand in neat lines on both sides of the street. The roads have been recently paved so the asphalt is coal black and makes the green of the grass yards and the colorful fall flowerbeds bitingly vibrant. The streetlamps have an old-fashioned oblong glass that suggests folks have been raising their families here for a long time. The damp earthy smell of fallen leaves hangs in the air along with the dying honeysuckle. In this traditional Midwestern town with its huge oak and sugar maple trees life feels settled and yielding, as if it knows where it is going; the path is trodden and soft on the feet.

Inside Alison Kraft's classroom with its dangling solar system made out of Styrofoam balls, and its encouraging aphorisms pasted to the walls, the majority of the third graders are listening to her. She considers the majority a victory. This generation is accustomed to sensory deluge; they splash through the rising tech tide with instincts the generation before them just don't have. Her generation debated the efficacy of multitasking; these kids never do one thing at a time. They carry the world electronically in the palm of their hands: they text, and shop, and do homework, watch movies, and download music all at the same time. She feels successful if half of the class pays attention to her at one time since she is limited by not being a multimedia purveyor. Alison is a popular teacher. And when this year's crop of scruffy boys and American Doll girls look at her, she sees their potential. These are the faces of tomorrow and she is aware of that truth every day she teaches them. She knows that one of them will do something special. There is no way to know which one, so she committed years ago to teach each child as though *they* were the one. Her students sense her belief in them, and they love her for it. She has "cheery eyes" they say. Their parents like her because she's tender, and even with all the inherent lunacy of grammar school, impatience is not in her nature.

Alison and Hank moved here to Hank's home after college. They married here and he started a business with his high school buddies. Alison likes this little midland town in Minnesota, but she does wander the streets sometimes wishing the donut shop were a pâtisserie, and that the movie selection at the fourplex would try something without gunfire, and she jokes that she would give her right arm for a piano bar. She misses the city world she grew up in, but she knows this is the ideal place for Hank and her to raise their son, Jimmy, and that's the priority. Life comes in phases. This is Jimmy's time to learn and run free. Watching him is fulfilling. It is the most fulfilling and joyful experience of her life. The piano bar will wait for her. She assumes there will be time.

Moving down the aisle between the school desks, Alison points to the large colorful poster of predators all along the wall: coyotes, bears, and cheetahs. "A mom animal will use her teeth, horns, hooves, stingers, whatever. Some mothers divert predators from their babies by using elaborate movements or by changing their appearance." She turns down the aisle in a deceptive stroll toward one particular boy. "Others rely on speed or surprise." She yanks the iPod earphones out of Tanner's ears. He looks startled and a little scared for having been caught. They look at each other for a moment. She holds his eyes.

"Uh...oh...sorry, Ms. Kraft."

"Okay, Tanner, but one more time and I'm keeping these for myself. They're really cool."

"Yes, ma'am." She hands him back the earphones. "Now," addressing the entire class, "for your homework for the next few days while the substitute is here." Loud groans from the instantly gloomy children. Howie Hunter drops his forehead down on the desktop in despair. She tries not to smile at him, so cute, so bereft, his shaggy blond hair covering his face. "Oh, right" she teases then, "these substitutes really are creatures from the Black Lagoon."

"Where is the Black Lagoon?" Sarah asks Joey.

"France."

"Oh, Ms. Kraft," Sarah whines, "I don't speak France."

Keeping a straight face with difficulty, "I'm quite certain the substitute speaks English."

Howie adds, "I knew a kid who spoke France. He was annoying."

"Howie, just because someone is from France does not mean they're annoying. France has a beautiful language, lovely museums, pretty countryside, and the biggest erector set right in the middle of the city."

"Really?" Howie asks excited.

"Yes. We can see some photos of the Eiffel Tower and learn more about France when I return. Now, the homework. I want each of you to pick a book from the library, absolutely any book, even a comic book, if you want, and read—that's all—just read and then tell the class about the story when I return. Okay?"

The bell rings and gleefully the kids fly out of the classroom. The room empties in seconds leaving a sudden complete silence after the last fleeing footstep. Alison remembers being their age and watching the clock as is ticked toward freedom. She was, and still is, a daydreamer. Her imagination has always had a wanderlust. She scans the room for a moment, and sees the usual: orphaned hair ties on the floor, several lunch boxes (mold experiments by tomorrow) and inexplicably one pink sock. She muses there is something exceedingly poignant about an empty classroom. One empty classroom feels so much more forlorn than an entirely vacant office building. As she straightens up the room, she thinks that must have something to do with the impermanence of childhood itself—the moving on: the seventh grader who becomes the teenager who becomes the college kid and leaves the toys behind. Closing up her desk, Alison wonders if at night, when the janitor sweeps his way through the silence of these rooms, if the echoes of thousands of children's voices keep him company as he pushes the broom. They call the janitor Old Man Tinker, even though he's only forty years old. She wonders how old she looks to them. It makes her grin as she collects up her purse and a few papers. She flips off the classroom lights, steps out into the school hallway.

Denise and Gary are also heading for the door. Denise interrupts Alison's thoughts, "Hi, Alison. You look thoughtful."

"Just considering my old age."

Gary says, "I'm looking forward to old age, sitting in an armchair, watching the television, and reveling in being the full-time cynic I know I am."

Alison smiles wryly, "Gary, cynicism is an empty gesture of sophistication. Smirking at the world is a cop-out."

"I think empty is underrated." Gary holds the door open for the two women. They smile at him and walk through. Denise and Alison are fairly good friends even though Alison holds the minutes of her life closely, spending most of her time with Hank, Jimmy, and a good book. Still, they enjoy each other when thrown together by their daily lives or by school events. Denise has a nontoxic envy for Alison and Hank's relationship, the only two married people she knows who visibly, demonstratively love each other. She sees them exchange secretive smiles and she always has the feeling when around them that they are sharing a fun and private view of the outside world. While she can't help but envy them, she's happy to know a connection like that is achievable. She studies them. She judges all of her dates against them.

"Jimmy's birthday tonight?" Denise asks.

"Yes. Legions of in-laws eating like locusts and using my bathroom guest towels."

"Oh, you love it." Denise teases her.

"True. Hank's family is endlessly entertaining."

"And then you're out of town for the rest of the week?" Gary asks.

"Four days." They hear a wisp of reluctance.

"What?" he nudges her good-naturedly, "You'd rather be here scraping gum off the bottom of your shoes?"

"It's a close call."

Denise asks, "Where are you going?'

"Nowhere you would go in a million years." Alison gives them both a warm smile and turns left toward the parking lot. "See you next week." But she won't see them next week. And when she does see them again—they won't know her.

CHAPTER THREE

W ARDEN TUMMELSON KNOWS WHAT IT'S like to be God. He controls these men's lives—he controls their deaths. This penitentiary houses the worst the human race has to offer: the baby eaters, the dismemberment junkies. He's the gatekeeper on death row. After eleven years here, Tummelson does feel as though he's the one imprisoned. He does the best job he can, but long ago he stopped being able to get clean. No one knows he has begun to wash compulsively and last week in the shower, he scrubbed the skin off his left elbow. When his sister Amy gave birth, three weeks ago, to his first niece, he stood next to her white fluffy crib in the hospital, but refused to pick her up. He would not. He has been permanently and irrevocably sullied. He walks slowly over to his office window as Wilkins and Doctor Kim stand on the other side of his desk and wait. Tummelson wonders how he wound up here in this room making these kinds of decisions. How he wound up a prison warden at all. It wasn't something he planned for or worked toward. He thinks most people wind up capriciously in their life's work—it is a surprise instead of a thoughtful journey to a specific choice. It requires so much focus, and even more importantly, the suspension of derailing events to successfully follow a path all the way. He would love to know how many people, if asked, would say 'oh, yeah, I'm doing exactly what I planned,' or for that matter, 'exactly what I wanted.' Kids, when asked in grade school what they want to be when they grow up, answer something interesting, something important. All children think they're important. It will be years before they realize they are a tiny component in a big ugly human machine, and they are easily replaced. Some folks, he believes, never realize that, maybe those are the lucky ones. He would be willing to bet that no child, when asked to speculate on their future, says 'I want to be a middle manager at a packaging plant,' or 'a salesman in a discount clothing store,' or 'a prison warden? Tummelson believes most people cannot trace the path that got them where they are. It is circuitous and rife with intervening events, a sick parent, a pregnancy, an application denied, a broken heart, a lack of funds. The immediate necessity of making a living surely led him from one stopgap job (where he never planned to stay) to another, and then another, and so here he is today, standing in this stifling office with a desk drawer full of Purell antiseptic gel. He turns to Wilkins and the frustration shakes in his tone.

"Come on, Wilkins, every damn inmate on death row finds God at the end. Ben Burne? You've got to be kidding me."

"I've been watching him for a long time. He saved my life. I'm telling you it's genuine."

"During the First National Bank robbery, which he pulled with his brothers, he shot a twenty-year-old teller in the face for sneezing."

"I know."

"Two years ago at the Miami Brinks holdup he drove the truck over a three-year-old who got in the way."

"I'm not saying he's a good guy, I'm saying he's a guy with a chance to do something good."

Warden Tummelson turns his attention to the reserved, small-boned, Doctor Kim who waits quietly in his finely tailored suit. His refinement is an incongruity here. Tummelson is certain he would not last eight minutes on the inside. This is a man, Tummelson thinks, who probably did choose his life and he has a flash of envy.

"Why, doctor? Why can't you do it here?"

Doctor Kim raises his eyebrows, "In a prison infirmary? Impossible. Even if you could construct an appropriately outfitted operating room, I could never achieve any level of sterility in this environment. The danger of infection would be too high, and so it would not be a feasible alternative."

Not clean. Yes, that is surely true. No one knows that better than Tummelson. He swings around and paces back and forth while fighting a nearly panicked compulsion to wash his hands. The room feels hot and a drip of sweat crawls down his back underneath his shirt. Tummelson crosses back to the tiny window and pushes it open. Crisp heavy air wafts in. He breathes. It helps. "Doctor, I understand you're a normal person, and so, you can't really conceive of what kind of men live here."

Doctor Kim responds with calm authority, "Look, I don't care if he found God, lost God, or ate God. There's a young woman who's going to die if she doesn't get that kidney. If your prisoner is willing to donate it's unconscionable not to find a way."

"If I agree to this I want armed men inside the operating room."

"Again, infection. He'll be unconscious, Warden, under a general anesthetic."

"Not good enough."

"The guards could be allowed directly outside the operating theater looking in. There's a window. What if I arranged for that?"

"Jesus." Warden Tummelson is torn. He paces with a furious energy. He does not trust. How can this be done without risk? He didn't mind playing god with these degenerates, but he's furious and frustrated to be in this position with someone else's life, someone good and deserving.

"Look." Doctor Kim plays his trump card. Warden Tummelson looks over. He is holding a 5 x 7 of the pretty, smiling young woman.

"Aw, shit, that's unfair."

"No. That's reality, Warden. You're going to kill this man in a month and this woman is going to die without his help. This is a no-brainer to me."

"You don't live in my world, doctor." Warden Tummelson rubs his temples; they're just bursting. He can feel the blood pulsing through the veins. His blood pressure is probably soaring again. He pulls the Excedrin bottle out of his pocket and downs two pills without water. Then, he turns to Wilkins, "Okay, bring him in. Let's see what he has to say." Wilkins walks over to the office door, opens it and steps out of the room. Tummelson pulls open his top desk drawer, squirts Purell into his palm and rubs vigorously. He offers it to Doctor Kim who declines.

"You ever been to a penitentiary, doctor?"

"No, Warden, I have not."

"Not much in the way of curb appeal."

"No."

"You and I are alike in some ways, you know. We're both God."

"How is that?'

"You intervene to prolong life. I intervene to end it."

"I suppose. Although, Warden, I am not a fan of capital punishment."

Tummelson smiles and nods, "Yes, well, folks who spend their lives in friendly company, and who debate the death penalty during nicely turned out dinner parties rarely are."

"I am sure your perspective is different for very good reason. And while I agree there are those who do not deserve to live, humans are fallible, the legal system is fallible, and so we cannot implement permanent solutions with fallible hands."

Tummelson lays his eyes on Doctor Kim. Here is a face from the outside, from the other world. He knows Doctor Kim can see the damage in him. He just cannot care about that anymore.

Tummelson speaks in a whisper, as if he is imparting something terribly important, "Doctor, we tell our children, before they go to sleep at night, there are no monsters."

"Yes, we do."

"That's a lie."

"Yes, it is."

"The monsters are us."

"Sometimes."

"No. They're always us. Just not all of us—but us."

Wilkins returns leading Ben Burne into the warden's office. Ben's wrists and his ankles are secured in heavy chains and he shuffles in with his eyes lowered. Ben seems literally smaller and certainly less powerful than he did in the chapel. The palm of his left hand is completely wrapped with white gauze and tape but still a little red seeps through.

Warden Tummelson asks, "So, Burne, you want to donate your kidney?"

"After next month I really won't be needing 'em, Warden. You can take 'em both if you like."

Tummelson studies Ben: his posture, his expression, his demeanor— all submissive.

"You think giving away your organs is going to relieve your conscience?"

"Nothing can do that. Living with myself is much harder than dying will be."

Tummelson leans in and Ben can feel the warden's breath on his face. "You don't fool me, Burne. There isn't a civilized cell in your entire pathetic body."

"I saw the girl on the TV. Said she needed a kidney. Just thought she could have mine is all. Simple as that."

"You deserve to suffer."

Ben raises his repentant eyes to Tummelson and a tear forms, "I'm going to hell for eternity."

The warden exchanges a look with Wilkins who shrugs. "Hell will be a picnic compared to what will happen to you, if I agree to this, and you try something."

"There are no picnics in my future, Warden."

Tummelson's temples throb. He notices that his mouth is dry. Stress. He is pissed beyond rationality to be responsible for this decision. He glances over at Doctor Kim who takes that moment to hold up the picture of the girl.

"Maybe since you're feeling so holy and contrite," Tummelson asks, "you'd like to tell me where we can find your brothers."

"If I knew I'd tell you. I live every day in fear that they will hurt someone else. If I could stop it, I would. But they, too, will answer to God in the end."

"Right. Get him out of here. I need to think."

Wilkins takes Ben by the arm and they leave the office.

Doctor Kim, "Warden, I do not see your conflict here."

"Doctor, no offense, but you have no idea what you're asking."

Doctor Kim walks over to Tummelson's desk and tosses the picture on it. The young woman's face smiles up at him.

"This is Jennifer Booker. She has three children under seven. Look at this while you're thinking it over." Then, he leaves too.

CHAPTER FOUR

— — — — — — — — — — — —

YEAH, WELL YOU'RE SO UGLY when you walk past 'em, flowers die," Jimmy teases his best friend.

Alan counters, "Yeah, well you're so ugly you make my cat throw up."

"Yeah, well, you're so ugly your mom has to tie a pork chop around your neck so the dog will play with you."

The two-story Kraft home pulses with relatives celebrating Jimmy's birthday. Nine-year-old Jimmy is stringy: his legs are spurting out of his body with so much speed his weight cannot keep up. He looks like an egret, all limbs and long neck. At the rate he is growing, his own arm length is constantly changing, and so, he knocks over nearly everything he reaches for; one day last week, a frustrated mother volunteer, at school, called him clumsy and Alison got mad. She explained to Jimmy (within the woman's hearing) that if her arms were longer every single week she'd misjudge things, too. "Jimmy, your dad is six-foot three-inches tall, so you are definitely on your way up, kiddo."

Classic rock pours out of speakers all through the home. Every room is wired for sound; it was the only thing that was important to Hank. The two-story bungalow is brightly lit and the rooms are alive with arguments, tall tales, and laughter. Uncles tell the stories they have told for decades, and laugh in all the same places; some teens pay attention to the stories for the first time, and without meaning to, become tomorrow's carriers of the family's oral tradition. The littler cousins, in a never-ending loop of catch-me-if-you-can, and looking like chipmunks, dart from the warmly upholstered family room of rich gold and red hues into the petite dining room, barely clearing the legs of Alison's antique French reproduction table. And while Aunt Ruth constantly yells at them to slow down, sit down, calm down, Alison never does. She notices this evening that they look exactly like the DVD she played for her class today of the lion cubs socializing in the Maasai Mara. This is the Kraft pride—the tribe she married into and it has been tricky. She can decide the course of her own friendships, she can even turn away from her own family, if she chooses—but her in-laws have a permanence in her life that cannot influence or control; the spouse decides. Alison is an only child, so it is easy for Hank. He did not need to integrate with her brothers or sisters. He was not subjected to the treacherous dynamics of an unfamiliar family with its long-held grudges, inside jokes, and uneven affections. He did not need to understand why different allowances were made for different family members, why for instance, Cousin Keith was forgiven everything while Cousin Carl was forgiven nothing. For Alison, none of it was easy. She married into a sizeable and voluble tribe. She has found that with Hank's extended family there is a lot to adjust for, to compromise with, and to forgive. The forgiveness requires the most plasticity. Alison learned that it is compulsory to forgive in-laws for flaws and situations that would not generally merit forgiveness in any other association. Alison finds ways to balance herself around the harried, sometimes jagged edges of Hank's family, with its outbursts and its treaties, while always feeling a little unnerved by the pitch in the room.

Alison was raised by her father. It was just the two of them in a hushed world. She was eight years old when they buried her mother on a dazzling sunny day. Allie believed people should only be buried on rainy days and she never quite forgave the sun for its disrespectful behavior that morning. Losing her mother so young, and then learning she could not trust the sun, made her a cautious little girl most at ease inside her own home. And since little Allie had anticipated rain on that terrible morning, she had dressed wrongly. She had worn her heavy black wrap skirt and teal wool sweater, and even though she was not dressed for the weather, that was not the origin of her physical discomfort. She had woken up the day before with a rash covering both of her legs. Doctor Hartman called it idiopathic—but she told her dad (privately) that Doctor Hartman was the idiot because it was obvious she was allergic to burying her mother. Allie stood graveside, as still as stone, even though her need to scratch her legs was more pressing than her need to breathe. She stood still in her wool outfit, and did not scratch, because she was holding her dad's hand, and she would rather have endured the awful itch than let go. She bore the itch, along with the choking sensation in her throat, and an unreal floating feeling in her head.

Afterward, Allie and her dad clung to each other with ferocity. They were indoorsy people he used to say, fond of Scrabble, books, and an elaborate electric train set they'd worked on together all the time she was growing up. That train set with its little stations, plastic trees, and wooden fences now circles Jimmy's bedroom upstairs. On Saturday mornings, when the other kids were out playing, Allie would make scrambled eggs while her dad read aloud the local newspaper. Then, they'd set up the Scrabble board. For months after her mom died, neighborhood women would show up like the gustatory Red Cross primed to assist. They gave advice on how to raise Allie and they left hot casseroles. He ignored their advice, but always accepted the casseroles. They devoured them while rolling their eyes and feeling secretly naughty. The doorbell would ring. Her dad would race to answer and whisper "Allie, look hungry." Little Allie would put on her most pathetic expression and they would accept the offering, close the door, and giggle all the way to the kitchen where they'd enjoy the lasagna from Mrs. Betty or the baked shepherd's pie from Mrs. Eckhart. Having lost his wife, having lost her mother, they were so grateful to have each other. Their bond grew strong and it was fulfilling. Her dad lived healthfully until the end, and when the day came last year for Alison to say good-bye to him, she did so with a grateful heart, and with the hope she could be a quarter of the parent he had been. Alison carries a singular irreplaceable affection for her gentle father, and every time that train whistles upstairs in her son's room, she feels it all the way through to her bones. It makes her sad and it makes her smile—it is a paradox she can live with.

After ten years, Alison navigates with deft skill around Hank's extended animated family. What is interesting to her is the emotional continuity; grudges and arguments resurface year after year, are pulled out, addressed all over again, and in the end, everyone hugs and kisses and goes home until the next time. Alison is intimidated by conflict, but she likes watching them all—it's like her own personal reality show. Tonight Hank's entire tribe is in her home: laughing, arguing, eating, joking, complaining.

In her cozy yellow and white flowered kitchen, there is a butcher's block with a cabinet and drawers for a center island. Over the sink, four little ceramic spice pots line up along the windowsill, which looks out on the backyard. Rosemary and basil scent the air. Along the far wall, past the wooden country kitchen table, is the door that leads down to the basement. She read once in a women's magazine that a kitchen tells the tale of the woman who likes it; Alison's kitchen is understated, elegant, and meticulously clean.

Alison kicks open the back kitchen door, which leads in from the barbeque, and steps inside the room. She is wearing a two-piece sage green linen pants outfit, which highlights her green eyes. She looks radiant, relaxed, and in her element. She carries a platter of perfectly grilled chicken. Stepping inside, she bumps the back door closed with her hip and hurries over to the center island where she places the heavy platter on top of the butcher's block top. She rinses and wipes off the long sharp two-pronged BBQ fork and replaces it in the drawer under the butcher's block. As she passes the microwave, she hits one button without even looking and the timer automatically sets to fifteen seconds. It counts down as she grabs the tomato and oregano salad out of the refrigerator. She looks at the salad disapprovingly. It's not tomato season and so she wouldn't normally make this dish. Tomatoes have no taste unless purchased from local growers in season; however, it is Jimmy's favorite so she made it even though she knows it will be disappointing. When the microwave has counted down fifteen seconds, it beeps loudly and she removes the cup of tea she was warming. She stops for a moment and takes a sip as a loud burst of family laughter from the other room makes her smile. She looks around at her home, her family, and decides that no matter how unpleasant the coming few days might be, she will be positive. Really, she asks herself, how bad could it be? A few days in the woods, big deal.

Using her butt to swing open the door into the dining room, Alison carries the platter to the table, which has been set up as a buffet. The relatives have congregated around the table and are grabbing plates and napkins. The oval dining room table has a white eyelet lace tablecloth that sets a bright backdrop to the blue and yellow Italian ceramic platters and bowls Alison has carefully set around for the buffet. The room smells like warm cheddar biscuits and freshly cut oranges. Alison savors the scents and she does wish that Aunt Beth would not smoke inside the house, but she is too gracious to say so. Jimmy and Alan dip their fingers in the potatoes au gratin.

"Boys," Alison stops them, "fingers out of the food. Jimmy, please run into the kitchen and bring in the lemonade."

"Aw, Mom, I want soda."

"Soda?"

"It's my birthday."

"So you think you can just have anything you want?"

"No, just soda."

"You think because it's your birthday you can just gulp down a big ole glass of soda?"

"Yeah?"

"You're right. Go."

Jimmy flies merrily into the kitchen. Alan follows.

"Not you, Alan." Alan freezes at the sound of his mother's voice. Jill looks at Alison, "We don't ever approve of soda."

Alison smiles, letting the derision in Jill's tone slide off her, "Your prerogative as Alan's mother."

"We don't even have soda in the house," she adds with just a hint of judgment in her tone.

"I'm glad that works for you." Alison turns away but Jill continues.

"Well, you know, Jimmy is my nephew and I surely wish he didn't drink soda either."

Alison drops her head forward just a bit to give herself a brief second to get the ire out of her eyes. She finds her sister-in-law trivial, and self-righteous, and Alison does believe that Jill goes out of her way to bait her. Aunt Lydie looks over with her eyebrows raised hoping for a messy takedown.

Alison responds, "And I suppose that is my prerogative as Jimmy's mother."

"I suppose. I just don't understand why you'd continue to buy that poison when you know how bad it is."

"Well, Jill, I'm an enigma."

Jill hates it when Alison uses uncommon words. She knows she does that to test her. And truthfully, Jill doesn't have an exact fix on what enigma means and so rather than make an error she shrugs and walks away.

"Suit yourself," Jill says.

Alison makes eye contact with Aunt Lydie who grins exposing some missing teeth.

Uncle Wes, who is a pudgy red-faced man nearing retirement age, passes a plate to his twenty-year-old niece Eleanor. Aunt Beth reaches across the table for her spoon as she attempts to stir up conflict.

"Fry-'em," Aunt Beth says, "the death penalty is the only answer."

Uncle Wes agrees, "Two chairs—no waiting."

"Isn't that a little barbaric?" Alison can't help herself even though she has learned staying out of political discussions with Hank's family is the prudent course.

"Naw," Uncle Wes says, "it's nature. Bloody real nature."

"I think, we, as humans, should be above that."

"Read a paper, Alison," Aunt Beth responds, and blows a smoke ring. Eleanor can't keep quiet another second.

"You know, Aunt Beth, passive smoke is harmful to us all."

"So, hold your breath."

Uncle Wes laughs loudly. Alison shakes her head as she proceeds down the hall looking for her husband. She finds him in the den with his sister Emily, who is breast-feeding, and their mother, Carolyn, who is disgusted.

Hank insists, "Emily, a nipple's a nipple."

"Not true. It's a fact that breastfed babies are smarter."

"That's ridiculous," Hank replies.

Carolyn adds, "Neither of you were breastfed"

"Oh, so, that explains it," Alison says from the doorway.

"My wife knows us too well."

"Dinner." Alison smiles. Hank walks over to her in the doorway, but Carolyn has not quite finished her thought.

"Emily, I love you but you look like a cow."

"Mother, it's a normal part of nature."

"So is peeing and I don't want to share that with you either."

As Hank kisses Alison, "My family drives me crazy."

"They have a special gift."

"Did I ever thank you for putting up with them?"

"Not often enough."

He leans close and whispers into her ear, "Later I'm going to thank every inch of your body with my tongue." His moist warm breath is welcome on the side of her neck. It gives her a little thrill. He still makes her crunch her toes. Hank runs his hands through his bangs. His caramel hair is long for a man in his thirties, but it is nicely trimmed and has a natural cowlick in the front, which is really attractive. He has a broad grin, which he employs constantly to keep those around him smiling, too. He can be lazy about shaving and so the five o'clock shadow that the macho movie stars try so diligently to achieve, comes naturally to Hank. Women always notice him. He only sees Alison. Sometimes, he wonders why this refined lovely woman puts up with him: his constant need for music, his quirky sense of humor, and his relatives. He doesn't appreciate how entertaining a large vivacious family could be to a girl from Alison's quiet world.

He kisses her on the neck, turns and walks toward the dining room singing "Beautiful" in falsetto. Alison looks back at her mother-in-law and they smile. Wife and mother—yes, they both love that man. That is their bond.

After dinner, all of the relatives gather around Jimmy's birthday cake to sing. His parents flank him. He blows out the red and white swirl candles, which relight over and over. He's too old for that trick. She knows that, of course, but the sentimental strain in her refuses to stop buying them. She joked with him last year that when he's forty years old she will be lighting those same candles so he should get used to it. She leans in and kisses him on the top of his head. She knows he will allow a small public kiss since it is his birthday, and his cool friends are not at the family party. She lingers for a second, smelling his freshly washed hair and wants to submerge herself in the disheveled mess of it. She remembers the afternoon he marched off the grammar school playground and announced with gritty six-year-old determination she could no longer hug or kiss him in public: it was too embarrassing. And she knew there would quickly come a time when he would be too tall to kiss on the top of his head. What a series of wrenching trade-offs: each year he becomes more interesting as a person, but less hers alone.

Jimmy beams since he knows the gifts are next. He grabs for a box and rips into the wrapping paper. Alison and Emily return together to the kitchen to divide the cake.

Emily asks, "What did you get Jimmy? Hank said it was really special."

"We told Jimmy for his birthday he could pick where we would go on our family vacation."

"Great idea."

"I figured, you know, Disneyland, Universal Studios."

"And?"

"And he picked a ragged outback fishing camp in the middle of Lake Superior."

"Let me guess, no room service." Emily grins.

"No indoor plumbing."

"So Hank and Jimmy are going without you?"

"No. All for one."

"Well, at least you'll get some fresh air."

"Fresh air gives me hives."

"Didn't you go to camp as a kid?"

"I went to camp one time. I got a staph infection from a mosquito bite and my dad had me airlifted out."

"Well, aren't you Dora the Explorer. I'm kinda sorry I'm going to miss this adventure."

"There will be nothing to see as far as I'm concerned. I bought two eight-hundred-page novels and enough bug repellent to maintain a defensible perimeter." They each grab cake plates and head back into the dining room to distribute the cake.

Alison hands a plate to Jill who recoils and asks, "Is that Red Dye Number Two in the icing?"

Aunt Beth retorts, "Could someone please get the duct tape, Jill's ruining dinner again."

Jimmy pulls a two-foot remote controlled robot out of the box. He's ecstatic. Everyone watches. He presses the controls and the robot scurries around the room with bells ringing and lights flashing.

"Cool. Really cool. Thanks, Uncle Wes."

Uncle Wes beams, "Cool. You see. I always get the best gifts." He turns to Hank, "Remember when I got you that hockey stick?"

"Uncle Wes, that was 1979."

"See. You remember."

Jimmy's robot is followed by a new Xbox game, a skateboard, from his Aunt Emily and Grandma Carolyn. And from Aunt Jill two bottles of extra strength sunblock and a documentary titled *Food, Inc.*

While the Kraft family celebrates Jimmy's birthday, Ben Burne's family also celebrates. They, too, have a birthday today.

CHAPTER FIVE

— — — — — — — — — — — —

GRAVEL BURNE WALKS DOWN THE narrow windowless hallway toward his mother's kitchen. His feet are flat and heavy. He is a gristly fifty-year-old with wiry arms and legs, and a mess of cheap hair plugs that look like clumps of dead grass. Long on anger, short on thought, he is the authority around his two other brothers while Ben is in the pen.

Small table lamps, with yellowed onionskin shades, shed the only light in this dreary apartment. City buildings rise up tall on all four sides blocking out the sun's natural light and turning the room a bitter color. The windows don't open so the air instead is stale and smells of mold and Bengay. The paint peels on the door moldings. The furniture resembles its owners: dysfunctional and warped.

In the kitchen, Theo Burne empties the jar of Ragu into the pot on the stove. Theo is an overly muscular, mildly retarded, mute man who follows his brothers like a puppy and has been trained well by them. Kent Burne, who is a year younger than Gravel, sits at the small table complaining to his mother.

"Most the trouble with women is they got no sense of humor, except for you, Mother." Sitting across from him, the wisp of an old lady grins exposing a gaping black toothless hole. Kent continues, "I was at the Lenny's BBQ with a prime piece-a-ass I picked up at the Walmart, and I let out this earth rockin' fart, and the bitch don't even crack a grin. Instead, she looks at me like her shit don't stink."

Gravel enters, "You might have more luck if you stop dating girls with hair on their back."

"Great. Advice from a guy who owes a fortune to 976-U-CUM."

A muffled grunting noise comes from Theo over at the stove. From the look on his face, it must be amusement. With the addition of Gravel, three of the four Burne brothers are present for their mother's special eightieth birthday party. They are only missing their oldest brother Ben.

Theo spoons out macaroni from the pot on the stove, pours some Ragu over it and plops it down on the table for the family. He takes a couple of used, dirty spoons from the sink and hands them out. The four of them sit around the beaten up plastic table and for a moment or two there is only the sound of the spoons hitting plates and sloppy chewing.

Then Gravel says, "Mother, in honor of your special birthday, Theo baked you a cake."

"Theo," she pets him like he's a dog, "you were always my favorite—after Ben, of course."

"Of course, after Ben." Gravel's lifelong envy comes alive in the room and it's ugly.

Mother continues, "Yes, Theo, you were always a good quiet kid."

"He's mute," Gravel says annoyed.

"He's not mute. He just doesn't have anything important to say. You could learn from him."

"I learned everything I need to already."

"You know, Mother," Kent says, "all the shrinks on the inside told me you're not supposed to have favorites 'cause it sucks for our development."

"Yeah, so, some people prefer other people. Get used to it." The old woman looks around the kitchen and then says, "Let's do this. I want my cake in the bedroom." Mother gets up and heads for the bedroom. The three men each grab some cake for themselves.

"Fried that guy at the state pen last night," Gravel says.

Kent answers, "Firing squad's a much better way to go than the chair."

"Nah, a good old-fashioned hanging—that's the way."

Theo cuts and puts a nice piece of cake on a plate for Mother Burne.

"I heard when you hang—your dick gets hard."

"Damn right." Gravel grins at him.

"Okay, so that's one good thing." They share a brotherly chuckle.

The bedroom has a twin mattress on top of the metal frame with no box spring. The sheets are grimy. Mother Burne is propped against the dingy pillow. Theo, Kent, and Gravel take seats on the sides of the mattress surrounding her. Gravel has brought in his cake and he licks some frosting from his fingers. It's the closest he comes to washing his hands.

Mother Burne takes a bite of cake and confirms, "Now, boys, you know what you're supposed to do, right? You've got no confusion?"

"First, we get Ben. Then we go across Superior to meet up with Uncle Rafe in Canada," Kent replies.

"We've always been a close family. I'd like to think you boys will stay that way when I'm gone."

"Yes, Mother," Kent says. Theo nods. Gravel hovers like a predator.

"Listen to your brother Ben. He's got more smarts than all you put together."

Gravel rolls his eyes and swears under his breath.

She smacks his face. "Only idiots mumble."

Kent asks, "So, Mother, sure you don't want to hang around 'til we get Ben?"

"Eighty's enough." She turns to Theo, "Son, I trust you." Theo's eyes take in her words. He nods. She continues, "So, don't fuck up."

Theo takes one of the pillows and plunges it down over his mother's face. He presses out the air. In mid-bite, Gravel looks up from his cake. Kent leans in closer with interest. They watch as their mother begins to flail. Theo presses down harder. She kicks. She slaps the mattress. She grabs out into the air. She lifts her body at the hips. They watch. A long, long, cold moment, and then the flailing stops. Wait. The old woman goes limp. Wait. Wait.

Kent says admiringly, "She was a wiry old thing."

"Yeah, well, I never fuckin' liked her." Gravel gets up. "Good job, Theo." He's happy for the compliment. The three of them get up and leave the room.

"Did you know that 'fuck' is the only word we have that can go into any sentence?" Kent asks.

"Yeah?"

"Sure, it can be 'get fucked.' It can be 'cool fuckin' shoes.' It can be 'Hey, fucker.' Yup, really it goes easy into every fuckin' sentence."

"Then that's a useful fuckin' word." Gravel grins, pleased with himself. All three of them are smiling as they grab a bag left by the door and exit.

CHAPTER SIX

FOR HANK'S FAMILY THE SAYING of good-byes is its own unique time-consuming ritual. Each family member needs to hug and kiss each other family member. It is a mélange of motion with an underlying order. There is a lot of circling around and gushing; when it's done, everyone has been touched by everyone else. It is late before the last lingering family member, overloaded with leftovers, pulls out of the driveway. Alison closes the front door and leans up against it, tired. Hank's family is exhausting.

Polly is coming in the morning to finish the clean-up, so Alison takes the stairs two-at-a-time, and crosses the hall, into her bedroom. She tugs a suitcase out onto the bedroom floor. She stops in the doorway of her closet and scans the hangers: skirts, nope, dresses, nope, nice pants, all unlikely to be useful—she has a closet full of inappropriate clothing. She shrugs. Think. Cold dense rainy woods. Well, I don't know why I don't own the long wool underwear and neoprene yellow poncho that I evidently need. Really, what was I thinking last Christmas when I asked for a Kindle? Oh, I know, I couldn't imagine actually being somewhere without Internet. I wonder if I lay my cutest bikini on the bed if Hank and Jimmy would consider cutting this fishing thing short out of kindness, or even pity. She crosses to the bureau and pulls out a pair of sweat pants, two pairs of old jeans, and a sweatshirt; how attractive, I'm bringing my best in-case-of-freezing-flood-and-mud resort wear. She arranges the bulky items inside the suitcase, and adds a grungy shredded pair of sneakers she has kept, in case she ever had the desire to paint or work in a garden, which she hasn't, because both involve the potential for dirt under her fingernails, which she can't stand. What else? She looks in the closet. I need some arctic-level pajamas. She sees Hank. He is standing in the doorway. The grin on his face makes his eyes bright. His thick eyebrows are raised in a humorous question. A relaxed comfort exists in the space between them now, as it has for years, the way it does when the struggle is over and the coupling is complete; whatever, they're in for the long haul. They will grow old together, sit side-by-side between the arms of an ample loveseat, leaning on each other, and looking out at the world, reliving their shared life. They will be aware of each other's thoughts in the most intimate way, and they will enjoy the sustained blissful contentment of knowing another person thoroughly.

"What?" she asks. "What are you grinning at?"

"The vision of you in nothing but fishing waders."

She cocks her head, "It's a little sick the way you're enjoying this."

"You underestimate yourself. You always have. You might love it."

"That's true. Perhaps I've been hiding all my outdoor skills from you all these years."

"If they're anywhere near as good as your indoor skills I'm excited." They share a knowing smile. Hank walks over and takes Alison in his arms. "Seriously, honey, I can take Jimmy alone and you can go to the day spa and get peeled or hot stoned or kneaded like dough, if you like."

"And let you get all the glory? No way. I'm not backing out. It is exactly what everyone expects me to do and I'm a little tired of being predictable."

"In that case, I'm going to knead you like dough myself right now."

"Please tell me there aren't a lot of bad baking metaphors on their way."

"I'm going to grease the pan."

"Stop."

"Play with it until it rises."

"Really." She tries hard not to grin. "Stop."

Hank didn't always love Alison. They had been dating for such a long time that he got married because it felt like the next thing to do. He fell in love with her slowly over the course of the next ten years. It is the greatest secret of his life that when he said "I do" he meant "Why not?" He became aware of his love when it surprised him. He listens to his friends complain about their relationships, and he feels embarrassed by the extent of his luck. He marvels at how close he came to disaster by not realizing how important it was for him to have her. Perhaps there was some invisible inner compass guiding him into these arms, this life. And when he began to love her, it awakened a set of instincts he didn't know he had. He wanted to take care of her. Watch over her. Protect her. It made him experience being a man in a completely different way. He had never struggled to get a date: his tall frame and uncommonly soft eyes served him well. He had been a college athlete and women seemed to be plentiful. He felt manly running around scoring at will. He had been an active participant in the he-man bluster and locker room bragging, ten chicks, twenty babes, the quantity syndrome—and then, one day, he saw it for what it was: it was backwards. Any man can satisfy one woman for one night; it takes real skill to keep the same woman satisfied year after year, especially after the heightened sensitivity from newness wears off. A guy has to have game: new moves. His buddies needed new women all the time because they were throwing the same old passes and the receiver was bored. Last week, as Alison was slipping her sweater off over her head he grabbed her arms trapping her inside and laid her onto the bed where he then took his time. He had lit a candle and he began by dribbling a few drops of wax onto her bare belly. They made love like teenagers, like they were hungry. He was thinking now that this dough concept might have something going for it. Baking. Dough. Frosting maybe? Yeah. There's something there.

CHAPTER SEVEN

T HEO DRIVES. GRAVEL SITS SHOTGUN with one foot up on the dashboard. He basks in smug supremacy; for the moment, he's in control, which feels orgiastic. A sensation of well-being spreads over him. He is relaxed. He hadn't known what a liberation it would be to get rid of his mother—one less thing to bother with. Old bitch never liked him. She was a fuckin' thorn.

Kent sits in the middle of the back seat with his elbows crossed over the front in between his brothers. He looks out through the windshield. It's a coal black Minnesota night. The car's headlights reach out onto the opaqueness illuminating the road and a multitude of frenzied insects many of which splatter their guts all over the windshield.

Kent says, "When we get to Canada I'm gonna run the cock fights."

Gravel smirks, "You gonna raise birds?"

"They aren't birds. They're fighting machines. But first, you gotta get 'em in shape."

"In shape, huh? What d' ya tie little weights to their wings and take 'em to the gym?" Gravel asks, rolling his eyes at Theo who snorts happily.

"No. You run 'em around for eight hours every day until their legs get like little stubby tree trunks. Then, you put 'em together and just let 'em go."

"Sounds too much like work." Gravel looks out the window and sees the lights of the small rural hospital just coming into view.

"They fight to the death on instinct. Even if you raise 'em nice, when you put 'em together—bam! They rip each other apart."

"How many you gonna buy?"

"Only need two. I'll buy a male one and a female one. Put 'em together and let 'em fuck their brains out."

Gravel's tone drips with derision, "You're gonna get a female cock?"

"Sure. I'll have baby cocks all over the fuckin' place. I've been readin' about it a lot."

"For someone who reads, Kent, you sure don't get much right."

"You just don't like it when I know something you don't know."

"Yeah, asshole, if that ever happened, I wouldn't like it."

Theo wrenches the car off the main road and enjoys the dive into the ditch. They come to a jerky stop. He shuts off the headlights and the black sedan vanishes into the erasing darkness. Up ahead, Grayley Community Hospital is a blast of ugly fluorescence. The square three-story building has light pouring from every window. An alarmingly large blood red emergency sign points the way to admitting. Gravel and Kent silently slip out of the car with their weapons tucked into their belts, in black jeans and hooded sweatshirts they, too, disappear into the night. At this moment, when they fall into their lifelong roles, the synchrony of their movement is dance-like. They cover the ground with the relaxed competence that comes from experience, and from being inside their comfort zone. Here, together, running through the darkness, fully armed, they are in their element and supremely happy.

Warden Tummelson had chosen Grayley because it was outside of town in a rural area. He thought that would be the safest spot; that way Ben Burne would never be anywhere near a population. Tummelson hadn't considered what a benefit that would be to Ben's brothers who moved in on the hospital like hungry hyenas on carrion. No one considered that the brothers actually cared—about anything. It was the prevailing assumption that they had skipped the country. It was the expected behavior of the merciless. It was inconceivable that men such as these would enjoy a deep brotherly connection. These men couldn't have the capacity for real emotion. They were empty beings—must be empty beings. It was so much easier to deny them the essence of humanness, so that nothing was shared: they are nothing like us. No one considered that these men would risk everything to rescue each other. All of the psychologists reported that these men just didn't think that way. They were narcissistic. They were self-preserving. They were grossly misjudged. The bond between them is fierce. The raw instinct from their shared blood rages within them. There is nothing they wouldn't do for each other, and if pain is the price, then pain it is. They understand pain. Their mother taught them pain. They scoff at the brotherly affection others claim. Would they kill for their brother? Rip the skin off someone's face? Chop off someone's feet? They had no restriction, and no rules. The Burne brothers approached brotherhood the way they approached a big bank score: all or nothing; they had no capability for, and no respect for, moderation. They considered other brothers' assertions of solidarity anemic. It was all a matter of what you were willing to do for your brother. What exactly were you willing to do? If one thing could be said with absolute certainty, it was that no one understood the Burne boys.

To the right of the emergency sliding glass doors the prison van is parked. Kent and Gravel exchange a confirming look. It's a go. Gravel's blood thrills sending a surge of bliss throughout his body. He loves this, every bit of it, the sneaking, the knowing, the teamwork, the weapons, the power. He slips up alongside the prison van and stuffs a cloth into the gas tank. He lights the end and darts back into the darkness.

Inside the operating room, Ben lies cuffed by both ankles to the hospital bed. Doctor Kim is checking the intravenous drip. The nurse stands nearby with a full syringe ready to administer the anesthesia. The chaplain from the prison stands next to Ben holding his left hand.

Looking through the glass into the operating room are two prison guards: Wilkins and Rodriguez. They stare into the room believing the threat comes from inside.

Doctor Kim asks a little impatiently, "May we begin?"

Ben replies, "Just one more prayer to the holy virgin."

Doctor Kim tries hard not to roll his eyes and steps back. The chaplain begins another prayer. "Hail Mary, Full of Grace, the lord is with thee. Blessed art thou…" Ben steals an impatient glance at the clock. Just as he does, an explosion rocks the building. The muscles in Ben's face relax. He smiles. Yes.

"What the hell?" Doctor Kim runs out of the room followed by the nurse and the chaplain. Wilkins and Rodriguez burst into the room to watch Ben. Wilkins sees the grin on Ben's face. He feels the shift of power. He pulls his weapon.

"Stay still, Burne."

"Wilkins, really, I'm chained to the bed."

"Stay still anyway."

"Unfortunately, my friend, I'm afraid it's too late for that. Have you met my brothers?"

Wilkins and Rodriguez spin around. They're face-to-face with Gravel and Kent. Bang! Bang! And the two guards sink to the operating room floor. Kent gets the keys from Wilkins' bloody pocket and uncuffs Ben. Ben rips the I.V. out of his hand.

"You're late," he says.

"Traffic," Gravel answers blandly.

"Yeah, and we took the expressway, so we were surprised." Kent hands a weapon to Ben. "Hey, bro."

They turn, exit the room and move together down the hospital hallway—blood harmony.

Ben asks, "Where?"

Gravel replies, "Second floor, southeast window."

Ben takes the lead. It has always been his role.

Consistent with Gravel's style, the explosion took out half of the emergency room blowing out one entire wall. Chaos reigns and injuries abound. Ben, Gravel and Kent slip easily through it, onto the stairs, and down to the second floor. They enter an empty room and cross to the window. In the distance, the fire trucks and police cars approach. Gravel takes a small flashlight from his pocket and signals. Flash. Flash.

Theo sees it. He throws the sedan in gear and pulls back onto the road. Two police cruisers speed up on him. He stops politely and waves. They pass by, sirens blaring. Theo drives up onto the lawn at the corner of the hospital, directly under the window. Kent, Gravel and Ben leap to the ground and roll. They dart to the sedan, climb in, and Theo floors it yanking the wheel hard right, driving back up onto the pavement, and they speed down the country road and into the darkness.

Ben now rides shotgun. He takes the power position between his brothers. It is his right. He gets dressed as they move.

Kent gushes, "Jesus, Ben, you look good, bro."

"I've had a nice rest. Did some reading. Worked out in the yard. Hey, Theo, shut up." He hits the back of Theo's head. Theo grins. "Nice pick-up boys."

"My plan," Gravel says.

"And full of your usual subtlety."

"Thanks. Be at the lake by dawn."

"The boat?"

Kent answers, "Waiting."

CHAPTER EIGHT

T HE MORNING COMES TOO SOON for Alison. The aggressive sun creeps skillfully in through the windowpane, up the mattress, onto the sheets, and then elbows her right in the eye. Without opening her eyes, she wonders how the sun does that, finds the one crack in the drapes and lands exactly on her eye. A few moments ago, she heard Hank and Jimmy lugging their suitcases down the stairs and she snuggled deeper into the covers.

Polly knocks on the bedroom door and then sticks her head in. "Hank asked me to tell you it's time."

"Ugh." Alison buries her head back under the pillow. How can this be a vacation if someone is waking me up? Aren't those mutually exclusive events?

"Alison?"

"Okay. I'm up."

Polly Steiner likes her job. At sixty-years-old, she has no patience for the drama of other families she's worked for—the Kraft family is a good fit. She's been with them two days a week since Jimmy was born, and an ease of life has developed between them.

Polly straightens up the bedroom as Alison heads lazily for the bathroom. Polly organizes the magazines neatly on the bedside table. She picks up Hank's black socks, which were left in a ball on the floor on his side of the bed, and she tosses them into the hamper. Alison rinses her face in the sink, and brushes her teeth. She slips on her light blue jeans and a long-sleeved white sweater.

"So, Polly, you will water the plants?"

"All except that ugly creeping Charlie in the downstairs hall. I hate that plant."

"Yeah? I didn't want to tell you, I heard it saying bad things about you to the other plants."

"I knew it."

"Oh, no. I forgot I have a dentist appointment scheduled this week."

"They called to confirm yesterday and I canceled it," Polly says.

"Oh, good. What else?"

"I stopped your mail."

"Oh, right."

"And the newspaper."

"Perfect."

"And I finished the novel you were reading."

"How'd I like it?"

"You cried at the end."

"Oh, I love a good cry."

They smile at each other. Polly hands her the small travel case.

"Have a good time."

"Actually, I woke up feeling a lot different this morning."

"Yeah?"

"This will be an adventure. I think I'm going to have a good time."

"That's the pioneer spirit. I slipped the bug spray, the aspirin, and the anti-itch lotion inside your rain boots."

"Oh. Good thinking."

* * *

A few hours later, the tiny grey speedboat, which from Alison's perspective is in questionable condition, and barely qualifies as a floatation device, bangs across the surface of Lake Superior. Hank sits in the aft next to the captain, who Alison is quite certain isn't old enough for a driver's license yet. The teenager has kept the boat relatively close to land. They've been speeding along since late morning without a single sign of civilization on the shore. Hank looks off at the distant horizon and invigorated, starts singing Proud Mary. Even the gathering storm clouds cannot wipe the grin from his face. He remembers the envious looks from his two partners, Scottie and Newt, at work yesterday. He knew when he got back he was going to hear about plans from each of them to do something out of bounds—something exciting. They are all ready for a break. They have worked hard and long on their business.

Two years ago, the three of them started Pump Up The Volume, a sound and lights equipment company. Hank is the first to actually take a vacation. They have worked like crazy for professional gigs, and they love it when a real band comes to town, but the bread and butter of their business is still high school musicals, bar mitzvahs, and weddings. Hank doesn't mind though, because while there is always stress when the special night arrives, he works all the time with people who are planning happy events and that fits with his nature. It has been fun starting a business, in his hometown, with his best buddies, and being able to work all day long with the music blasting. Music is as essential to Hank as breathing. All kinds of music: Hip-hop, Reggae, Blues, Rap, Rock—it all works for him. The only improvement he made to their home was to wire every room for sound; even if he is out in the backyard, there is a speaker. When there is no music playing he is constantly looking around the room as though he's lost something, and much to the misfortune of those around him if the music is turned off, he sings.

Business is good, but not too good as Newt says happily. Newt sees work as something one does in-between parties, something that pays for one's life, but not something that is necessarily interesting. He could have been in the business of making dog treats and it would be exactly the same. As long as he is working with his buddies, he is okay with working. He prefers a nice easy pace and doesn't like it when they get too busy. Scottie is a tech junky and loves the equipment, the more complicated the better. He shows up wide-eyed and excited at every tech convention within 500 miles. He races back to the store after each event like a teenager with a list of sound equipment they have to have. Newt keeps him in line economically. Hank just wants the music in every hour of his day. They have a comfortable partnership.

"Hank, you're singing again," Scottie complains.

"Am I?'

"A dismal rendition of Wild Thing," Newt adds as he lifts a soundboard onto the countertop.

"I rock and you know it."

"There's a reason why Mrs. Kravitz in the seventh grade put you basically under the bleachers for the Spring Show."

"Hey, don't talk trash about my glory days."

It was Alison who suggested the name for the business. It is an inside joke. Hank liked Pump Up The Volume for the obvious reasons. Scottie, Newt and Alison liked it because whenever you're around Hank you need to pump up the volume to drown out his singing.

Lake Superior suddenly rears up like a spooked horse. The speedboat pitches left and slaps back down on the water.

Hank keeps singing, "Big wheel keep on turning. Proud Mary keep on burning."

"Dad, so uncool."

"Uncool?"

"Completely."

"Oh, yeah?" He stands and starts to rap T.Pain, "I'm on a boat. Hey ma, if you could see me now…" Jimmy laughs as Hank continues and adds ghetto gestures, "Arms spread wide on the starboard bow. Gonna fly this boat to the moon somehow."

The boat shoots off a crest and out of the water, suspended, and then, smack down hard. Hank hits the deck and grins sheepishly flat on his ass.

The captain rolls his eyes and tries to keep his grin small. Alison bites her tongue hard. She scrunches her face, as she tastes a drop of blood. In only a few seconds, the water conditions on the lake have worsened dramatically. The boat begins to feel even smaller to her. She looks out at the expanse of water; the lake has no end whatsoever. It is so vast that it looks no different from the ocean, except the ocean hasn't ever looked this angry to her. The water is not a comforting azure with foaming whipped cream dollops, but an icky truculent green. She knows there will be no soft sand between her toes, no pedicures, or pleasing rum drinks in her immediate future. She notices Hank's expression. He is so engaged, so happy.

Up and down. Side to side. The boat rocks, and tosses, and shimmies. In her seat, Alison sways back and forth. Her stomach churns and the skin on her hands turn bluish. She sinks down in the seat. There is no relief from the pounding of the boat on the waves as the wind picks up. Pregnant clouds, bulbous and ash colored, press down on them. The captain eyes the sky, and then jams down the throttle, jacking up the power and racing to get to the camp before the deluge. Alison can't imagine why it matters to hurry, as she is already wet to the bone. She does not know about the unforgiving fury of this lake during a storm. The captain knows it well and this is why he is pushing the boat's engine to its limit. She glances at her husband and son. They are in the same boat, at the same moment, experiencing the exact same thing and they look energized. I'm such a fuddy duddy, she thinks, dismayed.

Jimmy enjoys the tossing from crest to trough and watching him reminds Hank of when he used to toss his son up in the air and catch him. Was it so long ago when he was that small? They all grab the rail as they hit a particularly large swell. Hank and Jimmy's faces are splattered with mist and glee.

Abruptly, Alison spins, leans over the edge of the boat, and throws up. It is a gut-wrenching heave that sends her chest smacking into the side. She opens her eyes. The water is only feet away and she swears it reaches for her. Its frigid spray clouts her face. She heaves again. The retching comes from deep in her belly, and she feels like her organs are coming out. With her chest against the cold wood, and her head loose over the side of the boat, she wonders which is worse, this actual all-encompassing sickness, or the stinging embarrassment. Even doubled over, ill as she is, she is still the lady her dad raised, and this is humiliating. And in front of Hank, and Jimmy, and this stranger. In ten years of marriage, her husband has never seen her shave her legs, floss her teeth, or go to the bathroom; she has always maintained her gentility and now this. She heaves again. It is the old seafarer's irony that she is now desperate for water to cool the acid in her throat and cleanse her mouth. She flops back into the seat. Her skin is pasty, her eyes are bloodshot, and the tip of her nose is mulberry. Cautious to keep his balance in the unpredictable lurching boat, Hank starts toward her, but she warns him off with a shake of her hand. She can't have him near her right now. He sits back down with no idea how to help her. He knows her well enough to know how she must be feeling. She places her head deep between her legs and her body sways limply, without resistance, as if she's been deboned. Hank looks to the captain.

"Is there anything we can do?"

"Nope" he responds with little interest, "them people just gotta ride it out."

Jimmy slides in next to his mother, "You okay, Mom?"

She responds without lifting her head. "Peachy."

Hank trades a sympathetic shrug with Jimmy and for the first time, all kidding aside, Hank realizes this is stupid. Look at her, crumbled up, sick, miserable. Shit, what was he thinking?

"How much farther?" he asks the captain.

"Almost there."

He yells over the motor, "Honey, we're almost there."

Alison doesn't move, or respond, but she thinks, somewhat prophetically - just shoot me now.

A few minutes later, the captain's gloved hand turns the tiller and angles the boat toward shore. He spies the small dock up ahead, and the raucous waves now pummel the side of the boat as he powers toward it. Alison looks up and sees beyond the dock a woodsy wall of green; woods so dense the ground never feels the sun's warm palm; a world that never completely dries out, damp and lush with birch, cedar, pines and wild orchids. The captain gestures to Hank to leap out. Hank bolts up and jumps off the boat and onto the shaky floating pier. He almost loses his balance as he lands one-footed, but manages to hang on. He knows that Jimmy is watching him with a son's eyes and Hank is excited to parade his colors. The captain tosses him the dock line. Hank snatches the rope out of the air with one hand. He is energized, something here connects him to other men in older times, men who worked the land, men who fished for their meals, men who provided in the most fundamental way for the lives of their families, and he feels the history like remembering something he never knew. He pulls the rope toward the dock cleat. He knows today's men have lost something being tied electronically to their lives, instead of through their bodies. How would he survive if confronted by the Earth's untamed elements? How would he light a fire in this dampness, or trap an animal for food. If he could trap an animal, how would he kill it? He's never killed anything larger than a spider. He has no clue which plants are edible or which are poisonous. He could never make a piece of clothing from an animal skin, and has little hope of constructing a viable shelter from twigs and leaves. Hell, now that he is being honest with himself, he doesn't even really know how electricity works—only that when he flips the switch—it does. If there were nuclear war, or a planetary disaster, he would be less useful than Stone Age man. His survival is built upon a foundation of knowledge that is so far removed from his life that it is inaccessible, even to his imagination. In this moment, on this rickety dock, he faces the fact that he is a completely dependent individual. He has no practical skills, and no idea how to survive. The sudden acknowledgment of his dependency makes him wonder if maybe he has lost a bit of what it means to be a man. He feels the fresh cold air fill in his lungs and he likes it. He feels bigger and taller standing on this dock with the bitter wind and the spitting lake. He likes the power in his hands, pulling the boat in by the rope, with its tough spine and coarse bristles slicing across his palm. He hadn't realized he was missing this connection. Civilized living with its take-out food and glossy magazine lifestyle precludes the opportunity to be a man in this fundamental way. Perhaps every man needs to go fishing in the wild with his son now and then. He is going to make the most of this. He gives Jimmy a thumbs up.

Jimmy smiles back at him. Hank knots the rope to the cleat on the dock. He looks up triumphantly to Alison...and...oh, her head is back between her legs. Damn. He will get her inside in front of the warm fire, pour her a glass of wine, and settle her down with her book. She'll be relaxed then. It'll be fine. He will make it fine.

"Okay, everybody out" the captain says. Hank steps down into the speedboat, takes Alison's hand, and helps her up onto the moving dock. Jimmy darts off agilely.

"Just follow that trail about fifty yards up to the lodge." The captain throws off their suitcases, reaches out, unties the knot, and starts to back the boat away.

"Wait." Alison asks, "You're leaving?"

"Yeah. Need to beat the storm. Easy, just up the path. Follow the sign." And he rooster tails back onto the lake.

Alison turns to face the wall of woods in front of her and is relieved to see that the sign and path are clear. She walks quickly toward solid ground. "I need to be on something not moving." She steps off the dock and plants both feet onto the ground. She takes a long deep breath. She bends over with her hand on her thighs and breathes deeply. Beneath her feet, the ground crawls with beetles, rolly pollies, spiders, mites, and the air is thick with mosquitoes so warlike they bite her through the denim of her jeans. Hank and Jimmy grab the suitcases and join her.

"Honey," Hank begins, "let's get where you can sit down and relax." He takes her hand and they start up the path. It is such a good feeling to have his fingers intertwine with hers. They wrap strongly around her skin-to-skin, such a simple act with tendrils directly into her heart.

Already she feels better. The dirt path is poorly maintained with large rocks and arthritic looking tree limbs splayed across it.

"Gives new meaning to the road less traveled by," she says. Hank looks over and grins as she continues. "Hopefully it isn't miles to go before I sleep."

"Dad, Mom's doin' poetry again, make her stop."

"Why would I do that?"

Exasperated he responds, "Because I'm on vacation."

"Oh."

"Okay, I get it." She answers Jimmy, "We're entering a poetry free zone. Although I'm pretty happy you even recognized it's poetry. Do you know who it is?"

"Stop."

She giggles. Hank squeezes her hand affectionately. After a few steps, the forest closes in all around them like a giant green fist. This is where green is born, she thinks. Here in this forest everything is soaked in lime and jade and covered with a thick verdant moss that climbs up and over every rock and every log. It is so vivid she can taste it on her tongue when she talks. She feels the green on her cheeks and on her eyelids.

As they walk up the trail toward the lodge the rain begins, a few drops at first, and then in earnest. The canopy formed by the trees serves as a living umbrella. When they become too sodden, they dump a bucket's worth on the path. Although it isn't far from the dock, up the path to the lodge, the distance she has traveled from her comfort zone feels infinite. Alison peers off to her left. She notices that even in the middle of the day, the darkness is edging in from the deep, and the woods appear foreboding.

CHAPTER NINE

MR. HOBBS MEETS THEM OUT on the porch to the main lodge. The lodge has a wrap-around plank porch that sits up two feet off the ground like the lodge itself. It allows for flood flow underneath. Stilts buried deep into the bedrock make the lodge sturdy and mostly level.

"The Krafts?"

"Yes, hello. I'm Hank. This is my wife Alison, and our son Jimmy."

"Hi," Alison is a little breathless but not from the exercise, she doesn't really know why, although it might be because she still feels nauseous.

"Hobbs. Follow me. Cabins are named. You're Cabin Four." Hobbs is a master of the short declarative sentence. Communication annoys him.

Hobbs waddles off ahead of them. Alison smiles to herself from the juxtaposition of this man and her expectations of him. This is not the mountain man type she had envisioned. He is crotchety, with a sour face, and flaps of sagging skin that nearly cover his deep-set raisin eyes. He doesn't look healthy, not like a man breathing clean air and living the proverbial outdoor life. He looks beaten up by wind, by rain, by cold, and by intentional neglect. She knows he can't be over sixty, but he looks a hundred and ten. She is feeling better about herself. If Hobbs is a model of the rugged natural life then her life is clearly healthier.

Hobbs smacks open the door to Cabin Four with his shoulder and they step in. It is an ascetic sight, three cots, a wooden dresser, and a naked bulb hanging from the ceiling. The walls are not finished, so the studs are visible, and it is devoid of insulation.

"Our best." Hobbs says proudly.

"It's great!" Jimmy beams.

"It's not finished." Alison can't help herself. She couldn't have imagined something this primitive. Surely, drywall and paint are not luxuries.

"Outhouse in back. Dinner at six p.m. Breakfast at six a.m. Easy to remember."

Hank steals a glance at Alison and whispers. "No reason why you can't sleep late."

"And really why would I ever want to leave here?" She eyes him.

"I use the P.A. loudspeaker to wake folks. Boat leaves by six-forty-five."

"Cool." Jimmy nods at his dad.

Hank says, "Took us longer to get here than we expected."

"Not near nothing."

"Yeah, felt far," Hank agreed.

"Getting' here's half the charm."

"Where's the other half?" she asks herself quietly. She smacks the mosquito biting her through her sweatshirt. She begins to scratch. Hobbs shuts the door. Alison looks at her two boys.

"Okay." Hank starts with comically false cheer, "So, let's unpack then. I'm sure the main lodge is great." Alison stands motionless. Hank nods to Jimmy, "C'mon, buddy, let's move these cots together so we can sleep closer, I think we'll need the warmth."

Alison does not want to be the person this adventure is making her. She doesn't want to be the complaining wussy woman. It is simply a role she decides she will not play. She has always been flexible, sort of. If this is it, then she will pull it together and surprise them all. She rolls the suitcase over to the chest of drawers and begins to unpack their clothing along with her new attitude.

She says, "And I saw smoke, so there is probably a great fire going in there, too. It'll be nice. I'm sure."

An hour later, when the storm starts for real, it screams like the Greek Furies. Hysterical winds whip through the trees and torrential downpours pummel the fishing camp. Inside the main lodge, there are no happy campers.

The lodge is one large wood-paneled room, a door on the left leads to a small kitchen. Covering the floor are a number of Chippewa rugs, geometric in design, with once bright colors now badly faded. A titanic fire rages in the brick fireplace warming the room. Two stuffed sofas and eight armchairs, comfortable from age, surround the hearth. Along the far wall is a bookcase jammed with old fishing magazines, and in front of that, is a circular game table with a half-finished puzzle on top. Over by the kitchen-side of the room is one long rectangular dining table where the meals are served family style.

Tonight ten people sit around the table. Bella Connors is the only one who has opted out of the evening meal. A thirty-year-old writer for Outback Magazine, she came prepared, and she had some granola in her cabin before venturing out toward the main lodge. Experience has taught her caution. She has done too much wilderness traveling not to be wary of unknown food sources. If everyone stays healthy, she'll eat tomorrow. Presently, she leans against the stone hearth, looking over into the warming fire, with a cup of hot coffee.

Around the dinner table are the Krafts, Hobbs, two college boys named Grant and Bruce, the Hutchinsons, a young married couple, and two hard-core redneck fifty-year-old fisherman named Dan and Mike. On the table is a bowl of hearty looking beef stew and a loaf of brown bread. Alison does not eat meat, but would never admit it with this crowd. She notices there is no green anything, no salad, no string beans, no asparagus…nothing. Ironically, she thinks, all of the green is outside. The bread looks okay and she could eat that if she could eat—which she can't.

Grant continues, "Hey, look, we're all disappointed, but only a moron would go out in a boat in this kind of storm."

"Are you calling me a moron, college boy?" Dan riles easily.

"It's a general comment. Not specific to anyone here," he answers coolly.

Mike talks to Dan, "Calm down. The kid didn't mean anything by it."

Bruce joins in, "Maybe it'll blow through by morning."

Dan looks to Hobbs for input, "Will it?"

"Dunno."

"Yeah," Dan looks dejected, "I sure as hell didn't come all this way to play Parcheesi."

Jimmy says delighted, "You have Parcheesi?" Hank laughs and Jimmy looks at him confused.

Julie Hutchinson says, "Have you ever been fishing, Jimmy?"

"No, but so far, this is the coolest vacation we've ever had." Hank and Alison exchange smiles. "Last year we went to this boring hotel in France."

Julie holds her grin, "Yeah, sounds awful."

"Nothing to do there. Mom liked it 'cause at the beach she got to take her top off."

"Jimmy, I did not." The group looks at Alison who reddens.

"Okay you didn't but other girls did. It was gross. They were all old."

"Clearly the wrong child to take to Nice." She looks back at her plate with the one chunk of bread on it. Her stomach lurches again. "How can I still be seasick? I'm on the ground."

"Sometimes it takes a couple of hours to feel normal again," Bella says kindly. It only took Bella seconds to recognize this is not Alison Kraft's idea of a vacation. She is so obviously the gentle bookworm type.

Bella doesn't usually run into women like this when she travels. They are usually more like Julie Hutchinson: Patagonia jacket, hiking boots, scrubbed face, no nail polish. Yes, there is most definitely a type of woman for this kind of travel. Maybe that should be the angle for her story, she thinks.

CHAPTER TEN

O UT ON LAKE SUPERIOR THE defining edge between air and water has become indistinguishable. The lake is apoplectic: spastic water reaches up white-armed toward the sky as saturated charcoal clouds spit back. The storm batters the speedboat carrying the Burne boys. Gravel, Theo, and Kent sit stoically and completely relaxed. The crushing natural display bores them. They are accustomed to sharper stimulation. Ben is calm at the controls. He revels in the icy slap of the elements on his bare cheeks and forehead. He smiles. His biggest complaint about prison is that it was dull. Now, he is moving again and he likes moving. Who was it who wrote, "How dull it is to pause?" Something someone read to him on the inside, probably that annoying librarian who spent more time fucking inmates than lending books. He remembers that poem though because he had liked something about it; it stayed with him. He's proud of his memory: exacting and steely. He remembers things in distinct detail. He remembers plenty of storms exactly like this one when they were growing up. His mom used to make them stand outside and yell at the lightning. Four little boys, out in the pouring rain, screaming at the sky. It was empowering. She prepared them so well for life. He is so grateful to have been home-schooled, and not contaminated, or brainwashed, by the fairy tales they stuff down the throats of little kids. Mother taught them the truth: beyond each other, there is no one and no thing of value. "Civilization is a pretty dress on a snake," Mom used to say. "There's no right or wrong, just winners and losers, and the winners get to write the books to make 'emselves look good, but the bare-assed truth is any human starving in a snow bank will eat his neighbor. They don't tell you that in school." Ben thinks fondly back on his mom. She would say, "There are groups a folks with different ideas 'bout what is good, and what is evil, and if that's not proof enough that it's all a crock of bullshit I don't know what is." She was so practical and real. "Worry only about each other, take whatever you can, and don't be a fool."

The only interference the Burne boys had growing up was when the school would send a spy to check on them. Ben grins recalling how they would laugh after each visit. The spy, invariably a woman social worker, would stop by and say, "You know, Mrs. Burne, those boys need to play with other kids, be socialized, learn camaraderie and compromise." Ben remembers how Mom would listen with that I'm-so-interested-in-what-you're-saying expression on her face, like she was getting superior advice, and after a thoughtful pause, she would talk about music lessons they never really took, and athletic teams they didn't actually join. And then she'd drop the big bomb; it was religion after all that didn't allow public schooling. She would invoke Jesus Christ and the social worker would shift her little ass around in the seat and look like someone shoved a gag in her mouth, which of course, was exactly it. Mom had raised all four of them to be God loving. She followed the Bible, as she used to say, religiously. She taught them that they were made in God's image and so were meant to be all-powerful. She explained how Jesus would forgive them anything as long as they said sorry after because this was what he said over and over in the Bible—the forgiveness thing is your free ride. She did prefer the Old Testament's clarity, although Revelations was awesome with all those infants damned (because really how could one enjoy heaven with a bunch of screaming babies) and that everlasting torture stuff, now, that was a good read. How could you not respect a God who came up with ever...lasting...torture? Still, she did explain to them the Jesus forgiving element was goddamn useful. She showed them in the actual Bible verses for the justification for everything: rape, infanticide, slavery. "Just learn your Act of Contrition," she would say. And they would recite it every night. Kent is the most religious of the brothers because he always liked the idea of saints and spirits, ghosts and witches.

Mother Burne kept her four boys close so she could teach them what they really needed to know. With her gone now, Ben knows that his brothers are truly his wards. Theo is easy. He's always been more of a pet. When Ben was nine years old and he wanted a dog, his mom gave him Theo. It was a perfect compromise. No one really knows how much is going on inside Theo's head, but to Ben he really is better than a dog because he's like a dog with hands. There are times when he does think Theo's his favorite. Kent is okay, although he's not too smart, and Gravel has a lot of issues, but the best head of hair. They are brothers. They are blood.

A sputter. A cough from the boat's engine. Ben looks down at it. "Shit." He looks out to assess the shoreline and possible landing spots.

Inside the lodge, Alison has abandoned her chunk of brown bread on her plate and joined Bella over by the hearth. The rest of the group continues with the meal. The atmosphere has loosened a bit as these strangers triangulate each other. It is a process as each finds their proper spot in a new assemblage: verbal jockeying, body language, informational downloads including jobs and residences serve to establish strengths, weaknesses, and put into place the requisite social hierarchy. They smile and nod politely while testing each other to precisely gauge who is successful, who isn't, who is educated, experienced, conservative, liberal, sophisticated, rich. We want to know, we need to know this to determine how the group is to be configured for the week ahead, each member of the new group subconsciously wondering where is my proper spot; where is yours? So much is decided in those first seemingly casual moments: the roll of an eye, a certain vocabulary, the tilt of one's head. And how often these decisions are accurate one rarely knows because these determinations are sticky and subject to confirming bias. Alison has always seen this weighing out process as blatant, even as others proceed ahead at the subliminal level.

Alison asks, "Not hungry?"

"Always dieting." Bella lies. "It would be good if you could get something in your stomach."

"I'm still having nausea. It comes in waves. Ugh…" Alison holds her stomach, "shouldn't say waves." Even sick, she manages to connect on a personal level with Bella. Alison is so plainly likeable. She has an innate softness that touches others gently. She is as naturally warm as the blaze in the hearth.

"So, did you lose a bet or something?' Bella raises her eyebrows.

"Oh, no," she grimaces and runs her fingers through her hair, "Is it that obvious?"

"The French Tips were a dead giveaway."

"You know what? I'm going to fix that. I can play with the team," convincing herself as she tries to convince Bella. "Sometimes don't you just get sick and tired of being exactly how everyone expects you to be?"

"Yeah, I guess. Although people don't expect much from me. I'm a writer so they expect me to observe and then huddle in front of a computer screen in a room by myself. And they're actually not far off."

"Yeah? I'm a middle-class, middle-aged, married, elementary school teacher, and I'll bet a whole bunch of prefab characteristics popped into your head when I said that."

"Yup, they did. With those statistics I guess I now know everything about you." She teases.

Alison says, "And look over at the table each of them in their little bubble of stereotypes: outdoorsmen, frat boys, newlyweds. I wonder if we construct those stereotypes or if they construct us."

"Already a deeper conversation than one usually gets on a fishing trip."

Alison tosses her head and smiles at Bella, "I'm not really prepared to talk about bait."

"There will be a lot of talking about bait here unless this storm keeps up, then, the entire week may really be about Parcheesi."

"Hey, I rock at Parcheesi."

"I kinda knew that about you."

"You see?" Alison smiles honestly and Bella genuinely likes her.

Back at the table, Ed Hutchinson asks, "Hey, Hobbs, there's no cell service so where's the phone?"

"No phone."

"No, phone?" Hank asks surprised.

"Got a shortwave for supplies."

"A shortwave?" Bruce glances at Grant.

Grant responds, "And here we are inside a living anachronism."

Hobbs continues, "Shortwave. This storm. Only static."

Julie says shyly, "It's kind of romantic being isolated like this."

Mike says, "Hey, I ain't that attracted to Dan." They laugh. And nothing brings a disparate group of individuals closer faster than a shared laugh.

"You ain't my type either," Dan responds with his voice booming, "You got less hair on your head than you got on your earlobes." Mike laughs so hard his eyes scrunch up around the outside and look like little squinty slits.

Alison has a sudden wave of nausea. "Oh."

Bella asks, "Hobbs, where's the head?"

"Through the kitchen."

Alison makes a dash for the kitchen and disappears into the other room.

Dan says to Hank, "Maybe you should've left her at the spa."

Hank defends, "Hey, she's a trooper. She came along and it—"

The front door bursts open! Violent winds and sheeting rain blast into the room along with the four Burne brothers. Around the dinner table, mouths drop open and eyes widen. Gravel slams the door behind them. Even with their oversized trench coats, they are drenched. Gravel's stringy hair clings to the sides of his cheeks. Kent's baseball cap sits sopping and tilted forward on his forehead. Their handguns are out of sight tucked into the back of their belts and in their coat pockets. Ben is holding the carburetor from the outboard motor. As the door slams, thunder claps loudly, and Julie jumps. Ben takes a quick measure of the dumbstruck group and begins genially.

"Gee, folks, so sorry we startled you. Our engine gave out and we were lucky to find you in this storm. A guy could drown standing straight up out there."

Hobbs ask, "You fishermen?"

Ben answers, "Yes, sir. Blue Marlin, Mako. My brother here (indicating Kent) held a record on a Giant Tuna for a while." Ben is calm, smooth, and believable to the core.

Dan looks interested, "That so?" Kent nods as the room relaxes. Theo crosses to the dinner table.

"Fishermen always welcome here," Hobbs says.

"Gee, thanks." Ben smiles. His blue eyes sparkle kindly and his grin is broad and sweet. "We're much obliged."

Theo has trudged over to the table where he sticks his fingers into the stew pot, takes out a large chunk of meat, and puts it in his mouth. Ben notices the disgusted looks and he adds, "Ah, sorry, about my brother, Theo, he skipped lunch and he's well…" affectionate emotion rises up in his voice, "he's special."

"He can't talk," Kent explains.

Hank experiences a rising alarm. Even with Ben's calming words, the guys just don't look like fisherman. A clutching feeling in the back of his neck travels down his spine. He will wait just a minute for Alison and scoot them back to the cabin.

"You fellas should dry out by the fire." Mike says.

"We're only staying a moment. Carburetor's dirty I guess." He puts the melon-sized carburetor on the floor of the lodge. "If I could just get a good toolbox so I can get into it and clean it out."

Off the kitchen, inside the tiny bathroom, between the noise of the pounding rain and intermittent thunder, Alison is throwing up. She hears nothing from the other room. With her head over the toilet, she rests her chin on her fist and wishes she could get it together. Why is her body sabotaging her this way? Where is her reliable sangfroid? This whole adventure is becoming one long embarrassment.

CHAPTER ELEVEN

I N THE MAIN ROOM, BEN is savvy enough and manipulative enough to make almost everyone comfortable, but this is not the case with the other Burne boys; even on their best behavior, their true selves seep out like pus. The air in the room is unstable with growing unease. Hank taps Jimmy's hand and says, "Let's go back to the cabin and finish unpacking."

"Okay, one sec." Jimmy lays out a napkin and reaches to put some brown bread in it to take back to his mom.

Kent turns to Dan and Mike and brags, "I caught a storm like this once off the coast of Guava."

"Guava is a fucking fruit," Gravel tells him derisively. The language is oddly harsh and suspicion crawls around the table. For Hank, dread settles like a fist in his throat. Gravel looks to Jimmy and says, "Uh, excuse my French there, kiddo." Hank slides to the edge of his seat as tension rises in his body. He doesn't want to spark anything but he knows bad when he sees it. His eyes roam as he considers his best move. He considers the brothers. The one with the carburetor seems reasonable, intelligent, calm. The mute one seems only interested in food. The other two—they are several clicks from normal—something is very wrong. Ed

Hutchinson moves his chair a little closer to his new wife. Ben doesn't want to waste energy, time, or ammo dealing with these people. Gravel is oblivious to the atmospheric shift in the room. He doesn't have an empathetic antenna and wouldn't care if he did. Bella has caught his attention and he can't ignore the rise in his pants. Bella takes a small step backwards.

Ben speaks a little too calmly to Hobbs, "So, where's that toolbox?"

"Porch."

Gravel leans into Bella inches from her shoulder; he smells her like an animal would. "You're a mighty attractive woman, there, honey."

Kent interjects, "Jesus, you got weird taste."

Bella doesn't know how to react. Her instincts are screaming. Hank sees the alarm on her face.

He says, "I think the lady wants to be left alone."

"Who asked you?" Gravel practically spits at him.

With a warning in his tone, Ben says to his brother, "Gravel, we're guests here."

Not taking his predatory stare from Bella, he responds, "Guests hoping for a little hospitality is all." Dan, Mike, and Bruce stand. They feel confident. There are only four Burne brothers and they are seven strong men.

"Look man," Mike says feeling his way, "we're on vacation. No one wants any trouble."

Dan's bristling middle-class macho adds, "But if you're looking for trouble."

Gravel snaps and turns on them with inappropriate fury. "Hey, you dicks find your own slot. I'm workin' this hole." The pretense of civility disintegrates. Dan takes a swing at Gravel. Bella jumps back out of the way. Gravel wrenches Dan's arm and snaps his wrist. Dan yells in pain. Mike jumps on Gravel.

"Aw shit." Ben says disappointed and annoyed by the ruckus. He exposes his handgun and shoots once into the ceiling. Everyone freezes. Jimmy jumps toward his dad who grabs him. He wraps his arms around his frightened son. Ben speaks calmly, "Okay, let's have a little order here." Terror is written on all of their faces. No one moves. Dan is holding his broken wrist and clearly in pain. "Okay," Ben says, "Better." Patiently he chides Gravel, "Jesus, Gravel."

"What? These guys jumped me. Didn't you see that? They jumped me."

Ben turns to Grant and asks calmly, "Is everyone here?"

Hank's eye catches Alison standing confused in the recess of the doorway to the kitchen. She is unnoticed. Ever so slightly, Hank indicates for her to step back. Bella sees her recede back into the kitchen.

With a raised voice, "You" indicating Grant, "I'm talking to you. Is everyone here?" Grant is too scared to speak. He manages a nod. Ben looks around. He wants to be sure. "Take your dinner seats. Everyone! Sit down in your chairs."

Jimmy says, "Mom?" Hank and Bella exchange an understanding. She walks over and takes Alison's seat.

"Right here, honey," she says to Jimmy as she sits. Acknowledgment passes silently between everyone at the table. They all agree.

Ben looks at the table. Since originally a place had not been set for Bella there are ten seats—ten people. Everyone looks accounted for but Ben is a careful man. He nods at Gravel.

Gravel says, "I'll check around."

No one at the table moves. No one breathes. In silent pain, Dan holds his wrist. Julie hides her face in Ed's chest. He has his hand on her head. Bruce and Grant look much younger than their twenty years right now. Hobbs' eyes trail Gravel. Gravel heads for the kitchen and Hank swallows hard scared for Alison. He squeezes his son's hand. It says be quiet, be calm.

From inside the kitchen, Alison sees Gravel approach. She tears across the kitchen and back into the bathroom closing the door. She has no breath. Her brain stutters. Shock. Think. Think. The rain pours like an open faucet onto the roof. It is loud and her gasping cannot be heard. She peeks out and sees Gravel opening the door to the food pantry. She turns and climbs onto the top of the tank of the toilet bowl. She slips her fingers under the tiny opening of the bathroom window and presses with all her strength trying to open the humidity swollen window. Her face goes red and her arms shake as she forces open the double-hung glass.

In the main room, Kent has taken off his coat and stands by the fire warming. Theo has grabbed the stew pot from the table and is eating in one of the armchairs. Ben stands, gun out, watching the table with a pleasant look on his face. Everyone at the table waits. They exchange glances tense with meaning, all hoping Alison is well hidden. She may be all they have.

From the kitchen, "Lookie what I found."

"No, oh, no," Hank drops his head and pain drenches his expression. Gravel pops his head out holding a box of Oreos.

Kent holds his hands up for the pass, "All right." Gravel chucks the bag over to him and turns back into the kitchen.

Inside the tiny bathroom, Alison's face is bright red and her teeth clenched as she pushes and pulls the window a few more inches. This is as far as it is going. This will be tight, maybe too tight. Shifting her weight, the toilet tank wobbles a little, she goes for it.

Gravel sees the wooden door to the bathroom. He walks over. He pulls his gun. Alison crawls out into the driving rain and reaches up to close the window. It comes part way down when the bathroom light flips on. She hits the mud and rolls up against the lodge wall lying on her side with her back flat against the building. Mud and water in her nose and mouth, she chokes but does not move. Gravel's pasty and distorted face appears in the window. She can see the outline from his head where it blocks the light coming from inside. He peers into the dark. She senses that he's directly above her. She closes her eyes and bites her lips. A moment. The light goes off in the bathroom. She lies there submerged in mud.

Gravel enters the main room and tells Ben, "Nothing." Covert glances are exchanged at the table. At least there is someone out there who knows what's happening.

Ben says, "So, okay, listen up. I don't particularly want to kill any of you. My brother Gravel wants to kill all of you because that's his nature." Gravel grins and shrugs as though Ben has said something charming. Ben continues, "So we've got a delicate balance here. You folks need to behave so as not to upset that balance. Now, you..." he speaks to Hobbs, "this your place?"

"Yeah."

"Where's your fishing boat? We'll be taking that."

"Storm like this, my partner drove it to safe harbor this morning."

"How far is that?'

"About two miles by water."

"Fuck." Kent says. Theo looks up from his pot of stew. He offers Kent a piece of meat. Kent takes it from Theo's fingers and pops it in his mouth.

Gravel asks, "Where's the nearest town?"

Hobbs responds, "No town."

"Fine." Ben looks to Gravel. "Let's just clean this carburetor and hope that will do it."

Behind a tree, near the front of the lodge, she stands. She is barely recognizable through the mud and the contorted expression. Her feet are parted, her knees taut, her arms straight at her sides, her unblinking eyes stuck to the lodge front window. It is dark outside and the lights from the lodge illuminate the main room like a stage play. She feels as though she is in the middle of something unreal. She stands indifferent to the pounding rain, the thunderous noise, and the flashes of violent electricity.

Inside, Ben's tone has taken on an eerie controlling calm. "How about you all move to the far corner over there by the game table and take a seat together on the floor."

"Why?" Gravel asks his brother.

"So you and Theo can tie them up."

"Tie them up? Let's just do 'em and be done."

Ben smiles nicely at the group at the table, "See, he's so impulsive, ever since he was a little kid." Then, back to Gravel, Ben explains,

"Currently, they are assets. Humor me. Tie them." Theo jumps up immediately. He pulls the table lamp from the wall and snaps apart its cord.

Kent stops him, "Theo, here." He holds up a spool of fishing wire. Theo smiles.

Alison watches her husband and son get up from their dinner seats and move toward the game table. Over and over in her mind she hears, this isn't happening, this isn't happening. She watches them all sit together on the floor.

Theo and Kent unspool fishing line. Kent kneels down next to Jimmy who presses back against his dad's chest.

Hank tries, "He's just a kid. You don't need to tie him."

"Yeah? How old are you kid?"

"Nine." Jimmy's voice is barely a whisper.

To Hank, "What are you raising some kind of wimp for the world to shit on? When I was his age I'd already killed three dogs, five cats, and the annoying kid next door."

Outside, Alison digs her nails into her head with terrified bewilderment. Her whole body bursts and shakes. Help. I need help. She turns around in a frenzy. What to do? What do I do? The instinct to find help engages and sends her running through the woods. The ground is muddy and hard to maneuver. She loses her footing, slips, and slides down a small embankment. She stops, looks ahead, realizes she is only a few feet from the edge of a cliff. She can barely see it in the darkness. A flash of lightning shows her its depth. She scoots back from the edge on her ass. Sitting there on the ground the near miss actually calms her. She talks to herself. Stop. Where are you going? What are you doing? Focus. Calm. What can I do? Think. Plan. Smart. Be smart.

The hostages are corralled uncomfortably in the corner. Theo has pulled over a chair and sits facing them with his weapon in his lap. Ben is surrounded by tools. He is taking apart the carburetor. Kent throws some logs on the fire. Gravel lies on one of the sofas with his feet up. He and Kent are in the middle of a discussion.

Gravel says, "It's dandruff."

Kent corrects him, "Doctor said it's stress induced scalp flakes."

"What kind of stress have you got?"

"Bein' your brother mostly." Kent laughs at himself.

"It's dandruff."

Theo stands suddenly and walks over to the hostages on the floor. He looks at them slowly. No one moves. No one breathes. His eyes stop on Mike. Theo bends down over Mike's feet. He sizes them up. He unties and snatches Mike's shoes. He takes them back to where he was sitting and puts them on.

Ben asks, "Is there any music in the glorious rustic hideaway?"

"Radio over there." Hobbs uses his chin to indicate the bookshelf.

Ben signals to Gravel who gets up and turns on the radio. He flips through the dials.

"I can't believe there's no TV here," Kent says and then to Ben, "Did you get to watch TV in the pen?"

"Not too much." Ben concentrates on the carburetor.

"We were a Nielson family for a while."

"Oh, yeah?"

"Such a cool feeling. If I didn't like something, I just cut it off. Bam! Gone."

Gravel is nothing if not impatient. He walks over to Hobbs who sits on the outside of the circle of hostages, slits the wire around his hands, and says, "Find something good on this fuckin' radio."

"Hard in a storm like this." Hobbs gets up and walks over to the bookshelf. He puts his ear close and slowly starts to move the dial.

Kent continues, "The Nielson thing was kind of like being on a jury. You sit there and then if you don't like the guy, bam, he's history."

"You've never been a juror," Gravel says.

"They don't take you if you've gone down for a felony. You'd think they'd be wetting their pants for a guy like me with experience. Some asshole's up for murder one. Hey, I'm your guy. I'd know it in an instant."

Over in the corner, quietly, Dan whispers, "We have to do something."

Bruce responds, "Lay low and stay alive."

"Wait for help," Hank adds.

"Help from where?" Mike asks.

"Alison's out there," Bella reminds them.

"Oh, great, we're relying on mountain woman in the high heels?"

Hank lunges for him forgetting he's tied. The wire secures him and he's pulled back down.

The commotion gets Ben's attention, "Now kids, let's not fight over there. We don't want to gag you."

Hobbs has finally landed on a relatively clear station on the radio. He fine-tunes it. It's a country station. Satisfied, he turns it up. Country music floods into the room. Gravel grabs his gun and fires repeatedly riddling Hobbs with bullets. Julie, Grant, Jimmy scream. Bella begins to cry. Hobbs, his eyes wide open in astonishment, collapses bloody to the floorboards. Jimmy buries his head in Hank's lap. Even with his hands tied, Hank manages to cover Jimmy protectively with his body. And then silence. The kind of silence that accompanies sudden tragic shock. Brains pause. A deafening clap of thunder fills the soundless void.

Then a calm, inquiring voice, "Uh, bro?" Ben asks.

Gravel recognizes the criticism in Ben's expression. He shrugs "I hate country music."

CHAPTER TWELVE

ALISON STEPS BACK FROM HER view into the lodge. Her soaked face registers the inescapable horror of what just happened. Helplessness, like weights, sends her to her knees on the forest floor. Why? Tears fill her eyes. She would rather give herself up and join Hank and Jimmy; she would rather share whatever their fate is than watch it from the outside. Seeing them collapsed together on the floor, she can hear the words of comfort that Hank is most certainly whispering into their son's ear right now. She wants to hear those words, too. She wants the sound of Hank's voice in her head. She needs it. She buries her face in her hands overcome and sobbing. Why? She rocks back and forth on the ground surrendering to the primitive drive to rock when in deep pain. And then, she does hear a voice. It is Hobbs' voice. It says "shortwave." Her head snaps up. Shortwave. She stumbles to standing with her body already moving and her feet catching up she runs toward Hobbs' cabin. She slips here and there in the mud but keeps her footing much better with experience. She has already learned which rocks to jump, which ones are deceptively slippery, and which ones to rely on. She is thankful all of the outside lights are on for all six cabins casting beams of wet light around the camp. She bursts through Hobbs' cabin door. This is a cabin well lived in. It's more of a home. She sees the shortwave on the end table. She races over. She looks at the unfamiliar contraption. She studies the dials. She cautions herself to calm down and let her brain work. She can work a cell phone, GPS, camcorder. She tells herself this is just another device. Relax. Figure it out. Relax.

She switches it on. Instantly static. Good. Okay. With trial and error, she locates the volume switch and turns it up. She flips through the dials slowly. When the static seems to lessen, she pushes the talk button. "Hello?' She waits. Static. Again and again, she tries. "Hello. Can anyone hear me? Hello? I need help!" She turns the dial, wiping her tears with the back of her hand, and continuing to speak, repeating the same message over and over... She hears Hobbs' voice again, "only get static in storm like this." She swallows the scream that is rising up from her very core.

"Hello. Can anyone, anywhere, hear me? Hello?"

A male voice responds from the ether, "Hello, I love you. Won't you tell me your name? Hello, I love you. Let me jump in your game."

A surge from her gut, "I'm at the fishing camp. Men with guns have taken hostages. They've killed the owner."

"Hobbs?"

"Yes. Yes."

"That sucks."

"How do I get the police on this thing?"

"Won't get shit in this storm."

"I got you."

"Yeah, but I'm the only other person on this rock. A quarter mile down the path."

"You're here. Thank god."

"Even my mom wasn't that excited."

"Hurry. Please hurry." Her entreaty is followed by a long pause.

"Look, lady, I'm sorry about your troubles, but I don't go out in the rain."

Alison stares at the shortwave. What? Maybe he didn't understand.

"They have my son, my husband, and other people."

"It'll probably be fine. Just wait it out. I'm sure they'll leave when it clears up."

"No. No. You've got to get over here and help me."

"Good luck."

She hears a click and the static gets louder. She whirls around in frustration. Her body goes rigid and she clenches her teeth maddened. What do I do? She sees the large hunting knife on the dresser. She walks over and picks it up. She tries to imagine herself plunging the knife into someone. She thinks about the blade sinking through skin and muscle, what would that feel like? What kind of resistance flesh? What if she hit a bone? She imagines it. Her hand falls to her side and the blade slips out of her grasp and onto the floor. She is not that person. She is not capable of killing. Kill or be killed, she would probably be killed. Does that make her more highly evolved or simply stupid?

Back at the lodge, Gravel and Kent have become bored waiting for Ben to repair the carburetor. They've devised a little game. Jimmy is standing with his back up against the wall. He has a red bandana tied as a blindfold. Hank is bound, face down on the floor, with Theo's foot on the middle of his back. He continues to struggle uselessly.

Gravel stands across the room. Kent places an apple on Jimmy's head.

"Don't move kiddo."

Gravel aims at the apple from across the room. He shoots. "Whoo hoo!" He splits the apple. Congratulations from his brothers.

"Really," Kent says, "that's so cool."

Inside Hobbs' cabin, Alison hears the shot and bolts. She easily avoids the slippery spots next to the cliff now. She leaps. She finds a spot where she can see into the main room. She sees her son backed up against a wall. Her stomach drops. "No. No."

Fishing wire cuts into Hank's already bloody wrists as he pulls with all his might to free himself. He is wild with emotion. Ben is absorbed with the carburetor.

Kent says, "But still bro, William Tell used his own son and so it's not the same. If you miss there's no downside like he had."

"I'll bet he couldn't do this?" Gravel grabs a grape from the fruit basket on the table. He walks over to Jimmy, who cannot see and so has no idea what is going on.

"Don't move kid." Gravel puts the grape on the boy's head.

Hank, unable to budge, starts to bang his head against the floorboards. "No."

Gravel complains. "Quiet. You'll screw my concentration."

Outside, Alison's eyes widen in horror. She will not watch this. She will not. She will not. Instinct takes over and without thinking, Alison picks up a large fallen tree limb from the ground. Gravel extends his arm and closes one eye aiming. Julie sobs. Bella hides behind Mike.

Gravel's finger on the trigger begins to squeeze and Alison swings the massive limb through the front glass window. Smash! Glass crashes everywhere. The hostages cover their faces. Ben stands up abruptly. Everyone looks at the shard-covered floor as the wind and rain howls in through the opening.

Kent yells, "What the fuck?"

Jimmy bends down to his knees and crawls over to his dad where he is immediately encircled by the group. Hank removes his blindfold with his teeth.

"You think that was the storm?" Kent asks Ben.

Ben's eyes narrow as he calculates the possibilities. He is not satisfied. He is not a big believer in random acts.

"Theo, go make sure."

Theo slips his arms into his coat. He grows monstrously bulky in his trench coat. His shoulders are forty-six inches. His chest muscular and barreled. He is not a man who would need the handgun that he slips into his belt buckle; he could break most men in half with his bare hands. Hank has these thoughts as Theo opens the front door and steps out onto the porch. Hank knows it was not the storm, not the wind. He knows the love of his life is out there—alone—and that she just saved their son's life.

Theo walks with slow even steps on the wooden raised deck that forms the porch, which encircles the lodge. He peers into the night scanning for movement. The beams from the lodge and six cabins form a crisscrossing lattice of light. His eyes and ears are acutely receptive. Theo likes hunting. He always snares his prey.

Underneath the porch, in the two-foot crawl space, Alison stops moving as Theo steps directly above her. She holds her breath. She cranes her neck around to look up and sees the bottom of his shoes through the little gap between the slates of the wood porch. Theo's instincts are keen and he senses her. He knows for certain someone is near. They both hesitate: Theo above, Alison beneath. Slowly, he turns his head from side-to-side. He feels her presence and even in this driving rain, he smells her. She is trapped. She feels it. She closes her eyes for a second and focuses on taking a long slow breath to try to calm her thumping heart. Theo steps. Lightning. She knows the thunder is coming. She hesitates. Then, boom. The thunder growls, and on her stomach, she stretches out her arms and pulls her body along in the mud during the rumbling. Pulling, she heads for the backside of the lodge. She reaches out her arms. She pulls. Theo takes two steps toward the edge of the porch. Her elbow moves against something soft. She turns to look. Her face is inches from Hobbs' staring bloody eyes. It is just the tiniest of shrieks—immediately choked off—but too late. Above, Theo looks down and smiles. He jumps from the porch landing his two big feet on the ground. He drops down and looks under the deck. Something is scurrying away in the darkness. He dives under the deck. With his long arms spread wide and his legs moving rapidly he crawls at twice the speed she does. She claws along on her stomach in fierce desperation, slapping her hands down, using her knees to propel her forward. Theo gains on her. His big flat hand reaches for her foot. She yanks it away with only a little gap now between them. With her knees slightly bent, and crawling as far up off the ground as the deck will allow, she speeds like a terrified spider. Her hands plunge into the mud up to her wrist, over and over, while her knees push at the ground frantically. The sharp edge of a broken twig smacks up and cuts her eyelid. She doesn't feel it. She gasps from the exertion and muddy leaves are sucked into her mouth. She spits. Theo's hand surges out and grabs hold of her right foot. Panicked, she kicks back hard with her left smashing Theo in the face. Surprised, he lets go and wipes the mud out of his eyes. This is fun, he thinks. He presses on after her. Alison emerges from under the porch at the back of the lodge. She staggers to her feet and darts into the woods. Theo bursts from the crawl space only seconds behind her. He springs to his feet and chases. He is mighty and physically fit; he knows he will catch her. But the ground is slick and her feet are more competent now in the mud than his are. She has a tiny advantage because she has learned some of the tricks of these woods and because she is running for her life and the lives of her family. Nevertheless, he is closing on her. She dodges left. He follows. She jumps over that slick flat rock she knows at her feet, dives to the ground and rolls down the embankment she recognizes. Theo's right foot lands directly on the sheer rock face, which is covered with mud. His foot slides unexpectedly throwing him off-balance. Surprised, he hits the ground hard and slides down the slippery mud path and off the cliff's edge. He grabs for anything as his body sails over and he manages a grip on an exposed tree root. He jerks to an abrupt stop—hanging. His expression changes as his body dangles dangerously over the rock bed below. He realizes. Alison stands only a few feet away. They stare at each other. He mouths, "help me." She is not a killer. She stands perfectly still panting, filthy, willing herself to think it through. He tries to climb up the tree root, but it is too slick, and the root too thin. He needs a hand. He turns his fraught eyes on her. She thinks what to do, oh god, what to do. He is helpless. Hanging. Death's razor sharp rocks like an open hand waiting below. For the first time since this night terror began she has power, she has a choice. She does not know this man, but he is a human being. Maybe if she saves his life he will be grateful and help her free the others. Maybe it will be the turning point in the horror for them both. Maybe all he needs is this one hand up. Maybe they are destined to save her family together. Maybe this one act of charity is all this lost man needs. Maybe there is good inside of him. Maybe she can reach that good with an offer of kindness. Maybe. She muffles a reflexive cry as she lifts her right foot and stomps down hard on his hand because—maybe not. Theo plummets with his mouth wide open forming a soundless scream. His back and neck shatter on the unforgiving granite and even over the noisy storm, somehow she hears that ending crack. She scrunches her face, drops her head, and trembles as the pattering clap of the rain on the stones builds to a crescendo of applause. She raises her eyes, the giant pines and oaks wave their limbs at her and she imagines the woods alive and clapping—a hideous ovation. And in the core of her, a private empty space forms like a point of dark: a black hole that sucks in those elements of her that are the furthest from her raw essence: her life, her tribe, at the very center. A metamorphosis has begun. She gasps, not realizing she was holding her breath. And then, again, she runs.

CHAPTER THIRTEEN

— — — — — — — — — — — —

ALISON BURSTS BACK INTO HOBBS' cabin. Her shirt is torn. Mud and wet leaves have bonded with blood from pine cones, rocks, and twigs that have scratched her. There is a nasty streak of blood above her eye. She uses Hobbs' bed sheet to wipe clean the mud from her face and some of her cuts as she hits the talk button on the shortwave.

"You. Where are you? Talk to me."

Curtis replies, "Doesn't this kind of rain just make you itch?"

"Do you have a gun?"

"You'd just hurt yourself if you don't know how to use it."

"Listen to me, you sonovabitch, I just killed a man." Her voice breaks at the end, but she does not cry. She would love to cry, to sit down and sob the night away, but that will have to wait.

Inside the one-room log cabin a quarter of a mile away from her, the sixty-year-old, bearded, pot-smoking, misanthrope, Curtis Wells, sits with his hand on the shortwave. He is not sure what to think about this whole fiasco other than that it is mildly entertaining and something he is not getting involved in. His home is a mishmash of the 1960s: old peace posters line the walls, a macramé covered sofa is brown with age, a red lava lamp sits on the cock-eyed night table, a two-burner hot plate, a toaster oven, and an ice chest are within reach of the table. There are several bags of dried beans and some canned soups along with a couple of cases of Budweiser.

Her voice is steady, "Do you have a gun? Yes or no."

"I do. But you'd have to come and get it."

"How do I find you?"

* * *

Inside the lodge, the Burne brothers have nailed a few pieces of cardboard and some pillows over the broken window. The glass has been kicked into a pile. Ben is back to working on the carburetor. Gravel is in an armchair with his eyes closed and feet up. Kent plays solitaire.

The hostages sit in the far corner of the room in two rows. Hank, Jimmy, Mike, and Dan are in front; Julie, Ed, Bella, Grant and Bruce are in line behind them. Hank whispers. They speak without moving their lips in a very low voice, "We've got to try something."

"Yes, while they're missing one," Dan adds.

Grant leans in and says, "This is six-pound test line. We can bite through it."

"Julie, can you bite through Mike's line?" Hank asks.

She is directly behind Mike. She looks to her husband. Ed nods. She should try. She lies down. It looks like she has just put her head down in Ed's lap to rest. She rolls a little forward. Behind his back, Mike pulls his wrists as far out from his body as he can. Julie begins to chew feverishly.

Ben glances over. Mike drops his wrists. Julie freezes. Ben glares at them. Hank wonders what made him look. There was no sound. He has a freakish intuition. Ben turns back to work. Julie leans back in and chews. After a minute, snap. Mike's hands are free. He doesn't budge but a thrill of hope tumbles through the group.

Gravel jumps up, "This is boring. Who plays poker? Ben?"

"Gravel, I'm busy."

Gravel points to Hank and Dan. "You and you. We're playing

poker."

"I don't know how to play poker," Hank says.

"No shit? What are you a fuckin' pussy? Listen, kid…" Every time one of the Burne boys addresses his son, Hank has to suppress a surging rage. He stays calm only with great effort. Gravel continues to Jimmy, "If your dad can't teach you to play poker find someone who can." Gravel looks at Bella, "Maybe your mom. My mom taught us." Jimmy starts to say something and stops. He looks at Bella, turns away, and buries is head in his dad's lap. Ben sees this. Ben and Hank make eye contact. They hold for a moment. Even with his attention buried inside this carburetor Ben can tell something isn't right over there. Something is off with this little family. He will have to figure that out soon as he is done with this.

Gravel says frustrated, "Where the hell is Theo? He plays a good game."

Kent agrees, "No one can bluff like Theo."

Ben says to Kent, "Go check on him. Maybe he needs a hand."

"Not as if he can yell if he needs help." Gravel finds himself funny.

"Hey, yeah," Kent adds excited to show off his knowledge, "if a mute yells in the forest and no one hears him, did he still yell? Wasn't that a Zen thing? I don't know if you noticed Ben, but I'm very well read since you were gone."

"Yeah, I did. And obviously saving time by reading every other word. Go check on your brother." Kent throws on his trench coat. "And take the flashlight." Kent takes the light from the table. He walks to the door buttoning his coat and leaves. Over in the corner, the hostages recognize their advantage. Only two Burne brothers at the moment and Mike's hands are free. Now. Now is the time. Hank whispers to Bella behind him. "Can you get him closer?" He indicates a totem statue he can kick with his foot. She gets it. They are instantly primed, encouraged to try something. The helplessness of waiting and the fear of what's coming are eating away at them.

Mike whispers to Hank. "I'm gonna go for the automatic on the chair." The large weapon lies on the wooden rocking chair not far from the hearth.

Bella makes a little humming noise. Gravel looks. Slowly, seductively, she licks her lips. Gravel doesn't need much encouragement; he is rock hard in his pants day and night. He grins and starts over to the group. She eggs him on with a look and a small knowing grin.

He stands near the group. "You know," he says to her, "I could be extra nice..."

Hank's leg juts out kicking the base of the totem. It crashes down on Gravel's left shoulder. Mike is instantly on his feet. He leaps over Jimmy and goes for the weapon on the rocking chair. Ben dives for his weapon on the floor not far from where he is working on the carburetor. Gravel throws off the totem, which hit him hard. Ben is too quick. Mike is in midair lunging for the gun when Ben fires one shot nailing Mike between the eyes and Mike is dead before he hits the floor.

Ben turns the gun on the group with an eerie calm, "Who's next?"

The hostages huddle closer together. Julie closes her eyes. Bruce and Grant drop their heads and wait, not knowing what will come now. Gravel removes his gun from his belt and as he points, "They're all next."

"Gravel, a moment." Ben's voice stops him. Gravel whips his angry face back toward his brother. Ben asks politely, "Please." Gravel drops his aim, walks quickly over to Ben and a quiet exchange ensues. Ben speaks slowly with a hint of condescension. "So this is the deal. We don't know who else is on the island, or who else might show up here. At present, these people are our insurance, our chips in the game so to speak. Understand?"

"Of course, I understand. I'm not stupid. I risked my ass to get you out of the pen. It was my brains, my plan."

"Yes, a good plan, a bit messy."

Gravel hates it when he talks to him this way. "We could've left you there."

Ben grabs his shoulder affectionately, "No, you couldn't." They grin at each other. No, he couldn't. Breaking through the rivalry is their affection. Ben acquiesces to satisfy his brother. "Okay, tell you what, go ahead and waste..." he looks over to choose.

Kent throws open the lodge door, "Theo's dead."

Ben and Gravel ask in distress, "What? What happened?"

Kent is visibly upset. "I found some tracks and followed them. Looks like he slipped off a drop into some rocks. I almost went over myself except I was walking really slow with the light."

"Did you check him?" Ben demands.

"Can't get down there."

"Give me the light." Ben and Gravel rush for the door. "Make sure they're tied. Tied sufficiently this time. And keep your gun on you." Left behind, Kent kicks one of the chairs. He cannot believe his brother is gone. He pushes and kicks each of the hostages around as he checks their ties.

Bella says sympathetically, "I'm so really sorry about your brother." Kent looks at her unsure of her meaning. "I had a little brother. He was hit by a drunk driver."

"Whenever we got drunk Theo always drove. He didn't drink because he was afraid it would blur is speech." Kent chuckles sadly, "Yeah, he was really funny."

She smiles warmly trying to engage him, "Yes, I could tell that about him."

"Awfully good thing Mother isn't here."

"Mother's do have special feelings for their sons."

"Mom was the best, most of the time. She didn't want to get old so we suffocated her."

Bella swallows hard, "Oh, how thoughtful."

"Mom would want us to pray. Yes. We should all pray. All say a prayer to Jesus for Theo right the fuck now." Everyone bows their heads. Every time Hank thinks he's getting some kind of useful profile on the Burne boys something like this throws him off. He begins to wonder if there is a way to get inside Kent's head if he's religious. Maybe he's the weak link in the Burne chain. And each of them on the floor realizes they again have an advantage alone with only Kent there, but their last advantage is lying with blood dripping out of the hole between his eyes.

CHAPTER FOURTEEN

RUNNING WITH PRECISE FOOTFALLS ALISON'S breathing has fallen into a heavy rhythm. She has followed the directions Curtis gave and sees the log cabin up ahead. She runs to it, bounds up the steps, opens the door, and steps inside.

Curtis sits at the table in front of the shortwave with a pile of books, and a mess of dirty plates. He levels his gaze on the woman in the doorway, muddied hair, ragged clothing, with various cuts and bruises, Alison stands gulping air and shivering.

"Well, well, Barbie goes commando."

She thinks are there only animals on this island? "Where's the gun?"

"Coffee?" He offers her a steaming cup. She looks at it not wanting to give in. "Come on, looks like you need it. No charge." She grabs the cup and drinks down the hot liquid feeling it like a warm palm running down the inside of her throat. She did need it, but she refuses to feel grateful. Not to him. Not to this guy. She looks at this strong able man, unwilling to get off his ass to help, and her mind goes icy. She would hate him but that takes energy and time, neither of which she has.

"The gun?"

"You look about ready to collapse there, lady."

"I don't have that luxury. Whatever it is you want, can we just get on with it quickly?" There is an implicit sexual connotation hidden in the words, assuming he is the lowest life has to offer. She challenges his hard gaze and a tear rolls down the side of her nose. It is peculiar because she doesn't feel like crying, or like she is crying, she feels like the whole inside of her is shut down. She would be surprised to learn tears are on her cheeks. Tears are so useless. There is no time for useless.

Curtis eyes her. She is about what he expected some middle-aged crazy chick hoping someone else will fight her battles. She pays her taxes and expects the cavalry on call. What could he possibly want from her? "I don't want anything from you." His tone suddenly tinged with ire, "I don't want anything from anyone. I would've thought that was obvious."

"I could use some help," she demands.

"My hero days are over." He points to the footlocker. "Gun's in there. Help yourself. Just bring it back." Alison kneels down and rummages through the footlocker. She finds a small caliber handgun.

She asks, "Is this big enough to kill someone?"

"If you've been taught to aim."

"I was absent that day."

"You'll have to dig around in there for the ammo."

She begins to haul things out of the trunk and onto the floor.

"I'm not a particularly neat person."

"What are you some kind of hermit?"

"Hell, no. I talk to people all over the world. It's the way I like it. Connected and yet blissfully uninvolved in the tribulations of others."

Every second she is away from the lodge, she is wondering if her family is still alive. She begins to feel panicky. "I can't find 'em. Where are the bullets?"

"They're in there."

She turns on him with palpable vitriol, "Look, I don't know if you're a psycho, an asshole, or just a damn coward, but I need bullets and some clue how to load and fire this thing." He feels slapped; it is jarring.

Alison's strength is born from quaking desperation. It impresses him. She walks over to where he sits. She puts her hands on the table so they are face-to-face. She drops the battle-edged energy and lets her voice come through, a voice that has the quality of all mothers in pain. Leaning in, "They are going to shoot my little boy." She reaches through the cobwebs draping Curtis' long capitulated conscience. "His name is Jimmy. He's nine years old." Curtis hears these words as though he were his old self, before it all. After a pause of connection, Curtis swings his chair around and cautiously lowers himself to the cabin floor revealing the utter uselessness of his legs. Alison stands aside as his arms pull him over to the footlocker. In another time, in another place, she would have felt genuine sympathy, but there is no room for that now. She is becoming a hunter; the aperture of a once expansive mind has closed down to a single focus. She feels no pain from her scratches and bruises. She doesn't notice the blood dripping down her cheek. All she thinks now when she watches Curtis crawl is that he will not be as useful as she'd hoped.

Moments later, on Curtis' dilapidated porch, Alison loads the gun. He remarks, "Hope this old thing works. Haven't tried it in years." Alison raises the weapon and aims. "Wait." he stops her.

"What?"

"Stop."

"Why?"

"The sound will carry. Might as well announce you're here over Hobbs' P.A."

"Thunder. I can use the thunder as cover."

"Good you're smart. You'll need it."

"I need the SEALS."

"You will have to separate these guys to have a chance. Take them out one at a time." She nods her head. Her chin shakes a little. It is the only visual evidence that she is holding back emotion. Curtis continues, "Course, they are stronger and better armed." A flash of lightning and she counts.

"One banana, two banana, three banana, four..."

Crash thunder.

She confirms "Four and a half."

"Storm's moving away."

"So I go on five."

"On five." And they wait. She stares into the night and waits for lightning. She waits for it. She wills it.

* * *

Back at the lodge, Kent has been left behind with the hostages. In frustrated moves of callous disrespect, he drags and kicks Mike's body out the back door. Hank exchanges a look of condolence with Dan who is dazed having just witnessed the murder of his best friend. Julie cries soundlessly with only her shoulders moving up and down slightly. Ed looks powerlessly at his weeping wife and wonders just how short their new lives together are going to be. Bruce and Grant who are sitting cross-legged have leaned all the way forward until their heads rest on their knees. Bella manages to stroke Dan with one of her tied hands.

This swimming feeling in Hank's head is counterproductive. He knows he must manhandle it and achieve rationality. He needs order and calm to function. Control. Review: Gravel seems to be the most violent and unpredictable. Kent could probably be talked into anything, he seems a little bit like a lap dog: easy to command and eager to please. Ben is a mystery, although he seems the most reasonable. He might be convinced to let Jimmy live. He's only a kid. They are clearly heading for Canada. Jimmy can't hurt them. Perhaps with the right words he can at least save his son, which could be okay since Alison is still out there and with this thought his head swims again. His wife. His tender wife who did not want to come. Who came for him. She is surely in shock, frozen in the icy rain, watching terrified and alone. He knows there is no help coming. This is his fault. This trip was his idea. Guilt begins to bury him and he stops it—no, not constructive, stop. He must do. Now is not the time to accept, but to keep trying. His last try killed Mike. These men didn't even flinch before gunning down Hobbs and Mike. It was as ordinary to them as tossing a ball. Hank's eyes drift out the window. Are you there? My darling, can you see me? Can you hear me? Forgive me for not being able to help you. Stay hidden. Stay safe. As he sinks into worry over Alison, he feels heavy and exhausted.

Gravel and Ben stomp into the room slamming the lodge door. They are pissed, which is how they grieve.

Ben paces, "Goddamn it."

"I made them all pray to Jesus. So we got that going for him." Kent reassures them.

Gravel responds, "His gun's still on him down there."

"So he slipped?" Kent asks.

"Looks like it." Gravel plops down on the sofa.

With affection Kent says, "Clumsy big-footed lug nut."

Ben, ever cautious, "What if he was pushed?"

Gravel asks, "You think someone's out there?"

"Something just doesn't feel right. Keep your guns on you." Ben goes back to the carburetor on the floor.

Gravel says, "Hurry up and fix that fuckin' thing so we can finish things up and get the hell outta here."

"Not just dirty, got a part problem, I'm working it."

Everyone on the floor knows perfectly well that finish-things-up refers to them, everyone knows this but Jimmy who thinks it means they'll leave and he'll be able to go find his mom.

"So, Dad, they'll leave soon."

"Yes, Jimmy, I hope so."

CHAPTER FIFTEEN

- - - - - - - - - - - - -

O N CURTIS' PORCH, THEY WAIT for lightning, knowing if it does not come in the next couple of minutes, she will have to go on faith that the gun will fire. Every second she wastes here, her son, her husband, and the others face the probability of being shot. She feels this responsibility in every cell of her body. In this brief pause, she admits to herself she will probably die tonight. Her family will probably die tonight. Please, for Jimmy, let him go first; let it be quick. How odd to know this in advance: to watch death approaching and to see that death comes not on a majestic pale horse at all, but on the wings of a whim, in a moment when someone asked shall we go fishing? How arbitrary. Who lives, who dies, each day—how arbitrary—and how pitifully frantic we are to make sense of it, to make order of it, to make it understandable when it simply isn't. And then, standing on Curtis' porch immune to the cold and the wet Alison asks for one thing from the universe—if Hank and Jimmy die, please me too. I cannot live knowing I had the chance and I could not save them. And I cannot live without them. I will not. She knows that it is this truth that is giving her the strength to fight. She doubts these men will leave witnesses. She will gladly take a shot to the heart rather than hold her dead family in her arms. She knows what her odds are against three vicious men. Her strength comes not so much from a belief that she will be able to kill the bad guys and save the day, but more from an unconscious resolution to live together or die together. That is her truth. She has no illusions about who she is, or about how this will end. And it is this understanding that calms her. It will play out as it must.

Curtis says, "You'll need to get close. You may only get one shot."

She nods. They wait loaded and ready.

Then, quietly, to no one, "Nothing in my life has prepared me for this."

"You can't prepare for this."

She cannot wait too much longer. Each passing second the drive to confirm her family is still alive pumps more adrenaline into her body. One more minute.

She asks him, "What happened to your legs?" Odd, she thinks, this would have been a question she was too polite to ask before this night. Tonight there are no social rules.

"Firefighter."

"Oh. Something collapsed on you?"

"I was putting out a blaze in the hood and some gang kid used me for target practice." She turns her eyes to him and sees Curtis for the first time as a person sitting on the porch. The crusty delivery of his words does not veil the betrayal. He is looking away into the distant dark nothingness. She reaches out and touches his shoulder. It is a fleeting gesture. It is what she has always done unconsciously. Sometimes it is a gentle brush of her hand on another's arm as she engages in conversation; sometimes it is a little squeeze as she laughs, or a tiny push away meant to pull nearer. She penetrates the personal glass shell and just that simple contact draws people to her over the natural bridge it forms. He does not look back at her, but he feels being touched for the first time in years.

She turns her eyes out into the same darkness that holds his gaze as says quietly to herself, "The world is not what I thought it was."

"Me, either."

"How long have you been here?"

"Eight years."

"It seems it would be harder to live here without assistance than back in the world."

"The world's the problem."

"Yeah."

A crack of lightning strikes her to attention. She aims at a tree in front.

She counts, "One banana, two banana, three banana, four bana…"

She pulls the trigger simultaneously with the thunderclap. The timing is perfect. The gun jerks back and fires. Yes. It fires. She is thrilled and ready to bolt toward the lodge. Curtis stops her.

"Aim for the chest and keep firing until he goes down. Don't stop firing until he's down."

"Yes."

"If you can, find a way to use the gun as a last resort. Surprise is your only advantage right now." Even though her chin shakes, she is focused like a laser on what he is saying. "If you come up against one of them in close contact, go for the eyes. Anything else will be useless for you."

She repeats, "Eyes."

"Don't hesitate. Don't hold back. Take this." He hands her a knife. She puts it in her belt. "Check the storage shed. Hobbs had a lot of shit in there. Use your brain. It's your best asset."

"Yes." She leaps off the porch and vanishes into the woods. He will wait for the gunfire and then he'll know it's over. He, too, understands the odds. He has stayed reclusive in these woods so his mind and emotions would remain as insensate as his legs. He has been at peace here, but he has not been alive. Having Alison blast into his consciousness has clarified that. She is what alive looks like. Seeing her run heedlessly into the woods is really no different from when he would run into a burning building. And while it has been his life's goal not to care again, he cannot deny his need to see her survive, to succeed. He wants something today. He hasn't wanted anything in such a long time. It feels peculiar. He wants her to win and he knows precisely how unlikely that is. If there's any justice in the universe this young mom running around bloody and half-mad trying to save her family should win, but justice is accidental. Most of the women he's ever known would have crawled crying into a hole and waited it out—hell, most men would have, too. Maybe that's exactly what he has done.

In the lodge, Ben processes the problem with the carburetor float. Can he fix it? Should he try to replace it? He just loves puzzles. He decides to check the tool bench outside on the porch. He rises from where he's been working on the floor. Every time one of the Burne brothers moves the hostages tense. Ben feels their fear. He's embarrassed for them; what a pathetic little group of rodents. He opens the front door and steps out onto the porch. To the left, up against the building, is a tool bench. He lifts the top and searches inside. Alison creeps up onto the porch and aligns herself along one of the log posts. She slips the knife from her belt. She closes it into her fist, but wait, the stabbing needs to be down, and so she turns the grip in her hand so the blade points down. Jesus, she thinks. Oh, god, can I do this? Her throat is so tight she cannot swallow her own saliva. She closes her eyes and brings Jimmy's face to mind. Her arm and leg muscles contract. Adrenaline floods her forcing her heart to pump harder. Every pore in her body opens and she becomes instantly clammy. She prepares to strike.

Bent over the tool bench, Ben raises his eyes. He senses her. He spins around. Methodically, he scans the woods in front. She is not visible only feet from him. Ben smirks at himself; too much time in the pen has his antenna's working overtime. He returns his attention to the toolbox.

She runs through it: three quick steps, plunge it in. It'll be gory. He might yell. Have to hope he doesn't. So close though. Not like sending someone over a cliff. She lays her eyes on exactly the point in his back where she will do it. This is it. Go. She yells inside. Do it. She wills her feet to move. She grips the knife. Go! Frustration builds toward explosion. She is paralyzed.

Ben chooses a small metal piece he hopes he can make work. He flips the cover down on the tool bench and walks back inside the lodge closing the door. Alison smacks her head against the post in defeat. Her opportunity. She hits her head hard enough to bring a lump, but she doesn't feel it. Shit. Rage engulfs her. She wants to scream aloud. She screams inside so hard and long that her face goes red and then blue, her muscles shake with unrestrained energy.

Minutes later, inside Hobbs' cabin talking to Curtis, she is livid with herself. "He was right there. The first guy was chasing me. It just happened." She begins to whine in trembling anger. "I had the knife. I couldn't make my arm move, or my feet move." She is nearly hysterical.

"Don't melt down, Alison. Killing isn't easy for most of us."

"Goddamn it. God, god…"

"The other guy was kind of an accident. This is different. First, calm down."

"Ughhh…" an animal like cry.

"You have to outthink them. Use what is on hand. Check the shed. I'll keep trying to reach someone. The storm is lifting. It's all I can do. I'll keep trying. Go."

She hates herself. That may have been her only opportunity, her best chance, and she failed. She has failed to save her child. Fear has been replaced with fury. Anger is the framework now supporting her, now keeping her from collapse. Anger is at least useful. She leaves the cabin and heads for the shed, which is about fifteen yards from the lodge on the path up from the dock. Be smart. Be smarter. Her feet have learned the terrain with exceptional speed. She knows instantly what is solid and what only looks solid. Like any animal in danger, her awareness is heightened and her muscle memory is flawless. Moving with alacrity and experience she has become a competent forest animal. She sneaks inside the shed. It is a tin structure. A countertop runs along three sides and holds what must be hundreds of screws, nails, saws, tools of all kinds. She finds a flashlight, very useful, as the floodlights from the lodge are quite dim here. She covers the light so it only casts a direct beam. She flips it on. There are old motors, anchors, clamps, ropes, what looks like a generator. The side wall has hooks holding fishing nets and lures. On the far wall on larger metal hooks various fishing poles, a harpoon, and several axes all orange with rust.

Ben tries to make one of the little metal parts he found in the tool bench work in the carburetor. Gravel snores on the sofa. The hostages, worn from terror, sit together in the corner. Kent flips through a book. Ben glances at the group. He watches as Jimmy realizes his foot is touching Bella. He pulls it back and presses against his dad. Ben rises from the floor. He slowly walks over to Jimmy. Electrified, the group tenses.

Ben speaks to Jimmy, "Hey, kid." Jimmy looks up scared. "Is that really your mother?" He indicates Bella. Jimmy doesn't know what to say. "Because I'm curious why you'd say it was if it wasn't."

Hank answers calmly, "It's his stepmom. We've only just married."

Bella adds quickly, "Jimmy is having a problem accepting me."

"Yeah? Now he's got bigger problems." Ben turns away, "Kent?"

"Yup."

"Go out to the shed and try and find me some metal-to-metal epoxy." Kent puts on his coat, tucks his gun into his pant belt, and takes the flashlight. Ben continues, "And watch your step."

"Hey, I'm not Theo. God rest is soul." Kent makes the sign of the cross and leaves slamming the porch door.

The lodge door slams, instantly Alison flips off the flashlight. Her reflexes are sharpening. She peeks out the crack in the shed door. She sees Kent approaching. Oh, no. He walks slowly, stepping cautiously on the slippery rocks as his eyes adjust slowly to the scattered light and darkness.

She steps back from the door. What? She looks around. Here he comes. This time she will have no choice. Either way this is it. There is nowhere to hide. She looks at the axes and the harpoon. She grabs the harpoon and studies it in the dark. Her eyes are well adjusted. She finds the trigger. It is heavy. Here he comes. She rests her elbow on the countertop to steady it. Will it work? Here he comes. Is there a safety? Where's the safety? Here he comes. The rain has let up so she hears his sloshing footsteps. It is now. Kent swings open the shed door and steps inside. His flashlight scans the room and hits her standing there pointing the harpoon right at him. Kent stares at her stunned. She is drenched and filthy. He sees her finger on the trigger. "Shit!" He reaches for his gun. She pulls the trigger. Flump! The harpoon spear comes out with so much force it throws her back as it skewers Kent's chest and nails him to the back wall of the tin shed. His eyes are opened wide. His body jerks in spasms. She steps back horrified. It wasn't quiet. She had hoped for quiet. Someone screamed. She knows he screamed. Or she screamed. Someone screamed. She begins to tremble convulsively. Yes, he screamed.

Gravel flies out of the lodge his weapon drawn and heading for the shed and at dead run. Alison sees him blast through the opened shed doorway. Think. Gravel is inside shocked to see his brother's life oozing away pinned to the wall. He spins. And there is Alison.

Dramatically, "Oh god, those men killed this poor man!" She looks skinny and helpless.

"What men?" Gravel is in a fury. "How many?"

"Four."

"Where are they?"

"There!" She points behind him. He whirls around ready to attack. He peers out from the shed. Alison leaps forward and with what she is sure will be the last move of her life, and with all the force that she can rally, for her husband, for her son, she plunges her knife up to the handle into Gravel's back. She lets go and steps back expecting him to fall. He does not fall. He does not yell in pain. He turns his crazed eyes to her realizing. With manic rage and sudden speed, he jumps on top of her and they go down.

"Bitch. I'm going to strip your face from your skull while you're still alive."

He punches her in the face shattering her cheekbone. She reaches the knife in his back and twists. He rears up painfully. She pulls the handgun from her pants and flat on her back, screaming, she fires into his stomach, and again, and again, and again. He doubles over on top of her. He manages to point his gun at her and she shoots him in the forehead.

The shots echoed. In the lodge, Ben is instantly on his feet.

In Curtis' cabin, he knows what this means. Engagement. The end. He sweeps his arm across the table throwing everything to the floor. "Damn." Maybe someone is alive. Maybe her boy is still alive. Maybe someone escaped. What have I become here? What am I?

Gravel lies dead and hemorrhaging on top of her. His shocked and staring eyeballs are inches from her face. Her breaths are coming in short convulsive gasps. Off. Ah—off! She pulls herself out from under him. He is heavy but she slides because of the pooling blood. She continues to aim at his dead body and uses her feet to push away on her back. She sits. She is covered in blood and sweat. Her right cheek is turning deep purple and her eye swells. She struggles to her feet.

Ben slides up next to the front door and yells out, "Gravel?" "Kent?" No response. Wild-eyed, he walks to the hostages. "Who is out there?" No response from the terrified group. Ben grabs Bruce, jerks him to his feet, and shoots him dead. Agonizing screams from the hostages. "Again, who is out there?"

Alison hears the gunshot from inside the lodge. She grabs Gravel's gun from his dead wet hand. Suddenly, she feels so oddly calm; the lights have been turned off inside of her and she is at peace in the dark. She is not confused. She is not scared. Everything that hurt has stopped hurting.

CHAPTER SIXTEEN

– – – – – – – – – – – – –

O N THE FLOOR OF THE forest, approaching the lodge, hands are digging into the mud, a pair of strong hands, pulling through the dirt, grabbing the exposed tree roots and using them to propel his body. Moving at a powerful speed. Closing the distance. Released from a nihilistic void, Curtis crawls into violence.

Alison kneels down, gets some leverage, and wrenches her knife from Gravel's back. She meticulously wipes it on his jacket and slips it back into her pants. Abruptly, a blast of static and then, loudly over the camp P.A. system, Ben's voice.

"Listen carefully," Ben's voice fills the air.

Alison slinks from the tin shack and drops to the ground behind a rock between the shed and the lodge.

In the lodge over by the bookcase, Ben holds the microphone for the P.A. system. His tone carries the sureness that comes naturally from being the smartest one in the room. His chilling authority is implicit in every word. "I'm going to kill one hostage every five minutes until you come on in here so we can chat. And for everyone's sake, my brothers had better not be hurt. You have four minutes."

Alison considers her options. She could rush the main room

shooting. But Jimmy or Hank could be easily killed that way. Think.

Meanwhile, those arms, muscular and gnarled, pull, pull, over the ground and approach the lodge because Curtis is no longer numb. He feels it. He can't help but feel it. His breathing is thick and labored but he is not slowing down. He is almost there. To do what? He doesn't know. He knows only that doing nothing is no longer his life.

Alison analyzes in eerie stillness. She scans the area around the lodge, the path, the shed—all areas she knows thoroughly now. She sees with different eyes. The connections in her mind have been rearranged. What is left of her grip on humanity is screaming at her not to allow another hostage death. Rationally, she knows giving up kills everyone. She knots her fingers in her hair and it looks like she might yank it out by the roots and not even notice.

Over the P.A., "Three minutes."

And she lets loose. Alison utters a long loud wail, a wail that has been waiting, that has been gathering inside of her since that very first moment. It is an aberrant sound: not recognizably human yet not resembling any animal. The plaintiff yowl echoes through the camp with a searing rawness. Ben hears it and finds it exciting. It stirs the ugly stew at the core of him. He doesn't know what he's dealing with, but if it sent his brothers into hiding, it must be powerful and cunning. The possibility that someone could have killed both his brothers is unthinkable. He considers what tools are at his disposal. He knows he is missing something. Something has been bothering him. And then, what he can only attribute to divine intervention, as a gift from God it comes to him. A small grin crawls across his face. He locks eyes with Hank. Hank holds his stare defiantly, but he sees it: the shift, the twinkle of delight from a puzzle solved. Ben begins talking directly to Hank and walking over, "I think the lady wants to be left alone. That's what you said to my brother. I think *the lady* wants to be left alone. Like you didn't know her. Odd words for a husband." Hank does not give in to the force of Ben's gaze. He holds his eyes with strength and says nothing. Bella's stomach cramps and she fights a wave of nausea. Julie hasn't lifted her head for an hour and Ed fears she is in deep shock.

"Aw," Ben continues, "but this is easy." He takes the muzzle of his weapon and points directly at Hank's head. Hank does not flinch. He will not cringe in front of his son. He maintains. Jimmy begins to quiver. Without taking his gaze from Hank, Ben asks Jimmy. "So, kid, that's not your mother there, is it?"

Jimmy is petrified and can barely form a word, "Ah…"

"Your mother's out there isn't she?" Ben moves the muzzle of the gun to rest on Hank's left eye socket.

Jimmy cries out, "Don't please. Yes. Yes. Please"

Ben always feels such a pleasant thrill when he's calculated correctly. He loves that rush of superiority. He lowers the gun. He savors a moment of triumph face-to-face with Hank. Then, he bends down and grabs Jimmy by his arms, which are still tied behind his back. He drags him across the lodge floor as all of the hostages beg for him. Hank dives out after his son. With his ankles tied, his arms secured behind his back, all he can do is crawl on his knees and face. He saw the menace in Ben's eyes. He knows pleading is worthless.

Hank explodes, "I'll kill you! Let him go." Hank crawls. "I'll come back from the grave if I have to."

Ben responds coolly, "You'll have to." He stands Jimmy on his feet, opens the lodge door, and pushes him out onto the porch. Ben steps out and ducks behind using Jimmy as a shield. He slams the door leaving Hank flailing around on the wood.

"Bitch. I've got your brat."

Alison lying flat in some brush within sight of the lodge sees Jimmy. She sees his terrified expression and the tears on his face. She feels his fear and it feeds her fury.

Ben shoves Jimmy to the edge of the porch. "Woman, I am not a patient man."

Something catches her glance. Underneath the lodge, in the crawl space, Curtis is dragging himself through the sludge. He is now directly below Ben and Jimmy. Ben is unaware.

Alison yells to distract, "I have your brother. Trade?"

Hank is riveted to hear her voice. That's Alison. She's alive. He shimmies his body up to the window to try to see. The other hostages are chewing on each other's ties and making progress.

"I don't like trades. Get out here with my brother at the count of three or I'll start by shooting out this kid's knee and then work my way up excruciatingly slowly."

Hank lies flat out on the floor as Ed bites at his binding to free him.

Underneath the porch, Curtis sees the tips of Jimmy's sneakers. He rolls onto his back so both his hands are free.

Ben begins, "One...two..."

Alison stands revealing herself fifteen yards away. For the first time, Ben and Alison lay eyes on each other. They connect animal-to-animal. Jimmy gasps at the sight of his mother: battered, bloodied, armed. Ben reviews this skinny beaten up woman.

Curtis' strong hands dart up suddenly, unexpectedly, from under the porch; grabbing Jimmy by his shins, with all his might he pulls. He propels Jimmy off the porch and face down into the mud. Alison opens fire on Ben now exposed. Ben dives for cover rolling off the porch.

Inside the lodge, Hank yells wild with anguish. Bullets strafe the cabin: breaking windows, gouging chunks out of the bookcase. Hank crawls, staying low, to the door.

Ben returns fire as he takes cover. Alison darts into the woods reloading her handgun. Ben races to the shed and looks inside. Kent hangs limp harpooned to the wall. Gravel is dead on the floor. Ben's whole family is gone because of her. He takes off after her. He is enraged. He will hunt her until she's dead, and then, he will hunt her into hell.

Hank bursts out onto the porch in time to see Curtis untying Jimmy. He falls on the ground and hugs his son.

"Dad."

"Who are you?" Hank asks.

Jimmy says, "He helped me."

Curtis says, "Get back inside." Jimmy and Hank grab Curtis, haul him up the two porch steps and inside the lodge. All of the other hostages are free now. They are moving furniture, covering the windows, and setting up a barricade.

Jimmy is crying hard for the first time, "Dad."

Hank holds him, "Yes. Okay."

"I saw mom. She's…she's…" There are no words to describe his mom.

As they fortify the room Curtis tells them, "I got through to 911. They're sending helicopters. There's been some kind of manhunt for these guys."

Hank heads for the door as he asks Jimmy. "Where'd she go?"

Curtis answers, "She's out to get the last guy."

Hank finds this information hard to process. Why? What does he mean? On purpose? In the distance, shots are fired. Hank sprints for the door. Dan emerges from the kitchen with an ax and several butcher knives. Dan and Grant, both suffering from heartbreaking loss, are unwilling to sit and wait.

"Let's go get this motherfucker," Dan says.

Bella asks, "Are you sure you should go out there?"

Jimmy implores, "Dad, don't. Please don't go."

Hank looks into his son's face, "Jimmy, she's alone."

"Dad." Jimmy's confused, "She didn't look…normal."

Hank kisses his son on the top of his head and turns for the door. Bella steps forward and puts her arm around Jimmy. The three men head for the door.

Grant yells back, "Barricade after we're gone."

"Hey," Curtis yells after them, "Don't sneak up on her. Really."

Dan, Grant, and Hank run into the woods.

CHAPTER SEVENTEEN

A LISON GLIDES SUREFOOTED AWAY FROM camp, purposefully drawing Ben away from her family. Ben pursues. He will get her. He will absolutely get her. His rage is cold. Now, it is just the woods and them. Alison slows her pace. Where should she lead him? Ben listens for the break of a branch, the swish of a twig. He studies her tracks; deeper, closer footprints in the mud indicate she is walking now—strategizing. They begin a deadly mime dance for survival. She has one goal: to draw him as far away from Jimmy as she can and the farther she travels into the woods the safer she now feels. It is no longer her enemy, but her cover, her friend. The sky lightens. A red watercolor dawn spreads out along the horizon. The storm has ended. She dreads the light having come to rely on the erasure of night.

Adeptly, Alison uses a few rocks as steps and propels herself up to a tree branch where she can climb a little higher and look around. During last night, long buried animal instincts crept to the surface of her, and she knows now that Ben is there, just as he knows she is near. A mighty cord has formed attaching them, bonding them. When they caught each other's eyes, it was clear that both of them would not, could not survive: one of them will come to the end—and they must play it out—to that end—until it's over. They are joined in an epic fight: eye for eye, family for family, one winner. Perched on this tree limb, she begins to feel the ache in her bones. Her head swims and she starts to break down. She tells herself that even if I die now they will have had time to prepare back at the camp. They will be okay. She could give in, let go, and suddenly that is exactly what she wants. What if she just lies down in the brush? Maybe he finds her, maybe he doesn't. What if she just lies down still? She wants to lie down; she aches to lie down, please can she lie down and let be what will be. She is suddenly so tired. Her head falls forward. Her beaten body wavers on the branch. Her arms are too heavy to lift. Her legs throb. Emotion crawls up her parched throat. She's done enough. Hasn't she done enough? Two dark spots form in her mind's eye. Slowly, the illusion takes shape—they are the eyes of Ben. The eyes she saw right before she ran. Then, she knows. He'll go back. She knows this is the truth: he will go back and kill her family. He will drag back her body, show it to her son, and then kill them slowly. They do not understand him. She doesn't know why she understands him; she just knows that she does—deep in the core of her she knows who he is, what he will do. She opens her eyes. Something moves. Over to the left. She strains to see through the wall of green. Yes, a body, Ben's body moving cautiously because he senses her too, but he does not think to look up. This will end it. Her eyes clear and her hand steadies. She aims at his head. Confident. She will hit him. She pulls the trigger. Instead of the explosive bang she is expecting, a small clicking sound. She pulls again. It's empty. She pulls and pulls. The gun is empty. She thought she reloaded. She looks down at the weapon confused. Ben heard it. Was it a cricket? No, the sound of an empty gun. He looks up and catches sight of her as she drops from the tree and disappears. Ben accelerates through the forest after her.

Darting left, she realizes that with no gun she must hide. Moving around is making too much noise and she looks for a place. Ahead a couple of downed trees and a few rocks form a bit of a covey. She settles into it. Minutes go by. No movement. No noise. Ben learns very quickly, how to place his foot on the center of the rock, as he moves so if it is unsteady it doesn't buckle. He learns some leaves make crackling sounds when he steps on them and others are silent. He learns, like she learned, and at a staggering speed. Where Alison hides there is a small pool of rainwater in a cup of granite and it looks like life itself to her. Her throat is sticking together. She leans in and puts her lips to the pool. She drinks and it is heavenly as it soothes her. Ben sees a footprint near the fallen logs. Stealthily, he moves around the little cubby. From an angle to the right, he can get a view through some branches and he sees her bent over the water. He puts his weapon in his pants. He moves in. His hands itch. He needs to kill her with his bare hands. He will not deny himself that pleasure. He needs to close his hands around her throat and slowly strangle the breath out of her while she looks him in the eyes knowing what is happening. Alison lifts her head from the pool. The first rays of the rising sun break through the trees behind Ben and cast his shadow across the rock in front of her. He's right there. She lunges out of the cubby. He dives and grabs her shin. They both go down. She bends at the waist over a log. He goes down hard on the granite. He reaches to grabs her other leg. She clutches a medium-sized stone into her fist. Eyes. Eyes. She whips her hand back and strikes him in the eye. He recoils for a split second. She crawls over the log and stumbles to her feet. She goes. He is right behind her. She breaks out of the woods and stops just short of sheer drop to the beach fifty feet below. Ben emerges from the woods and walks deliberately toward her. Taking his time. Step after slow step, he walks toward her slowly, because she is trapped and he wants her to feel it. She drops her hands to her sides. They stand looking at each other. His family dead. Hers soon to be. The waterlogged ground shifts from Ben's added weight. She sees what's happening. In his rage and triumph, flooded with the euphoria of revenge, he sees only her. She jumps with all her might sideways and catches a small limb of a baby tree with one hand as the ground triggered by his added weight gives way to a mudslide that carries Ben down the drop. She pulls herself up to solid ground. On her hands and knees, she crawls to the edge looks down. He stands directly below, his entire body black with mud, his eyes white fire. His hatred sears her skin.

The roar of two helicopters interrupts the force field created by their keen singular concentration. They both look to the sky and see the police choppers zooming in. Then, locked eye-to-eye in a scorching intensity Ben speaks softly and even though his words are too faint to be heard over the roar and the distance, somehow, she hears him as if he were whispering directly into her ear. "It's not over." And in an instant, he is gone. Frozen on her hands and knees, she does not move. Her eyes remain glued to the spot where she lost sight of Ben. She waits. She watches. She could not tell you how much time passed before she hears something behind her.

"Alison?" Hank approaches with caution because while he can see it is his wife, something unnamable warns him to be careful. Alison doesn't move from the edge. Dan and Grant hang back as Hank crawls out to her on the shifting mud. Gently, Hank pulls her back to him. He looks into her expressionless face. He gathers her up in his arms and rocks her back and forth. He is crying. Her pants are ripped and what's left of her shirt is stiff with Gravel's dried blood. Her right eye is swollen almost shut. Her face and body are cut, bruised and filthy. They sit wrapped together in the mud. He does not feel her hugging back. He assumes this is exhaustion. He cannot see her face. If he could, he would see her eyes are still on the spot where Ben disappeared. She is still looking for him. "Alison." Hank holds her with all the force he can without hurting her further. He tries to reach her, "Alison...Allie?" Finally, she turns her attention to him. She sees him. It is Hank. He sees a flicker of herself in her face. He holds her rocking back and forth. "Jimmy is fine. Jimmy is fine." Hank scoots her back from the edge. Dan quickly removes his shirt and places it around her. She cannot move. And so no one moves for quite a long time. Dan and Grant sit down now too, and begin to grieve in earnest for their lost friends. They are a profoundly pained little group sitting in the mud. Just sitting. The three men crying. Alison staring, but not crying.

When they can, they start back. Alison, who is unable to support her own weight, is being physically supported between Grant and Hank. Dan has walked ahead clearing an easy path. They emerge into the small clearing by the lodge. The police are already in high gear. Each of the hostages is giving statements. Yellow tape surrounds the shed. Hobbs, Mike and Bruce's bodies are laid-out and covered respectfully with blankets while they wait for the body bags.

In a chair on the porch, Jimmy has been watching the woods, traumatized. And then, he sees them. He flies out of the chair. "Mom." He runs into her arms. She falls to her knees on the ground holding her son fiercely. He cries. She does not.

"You're hurt. You're so hurt. Mom, are you okay?"

"Are you?" she asks him. These are the first words she has spoken and it gives Hank a little solace to hear her voice.

"They killed Hobbs and Mike and Bruce, too."

"Yes. Terrible. Terrible. But you're okay."

"I'm okay, Mom."

Alison notices Curtis sitting on the edge of the lodge porch. She takes Jimmy's hand and she walks over to him.

"Hey." He nods at her.

"Hey," she responds.

He almost smiles, "You sure can kick-ass for someone unprepared."

"You sure can haul-ass for someone immobile."

"Yeah."

"Yeah. I thought your hero days were over."

"Some people never learn."

"Come back with us. You can stay in our home until..."

"Until I get back on my feet?"

"Metaphorically."

"And leave all of this?"

"All of what?"

"I think I'll run Hobbs' camp for a while. Break my way back into the peopled world slowly."

A stretcher passes them holding Kent's dead body. His chest is ripped wide open where the harpoon had penetrated and been removed. Jimmy grabs his mom around the waste and buries his face in her side. It is so gruesome, Hank and the others glance away. Alison stares like a predator. Curtis watches her and feels a little alarmed by it. She keeps her eyes on Kent until they have laid him on the ground next to Gravel. Then, she looks back.

"Excuse, me, Ma'am?" A young policeman approaches with Detective Coby. She moves her gaze slowly. She never lets go of Jimmy's hand. She never breaks down; she never cries; she never shows any emotion at all. Hank takes her hand in his. He is completely bewildered about what to say or do. He is helpless and he desperately wants to clutch her in his arms and let her cry, but something stands between them; something unseen has taken shape and is fixed between them.

The Detective begins. He is at a very high energy level. The scene in the camp is overwhelmingly gory even for a veteran Detective. "Ma'am, there seems to be some confusion."

"And a shitload of dead bodies," The young policeman adds. He gets a derisive gaze from the detective. "Well, there are."

Alison waits. She emits a strange vibration: an icy, unnerving fatigue.

Detective Coby prompts her, "I was told that you may know what happened to those two men?" He indicates Kent and Gravel. They walk a little way toward the two Burne brothers. When Alison begins to speak everyone quiets down to listen. Everyone wants to hear. Even hearing it from her mouth, it is hard to fathom. Dan, Grant, Ed, Julie and Bella move closer. Alison explains with a lifeless flat tone.

"I shoved the first one off the cliff." She points.

"There's another one?" He indicates for the policeman to check it out.

She continues indicating Kent, "I shot that one with the harpoon in the shed." Then pointing to Gravel, "That one, I stabbed but then I shot him over and over in the stomach and then once in the head." She looks at Detective Coby. "One got away." There is a silent pause as this sinks in. Then she says with powerful intensity, "You need to get the other one now. You have to kill the other one."

"We're searching. We'll find him. There's no way off here."

The policeman yells from an unseen spot in the woods, "Yeah. There's another one down there. A big one."

Detective Coby looks at this petite woman and all these corpses. It doesn't make sense and he asks, "Ma'am, are you a police officer?"

"No."

"Armed forces?"

"No."

"Do you mind if I ask what kind of training you've had?"

"I'm a mother."

She takes Jimmy by the hand, turns around, and leads him away. Detective Coby asks after her, "Ma'am..."

"It's Mrs. Kraft, not ma'am," Hank corrects him.

"Right, well," he starts after her to regain her attention. "So, Mrs. Kraft?"

She keeps walking toward the porch.

Hanks steps forcefully in front of Coby. "My wife is in shock, injured, and exhausted. Your questions will wait."

Alison sits down on the edge of the first porch step. Jimmy sits on the ground between her legs and rests his head on her thigh. One by one, all of the hostages stop talking and walk over. They settle in all around her. They are all damaged, and they all know no matter how impossible it seems, they are alive because of Alison. Dan rests his hand softly and in comfort on her shoulder. Bella places her hand on Alison's knee. Julie sits behind on the second step with her knees up against Alison's back. Ed puts his hand on Alison's hand. Grant rests his palm on her other shoulder. And in silence, they sit and breathe as one, forming a human bandage around Alison.

CHAPTER EIGHTEEN

T HE COAST GUARD BOAT CUTS effortlessly through the lake water. It is nothing like the trip to the island: with the storm spent, the lake is placid, almost friendly. Jimmy sits between his parents and all three hold hands. Alison has received some first aid. She has a butterfly bandage closing the gash by her right eye, and several sterile pads covering wounds on her knees, her elbows, and her stomach. Although she has changed into her sweat clothes, it is not enough because she is cold from the inside and so she is wearing Hank's coat, and still, in the bright sunlight, she shivers. Most of the mud is gone, but not all.

Back at the cabin, Hank had become concerned when she had stepped into the shower. He checked on her and he found that she'd forgotten to turn on the hot water and was standing inert and oblivious in the cold pour. He jumped in, wrapped his arms around her naked beaten body, and held on as he cranked up the hot water and waited for it to come through the pipe. Tenderly, he washed her body and her hair as best he could while cursing the teeny travel shampoo bottle that kept slipping from his hands. Jimmy yelled in every minute, "You okay, Dad?" He did not like that he couldn't see his mom and dad. He sat with his back up against the shower door waiting.

As the boat carries them along the water, Alison's head is angled back so she can watch the island recede. The others on the boat sit and stare at the floor. Grant's eyes brim with tears and Dan comforts him with a pat. His broken wrist is vigilantly wrapped. These two will never lose touch. They will know each other for the rest of their lives.

"Dad?" Jimmy whispers, "Mom's not okay."

"She needs some time, Jimmy. We all do."

Hank squeezes her hand. She does not respond. She can't take her eyes off the island. She wonders, where are you? I know you're there. I know you're watching. I feel you.

The Coast Guard vessel pulls into its slip. Coast Guard Officer Frank steps out and extends his hand to help the others get onto the dock. Once they are all off the boat, they begin the walk toward the Station House. Coming from the end of the dock a mass of reporters race toward the group. They are yelling. They've done their homework fast and know exactly which one is Alison Kraft. Coast Guard Officer Joe leaps quickly onto the docks and joins Frank. The two try to shelter and shuttle the group toward the building.

"Mrs. Kraft?"

"Alison?"

Guard Frank says, "Who let these guys in?"

Guard Joe responds, "Freedom of the press."

Hank yells, "What about her freedom?"

"This isn't freedom. It's harassment," Dan adds.

The hostages press through the chaos.

"Get back." Ed pushes one of them.

Jimmy's eyes are wide with confusion. He doesn't understand. One of the reporters reaches in and grabs Alison's shoulder to make her turn toward him. Jimmy kicks him hard in the shins. The reporter recoils. Another one says, "Oh, like mother like son."

A reporter yells "Mrs. Kraft. Have you ever handled a weapon before?"

Everyone seems to be yelling at her.

"Alison."

"Mrs. Kraft."

"Alison, were you scared?"

Alison puts her hands over her eyes. Hank takes the lead and pulls her through behind him trying to shield her and Jimmy with his body. A reporter reaches his arm inside the protective shell and clicks his camera near her face. Her eyes shoot up, and when they do, she doesn't see the dock she is on, she sees the woods. She is back in the woods, back up on the tree limb pointing her gun at Ben. She pulls the trigger and click...click. The reporter near her face...click...click. Alison flails out suddenly and violently smashing the camera away from her face and sending it to the dock where it shatters.

The reporter reacts angrily, "Hey. What the..."

She makes eye contact with him for a split second and the dead frost in her gaze shuts him up.

A police car pulls into the circular drive at the end of the dock. Officer Bill Thomas steps out of the driver's side and trots toward the group breaking through the swarm of reporters. Thomas is in his late forties, a tall stalk of a man who drinks milk shakes every night before he goes to bed hoping to put on some pounds. He is a no gloss guy with a serrated edge. For the department, politically, he's a nightmare, but he's an expert on the Burne brothers. He yells over the reporters to Hank. "This way, Mr. Kraft." A reporter slides in between them. Thomas says, "Get back or I'll arrest you."

"You can't arrest me." The reporter sneers. "Freedom of the press, baby." Thomas sticks out his foot and the reporter trips over it swearing as he hits the dock.

"Hey."

Thomas replies, "Oops, sorry." To Hank, "Did you hear me say sorry?"

Hank answers, "Sure did. I'd swear to it."

Hank grabs Alison and Jimmy and follows Officer Thomas to the police car. He opens the door for them and they slide inside. Officer Thomas has wide bull-like nostrils and he is breathing heavily as he gets into the driver's seat. It isn't from exertion but from irritation. "Damn vultures. I'm Bill Thomas. Chief asked me to pick you guys up and then do a quick debrief at the station and…"

"No, debrief. Take us home," Hank tells him.

"It'll only take a few…"

Interrupting, "Take us home or stop this car." Thomas meets eyes with Hank in the rearview mirror. He sees the three of them nearly on top of each other and he thinks they look like baby birds in a nest outside his window when he was a kid. Thomas picks up the radio. He has been working on the Burne brothers cases for years. He is the officer who found Mrs. Burne smothered to death. Ingesting each of their files, and predicting their moves, he has come as close as anyone could to getting inside their perverted heads. With his eyes now on this fragile twig of a woman, he cannot reconcile what she did with what he knows to be true about those men. He is dying to ask her questions—a ton of questions. And while he would not admit it aloud, he is disappointed that he didn't get his own shot at Gravel Burne. Several months ago, Thomas was honored by the force for tracking down Ben Burne and putting him behind bars. He was uncontrollably angry when the warden fell for the kidney ploy, which Thomas never would have bought, and now people are dead and Ben is loose. He stomped around the department yelling obscenities and ready to shoot the warden and the doctor for criminal stupidity.

Thomas speaks insistently into the cruiser's radio, "Nope, takin' 'em home."

The voice on the other end of the radio sounds stressed, "Thomas, Chief wants to see them at the station."

"I said I'm taking them home. Out."

Hank and Alison feel a surge of gratitude toward him. All they want is to go home.

"If you guys get a chance to jot down some notes, and things you remember, 'cause we're tracking Ben Burne right now and that'd help me out some with my boss. You, know, whatever you remember exactly."

"I remember everything exactly." Alison says sadly, as she looks off at the passing scenery. "Forgetting won't be a problem." Hank wraps his arms around Alison and Jimmy. They lean their heads in together and in a cocoon of their own bodies, they block out the world.

Half an hour later, they pull up in front of their home. News vans are parked on the street in front and several cameramen and reporters leap out and race toward them as the police car pulls into the driveway.

"Can't you get rid of them?" Hank asks distraught.

"They gotta right." Thomas shrugs.

"What about our rights?"

"You can keep 'em off your property. That's about it."

They get out of the car. The reporters surge forward.

Thomas yells, "Back it up. Back!"

The four of them hurry toward the front door. The reporters yell Alison's name repeatedly and she holds her palms over her ears as she runs inside. Once inside the foyer, Hank slams the door. Alison runs upstairs. Jimmy follows. They crawl into her big bed together, pull up the covers, and lie completely swept up into the sweet comfort of home. Hank is alone in the foyer with Thomas.

"My family is not public property."

"Tell me about it," he agrees sarcastically.

Hank goes to the front windows in the living room and starts pulling all the drapes shut. Reporters use their telephoto lenses to shoot right into his house and pictures of him closing the drapes hit the press.

"She's suffering. We need privacy."

"I can put a unit in front and keep them off your grass that's about all unless they break the law."

"This is harassment."

"They call it news now. The public eats this stuff up."

"What can we do?"

"Stay inside until it blows over and it will blow over."

For the next three days, Alison and Jimmy stay in her bed. They soak Alison's wounds in hydrogen peroxide and then coat them with Neosporin. Her bruises turn purple and yellow. Jimmy takes a colored pencil and makes a circle around one of them and adds petals so it looks like a flower. She smiles and tells him it's beautiful. They watch mindless cartoons, and eat in bed, which Jimmy knows was never allowed before.

* * *

Meanwhile, Hank fumes about the relentless dogs of the press outside. The "I'm a mother" comment leaked to a reporter and made front-page headlines. Then, it turned up on T-shirts by day two. The NRA immediately started a new website called "Mother-loaded." Jay Leno and David Letterman wove it into their monologues. Jon Stewart made fun of Leno and Letterman for weaving it into their monologues. Hank held onto his rage with a slippery grip, after everything they'd been through, to be subjected to this was heartless. What gave them the right to stalk them, to badger her, to hang around their yard, to peek in their windows, to talk to the neighbors, to follow their car? She is wounded. She is a victim. All three of them are victims. They are forever changed. Hank sees his life sliced into two finite sections—before and after. Before, he believed in a god and in goodness. Before, he believed in fairness and in human decency. Now, he believes there is a brutality beyond reason, and that it survives on the bloody edges of life, and there is a society of sofa slugs, whose lives are so tedious, they find that brutality entertaining.

On Monday, their neighbors Pam and Jessie fought their way through the frenzied group of reporters to deliver casseroles so that the Krafts didn't have to leave the house to shop. Hank passed a few words with them in the living room, but Alison never came downstairs. She can't chitchat. She can't talk about it and she can't talk about anything else.

The casseroles unnerved her. They reminded her of when her mom died and the neighborhood ladies would come by with food for her and her dad. A tragic association was cemented, which she never completely shakes off, and so the casseroles only serve to reinforce her belief that something is deathly wrong—why else would there be casseroles? The telephone rings constantly with relatives and friends checking on them. It becomes so intrusive Hank leaves a message for the people close to them and unplugs the phone.

CHAPTER NINETEEN

A THERAPIST WHO SPECIALIZES IN POST-TRAUMATIC stress arrived early the second week and spent a couple of hours. Doctor Cartwell is a restrained white-haired gentleman in a neatly pressed suit and tie. He speaks with a soothing tone and deserves his reputation for successfully treating victims of crime. Officer Thomas, who doesn't particularly believe in therapists, and who comes from the just-get-over-it-school-of-mental-illness, gave them Cartwell's number when Hank asked. The police department has recommended him for years. Hank and Jimmy found him easy to talk to and genuine. Doctor Cartwell felt good about the things Jimmy had to say and advised Hank that Jimmy should return to school and his usual routine immediately as the best course of therapy, but that he should let Jimmy pick the day. He found Hank already looking for ways to put it behind him, and felt that moving on was the best therapy for him as well. Then, he approached Alison.

Alison sits upstairs in the flowered lounge chair where she usually enjoys reading by the morning light on weekends. This morning the bedroom is dark because the news crews outside have forced her to keep the drapes shut. A book sits opened in her lap but she is not reading. She just sits. Doctor Cartwell knocks.

"Mrs. Kraft?" She looks over. "May I come in?" She shrugs. He enters and takes a seat on the edge of the bed facing her. "I'm Doctor Simon Cartwell. I spent some time this morning with your husband and your son and I do think they're doing okay. They are, however, both worried about you and so I thought perhaps we could talk?"

"About what?"

"About how you're feeling, about the experience, just work through it a bit together."

"Why would I want to do that?"

"It's been my experience with victims of violence it is a first step toward healing."

"I'm not just a victim. I'm a perpetrator."

"Is that how you see it?"

"That's the fact."

"We both know it's not that simple."

"I killed three men."

"And in doing that saved yourself, your family, and a number of other innocent folks."

"I let one get away."

"You didn't let him get away. It is the police's job to find him."

"He will kill us all now."

"Why do you say that?"

"I know him."

"Mrs. Kraft, may I call you Alison?"

"You can call me Shirley; I really don't care."

"I'll go with Alison. Alison, with all due respect to the horrendous experience you've had, you do not know this man." Alison turns her head away and stares at the photograph she has hung on the wall of Jimmy when he was a toddler. She drifts into it. Doctor Cartwell feels her leave the room and he waits. He knows this drifting in and out process thoroughly. It is a coping mechanism he sees often. He rises from the bed and walks over to the photograph. He looks at Alison pushing Jimmy on a swing. Jimmy looks about three years old; his hair is blown back, and his face is brilliant with glee.

"He's a beautiful boy."

"Yes" she whispers. "He is."

Cartwell takes the little chair that is pushed under the delicate wood writing desk against the wall. He pulls it out and places it closer, but not too close, to where she is sitting on the lounge. He reaches into her with skilled intimacy. "Alison, I've read the police reports about what happened, but I'd like to hear it from you. You're the only one who really knows."

"If you read the reports then you know the details."

"I don't know what it was like for you." Cartwell is only a few feet away from her and it is possible for her to whisper, so she does. He leans in and listens very intently.

"It was a progression," she tells him.

"How so?"

"The first one, it was mostly an accident. He was chasing me..." she breaks off. Her throat closes.

"Alison, sometimes it helps to tell it in third person. Try that. Let's try that."

"The first one was chasing her. He slipped. Slid off a cliff. He was almost an accident. She knew the cliff was there. She led him there. There was a moment when she could have saved him. She didn't. She thought about it, but then she didn't. She watched him fall. She heard him break. The next one, she planned it and she killed him. But it was from a distance. She didn't get her hands dirty. It was not up close. He was a good eight or nine feet away from her. But that third one was..." She falls back into first person, "that third one was in my face, bloody and gory all over me. I felt him die on top of me. I was wet with his blood. And then, the worst one got away."

"I see."

"No, you don't, you can't."

"You're probably right about that. Doesn't sound like something a person could imagine."

"Look, Doctor, you seem like a nice man and you can come and talk to Jimmy and Hank all you want, but unless you can call in the Marines to protect my family you really can't help me."

"Perhaps next time I come you will meet with me downstairs."

She let her gaze go back to the photographs on the wall. She falls into them. They are a sweet place for her to be.

At the bottom of the staircase, Hank crosses quickly to Doctor Cartwell and asks. "What do you think?"

"She's traumatized. It's going to take a while."

"Okay." Hank focuses with sharp intensity. He wants frantically to do all the right things. "What should I do?"

"Anything that feels normal."

Hank's head shakes, "Doctor, nothing feels normal."

"I understand. But anything that can be tied to what was normal before will help her reconnect with herself."

"Okay" Hank says. "Yeah, okay."

Abruptly on Wednesday at 1:30 p.m., the media siege ended: some teenager across town shot his friend two times in the chest and Hank regretted he lived in a world where for them that spelled relief. The news vans packed up and split in seconds. Hank was positive that now things would begin to fall into place. But the departure of the media had unexpected consequences. While the house was surrounded by cameras, Alison felt a limited safety, but when the media left, it became very quiet, very quickly. Then, she knew—he was coming.

CHAPTER TWENTY

F RIDAY MORNING FEELS FRESH WHEN Jimmy opens his eyes. The air in his bedroom is autumn cool and he hears his dad downstairs making coffee. He's always loved Fridays. He likes the assembly at school where all the students gather in the gym for announcements and sometimes they give awards. He sits on the wooden pullout bleachers next to his best friend, Barry, who can fart anytime he wants and always does when the principal is talking and that is hilarious. Then the principal asks why are you boys laughing, and tells them to stop laughing, which of course, they just can't. Yeah, he loves that. He throws off the covers and gets out of bed. Also, his mom, who always monitors everything he eats, lets him buy lunch on Fridays. Lunch at the school is cool because you can get nuggets, or pizza, or hot dogs, and there isn't anything green for miles, and even though his mom says it's disgusting, on Friday he gets to have it.

Down at the breakfast table Hank is sitting alone with his coffee and the newspaper. He acts nonchalant when Jimmy enters dressed for school, walks over to the pantry and takes out a box of Cheerios. Yes, Hank thinks, this is good—this is normal. He holds back the grateful tears in his eyes. Jimmy is turning the corner.

He asks casually, "Hey, buddy, you're up for school today?'

"Yeah."

"Cool." And that was all they said. It was perfect.

After breakfast, upstairs in Hank's bedroom, where Alison is lying awake in bed, there are no grateful emotions.

"Absolutely not," Alison says.

"He's going back today. It's his decision and it is what the therapist recommended."

"No, Hank, no, please."

Hank sees the fear on her face, walks over, and sits on the side of the bed. He takes her hand. "Alison, this is the right thing for him. He looks good this morning. It's what he needs. It's what's best for him. You have to support it."

"No, I don't."

Jimmy bounds into the room. He has his coat on, his favorite scarf and beanie, which he believes makes him look really "swa–eet", and his school books balanced on his hip. He practically skips over to the bed, kisses her on the cheek.

"Bye, Mom. See you right away when I get home."

Hank kisses her, too. "I'll call you when I get to work. I love you, Alison. Try to get out of bed."

* * *

Harbor Hills Elementary School ripples with excitement and then opens its arms to Jimmy. Denise, Gary, and a few of the other teachers surround and hug him, which embarrasses him in front of the other boys.

"Jimmy," Denise says, "you look really good."

"Uh, thanks."

She continues, "Honey, how's your mom doing?"

Jimmy shifts from foot to foot and then says, "Okay, you know, kinda."

"Did she say when she might come back to school?" Gary asks.

"Nope. She's awful tired."

"Of course," Denise adds, "I stopped by yesterday. But there wasn't any answer at the door."

"Oh, she doesn't answer the door."

"Okay, tell her we miss her, okay?"

"Sure."

Jimmy's classmates are mesmerized by his commando experience and while it certainly seems peculiar, Jimmy suddenly finds himself very popular and the center of attention. The boys pepper him with questions. So he tells the story again and again, the sting of it lessens, and it begins to feel only like a story. The school counselor observes him and she is encouraged by his ability to concentrate on his schoolwork and to play during recess. When she pulls him aside he tells her it feels like he was just inside a video game and that it really didn't happen. She sees this as a positive distancing mechanism and the report she sends home is even more encouraging than Hank had hoped.

Hank was sorely needed at Pump Up The Volume. He is the one who examines the demographics of the audience and creates the music playlist for the DJ events. He has an encyclopedic knowledge of music history and his playlists are a sought after commodity. Pump Up The Volume has started providing them over the Internet for a fee. They were almost making more money on that than on rental equipment. Sometimes when Hank is deep in the flood of chords and melodies he remembers his father, standing in the doorway of his bedroom yelling, "Damn it, Henry, turn off that music and study or you'll never get a job."

That morning, several clients called Hank, panicked with what they thought were emergencies. His definition of emergency has changed forever. All of this provided some distance for him, since it helped to place the island and its events, in time past.

CHAPTER TWENTY-ONE

ALISON REFUSES TO LEAVE THE house. Doctor Cartwell who has come to the house two more times told Hank she is still in shock. He prescribed medications, which she pretends to take. She tried them one time but it made her feel murky. She needed to be clear-headed. Of that, she is certain.

When Jimmy leaves for school each morning she gets up infused with anxiety. She paces back and forth in the bedroom. How can they not feel it? How can they not sense the danger? It is so loud—it is practically screaming at them. Her head begins to shake back and forth with aggressive energy. What to do? What should she do? Damn it.

Doctor Cartwell asked her if she was having hallucinations and she decided not to tell him about seeing Theo's eyes like two black bullet slugs glaring at her in the chrome of the toaster. Cartwell would not understand. How could she tell him that when she was cutting through the orange peel yesterday she felt the knife close in around Gravel's skin? How would that help anything? These are not hallucinations. These are warnings. And she has them all the time: in the glass door of the microwave, on the stainless steel hood over the stovetop, hollow-eyed faces take shape in the fog of her shower. It startles her, but none of those visions with their hellish dead eyes are as fearsome as the living eyes of Ben at the bottom of the mudslide—at the bottom of the mudslide where she heard him make a promise. He's coming. I know he's coming. She waits.

In the evening, Jimmy jabbers on about his school day. He is giddy with school news. It feels good to have things to say again. Hank listens happily to his son's tales from life on the outside. They have been imprisoned with each other, emotionally trapped on that island. Hank notices a genuine lifting-up in his chest.

Jimmy's face comes alive as he talks, "But that wasn't just it because..." he pauses for effect, "Alan likes Cindy."

"You mean likes?"

"He like, likes her. So that's why he let her have his spot in line at tetherball and I don't think it was any of Sarah's business."

Alison tries to focus. Exhaustion makes demands. Her mind hovers. She blinks her eyes forcefully and squints hoping to see Jimmy clearly but there is a film over her eyes she can't clear. She puts on a fake smile and her eyes begin to close involuntarily.

Hank asks "I thought Alan like liked Jennifer and you like liked Cindy."

"Gross, Dad, really."

"Sorry."

"I was telling Mrs. Davidson that English is definitely missing some words."

"Like what?" Hank asks.

""Cause if you like someone then you can like them, but if you like like someone you have to say like like because there's no word between like and love. How's a kid supposed to say they more than like but less than love a girl? 'Cause love is for grown-ups, and is scary, you know? And it's not like you just like her, and then you love her, there's a lot of space in between and there aren't any words for..." Jimmy stops. Both Hank and Jimmy notice as Alison's head drops forward and slowly she crumbles over with her forehead landing in her dinner plate. She's asleep. She sleeps only when she literally passes out and it never lasts, an hour here or there. Hank signals for Jimmy not to touch her. Two sets of compassionate eyes stare at her. And then they whisper.

"Dad, why won't she get better?"

"She will. She had a different experience than we did."

"It was bad for us."

"Yes. Bad, very bad, but different. We need to be patient. Just think how patient she would be if it were you or me."

"Yeah, but, I kinda need my mom." Tears roll down his cheeks. "I want her back."

"Me, too, buddy, me too."

They finished their over-cooked hamburgers and limp asparagus in a sad silence. Alison didn't move for forty minutes and then her head shot up. She looked around in bleary-eyed confusion. Hank had cleaned up dinner except for the plate she was lying in. Jimmy had gone off to do his homework. The anxiety of her husband's face touched her in the place where she loved him. And for a brief second they exchanged an affectionate smile and Hank felt a palpable rise of hope thinking it might be the beginning of her road home. He dared not speak, but he could see it was her. It was definitely her. He sat down next to the wife he knew and loved and missed and with a clean napkin, he gently wiped the ketchup from her forehead. She rested inside his warm eyes and it felt so good. It felt like a sip of cold fresh water, like a soft down pillow. Then, her eyes clouded, and he knew he'd lost her again.

* * *

Jimmy finished his homework and Alison tucked him into bed. She said nothing except good night. Jimmy rolled over and slept soundly. The content of Jimmy's dreams, which has been toxic with island memories, has been slowly changing. Instead of feeling vulnerable, thanks to the astonished reactions of his classmates he feels tough, cool, more like a survivor than a victim. Sharon Singler said he must be some kind of superhero. Relief and healing creep over him as he sleeps.

Alison stands stoically by the window. Dread stands with her. Sometimes it sits on her chest. Sometimes it stands right behind her. It always has a cold boney hand on her shoulder. The dread is a companion that presses down on her. Each day it accelerates with its full weight in a free fall toward her, and like the pull of gravity, it is inevitable and cannot be persuaded. She knows what she knows. Nothing can change that. She realizes that now she must keep her raw thoughts in a box, well wrapped, to ward off the scorn of those who do not understand, including Hank. So she stands lonely in the coal blackness and she waits for Ben.

At two a.m., the neighborhood goes dark. In an attempt to be conservation-smart the town elected to turn off all of the streetlights at two a.m. every night. The street outside the Kraft home sinks into black. All of the houses look like indistinct hulks.

The lamps on the nightstands in the master bedroom are off. Alison has plugged nightlights into every single electrical socket in the room throwing a lattice of beams, which eerily resembles the floodlights at the fishing camp. Hank is asleep. He is sleeping for longer chunks of time, but he knows that she is not sleeping at all. He knows every beat of Alison's personality and he is aware that she is not really home with them. She is not making progress every day in the same way he and Jimmy are. He wakes and looks at the clock. Then, he rolls over to see her. She is where she always is, every night, standing at the front bedroom window staring out into nothing.

Hank slides from the warm comforter and joins her at the window. He drapes his arm around her.

"Allie?"

She is stiff and nonresponsive.

"Alison, you have to sleep. We have all these sleeping meds. Take something. Please."

"I need to stay alert."

"No you don't. I'll stay up. Okay? I'll stay up tonight."

"No."

His frustration grows, "You need to eat, to sleep; you need to take care of yourself."

"I am taking care, right now."

"You've lost weight. You've lost hair. There are circles under your eyes."

"I've postponed my Cover Girl shoot."

"You know that is not what I mean. You are physically deteriorating. Surely you can see that."

"He's coming, Hank."

"They have witnesses that he entered Canada. He is gone, long gone."

"No. He's not."

"Alison, try and be rational." Doctor Cartwell warned him not to argue with her, but he can't help it. Someone has to bring her back to reality. Who will it be, if not him?

"I am being rational."

"You are staring out a window into complete darkness in the middle of the night looking for someone who is long gone. You're exhausted. You are probably hungry. How is any of this rational?"

No response. Frustrated, Hank pulls the little desk stool over to where she is standing. He gently pushes her down onto the stool so she is sitting. He thinks at least this way she won't literally fall over and hit her head. He stands for a few minutes feeling awkward in his own skin. By his sides, his arms hang long and heavy with uselessness. And that's it, he thinks, it's the uselessness. It has been the uselessness all along. He is utterly ineffectual. He was useless on the island. He is useless now as his wife comes apart piece-by-piece. Despondent, he climbs back into bed alone. He tells himself he must be the quiet strength she needs. He must stay in complete control. It is for him to provide a solid foundation. It is for him to rebuild a sturdy platform so she can find her balance. Time will be the key to releasing her back into his arms. She belongs in his arms. How can he make this world, this house, her reality again? He studies her over at the window. The crisscrossing nightlights in the room create an uneven design on her back. The beams swipe across her white nightshirt leaving a pattern of light with dark edges that resemble the pieces of a puzzle. He thinks that is what she is now—a series of broken pieces fitted together, appearing whole, but not whole. He takes his finger and holds it up at arm's length. He runs it over all of the edges of those pieces and as he does, he miraculously fuses her back together, it melts into one piece again, and then, he wakes and realizes he only dreamed that he'd fixed it. His heart aches and his chest feels heavy. He watches the back of his wife's nightshirt for an hour until his eyes close again. She senses when he drifts off and she stands back up from the stool to get a better look at the street.

CHAPTER TWENTY-TWO

A WEEK LATER, THE MORNING LIGHT is tilted and the air stays cool longer as winter's hand dangles over Minnesota. At first, the slinking cold creeps its way into the neighborhood during the night when everyone's sleeping, and then it hangs around through morning, and after a few weeks, it grips down hard as a fist until March. People are thinking about turkey, and butternut squash soup, and airline tickets for annual family gatherings. On Oakline Street, everything looks perfect on the outside. Inside the foyer of the Kraft house, Alison is explaining the brand new state-of-the-art alarm system to Polly.

Polly tries not to think about what Alison has been through. It all seems unreal to her. She can, however, see clearly that this woman in front of her right now is not the same woman she has come to know over the last nine years. Polly is no longer at ease in Alison's company. There is no humor in the home, no contentment. The home feels cold and edgy. She thinks Alison is like a zombie. Polly continues to show up on her scheduled days. She does her job and she listens.

"I want to show you how to work the system. It is important that the system is on constantly. It should never be off. Do you hear? Never."

"Yes, Alison, never."

"Every window, every door, inside and out, is wired."

"Okay."

"Every day I will change the code."

"All right." Polly's voice sounds heavy. This is all too much for her.

"When you enter and you hear the little beep you will have ten seconds to punch in the correct code."

"Yes."

"Good." Alison tries to smile because she knows she is supposed to, she searches around for a smile, but has none. So she spreads her lips, forces a grin, and shows some teeth. Polly leaves the conversation very sure now that smiling actually comes from the eyes and has little to do with the mouth, because Alison just looked scary.

Cautiously, Alison opens the front door and looks out. Seems fine. She walks quickly to the mailbox. Jessie, who is pulling out of his driveway, rolls down his window.

"Hey, Alison?" She looks over. She had hoped if she didn't lift her eyes he wouldn't call to her. No such luck. She continues moving toward the front door.

"Hi, Jessie."

"Can you and Hank come over for cards this weekend?"

"Nope, sorry. Don't think we can. Say hi to Pam for me."

She is at the door and inside. He drives away. She takes the mail into the kitchen. She flips open her laptop to CNN, and begins to scour the news not completely certain what she's searching for.

Later, having decided to work from home that afternoon, Hank puts his key in the lock and opens the front door. Nine seconds later, as he steps into the hall closet to hang up his coat, an ear-splitting alarm blasts followed by floodlights all around the property. Alison rushes into the foyer, opens the end table drawer, grabs the handgun she's stashed there and turns it on Hank. He freezes, confused by the alarm, stunned to see the weapon in his wife's hand. Her distant look. She doesn't see him. Doesn't know him. She aims. Polly screams! The scream shakes her and her eyes clear. She sees Hank. She lowers the gun. She takes a deep breath. Polly and Hank are paralyzed. Alison walks over to the alarm keypad. She punches in the code, picks up the ringing telephone, gives the alarm company the password, returns the weapon to the drawer, and walks back into the kitchen without a word. Shaken, Hank and Polly look at each other. Tears pool in Polly's eyes. Neither one of them knew she had a gun. They realize just how far gone she is.

"Hank…" Polly begins, "I just can't—"

He will not let her finish, "Polly, please." His desperation is so clear, so heartfelt. "Please," he begs. "I'll take care of it." Polly cannot add to his distress. She nods. He nods. They both turn away. He starts for the kitchen. She collects her coat by the door and as she leaves.

"I'll be back Monday."

His voice cracks with gratitude, "Thank you."

Once inside the kitchen he hears their car engine. He looks out the window above the sink and sees Alison driving away. He knows it must be 2:30 and so she is on her way to pick-up Jimmy. With his adrenaline pumping and his heart pounding, he thinks about her aiming a gun at him and he must face it: Alison is dangerous, dangerous to him and dangerous to their son. This may not be something he can wait for her to get over. It may take more than time. He wonders if there is something contagious about violence, if it's a virus, if her brain has caught something she can't shake. What if violence is infectious in the same way as laughter? He's experienced that. He has been in a room where someone is roaring with laughter and he has begun to laugh having no idea why. Maybe violence is like that. What should he do? Is he failing to help her? Is he failing to protect his son? What should he do? Who can help? His misery is mounting. He goes back to the foyer, pulls out the end table drawer, and removes the handgun. It is the gun his dad had and Hank inherited when he passed away. It's been in the safety deposit box at the bank for ten years. That's what they both decided. Neither one of them wanted a weapon in the house. He stands in the middle of the living room having absolutely no idea what he is supposed to do.

Alison parks the car in the red zone in front of the building. The crosswalk guard begins to wave her arms for Alison to move, then she sees who it is, and she backs off. Everyone has backed off. Some are giving her the time they know she needs, others fall back as their instincts dictate. Methodically, Alison scans the front lawn, play area, parking lot. There is too much to keep within her control. She hates this part of the day. She gets out of the car and walks up the sidewalk to the front of the school. Jimmy is standing right there waiting as he has done every day since he returned to school. She takes him by the hand and leads him quickly back to the car. He tries not to look around. Many kids in the packed schoolyard stare. He gets into the car and slumps down in the seat. He's no superhero this way.

"How was school?" She asks.

"Okay."

"Good."

They drive in silence because her vigilant attention is required to check into every passing car, to peer around every streetlight post, behind every trash can and mailbox and tree. She runs every yellow and only stops for a red when necessary. She pulls the car into the driveway. Jimmy jumps out and runs into the house. His dad is waiting in the kitchen. Angrily, Jimmy blasts past him without even saying hello and vaults up the stairs two-at-a-time slamming his bedroom door. Alison enters, closes the door and hits the code. She turns.

"What happened with Jimmy?"

"Nothing. He's good."

"What's with the alarm?"

"It's smart to have an alarm. I've got a series of codes worked out we can go over them together at dinner tonight."

"I don't want an alarm."

"I do."

"It's an overreaction."

"It is not."

"We live in an extremely safe neighborhood."

"No such thing,"

"Alison, do you even know you pointed a gun at me today?"

"Yeah. Sorry."

"Sorry?"

"The alarm went off and it was actually a good rehearsal for us."

"You almost shot me!"

"No I didn't. I saw you."

"You haven't seen anything properly since we got back."

"I see things in greater detail than I ever have."

"I don't want a gun in the house."

"You don't want an alarm. You don't want a gun. Would you just like us to roll over?"

"I can't believe what I'm hearing." It takes enormous effort not to start yelling. The vein in his neck throbs and he holds his temper. "I'm going to check on Jimmy; then we'll talk."

Hank sees it all descending into madness. He doesn't know if he really can continue to negotiate the craziness. Upstairs he knocks on Jimmy's door, opens it slowly, and walks in. He closes it behind him. Jimmy is kicking a stuffed giraffe around the room.

"I'm not going to school anymore. She took my hand—my hand."

"Jimmy, your mom does not mean to embarrass you."

"All the kids are laughing at me. I went from cool to fool in days."

"I'm so sorry, kiddo." Hank can't stand seeing the humiliation on his son's face.

"Why can't you pick me up or Polly?"

"Okay. I understand. Let me see what I can do."

The explanation of the alarm system during dinner went badly. Neither Hank nor Jimmy was in favor of the system, and the skin of patience they've had has been rubbed raw. After an hour of fury-tinged debate, Alison agreed to leave it off for a few days so they could get used to the idea.

The tension has not lessened as Hank and Alison get into their pajamas. The bedroom feels unusually hot and a poison mood hangs in the air between them. Hank pulls off his T-shirt.

"You have to stop embarrassing Jimmy in front of his friends."

"He'll get over it."

"It's not fair to him and it has to stop. Things need to go back to normal for him."

"Normal has changed."

"Normal hasn't changed—you've changed."

"And you're not changed? Get serious, Hank." The sarcastic tone is new for her.

"Serious? Okay, I'll get serious. You are scared to death one hundred percent of the time. You are exhausting yourself and hurting everyone around you."

"I'm not scared. I'm ready."

"For what? Ready for what? We're home. It's been three weeks. We need to get our lives back."

"We will. When it's time."

"Jimmy's nightmares are less frequent. The therapist says he's doing really well but he needs normalcy. You are making things worse for him, harder for him, harder for all of us."

"Keeping him safe comes first."

"Open your eyes. We're home."

"It's not over"

He erupts with aggravation, "Alison."

"I know what I'm doing."

Hank runs his hands through his hair. It is all he can do to keep from screaming at her.

"And I'm calling Polly to pick up Jimmy at school. You can't do it anymore."

"No way."

"I swear to god, Alison, this is going to stop."

"Polly doesn't know what to look out for."

"I will pick up Jimmy for the rest of the week then we'll see."

"Hank, he's coming back."

"No." He bores his eyes into her. "He's not." Hank marches into the bathroom and slams the door. But Alison is sure; she is so very sure she is right. Surely, she is right. She walks over to take her spot at the bedroom window. What if? What if I'm not right? For one slippery second she remembers life before, and then her reflection clarifies in the glass of the window. She does look different. She asks herself the question: is something wrong with me? Am I going mad? Hank gets into bed without saying good night, without a good night kiss. He turns away from her and faces the wall.

When Hank opens his eyes in the morning, his body aches. He feels chewed up into chunks. Never had a man longed more for normal than Hank. He was thirsty for an ordinary day. Several nights ago, their neighbor, Jessie, had called and invited him out to a movie, which they used to enjoy together. They'd steer clear of the chick flicks and find a great action feature. It sounded like such a nice little piece of normal Hank accepted. Ten minutes into the film the gunfire started. Eleven minutes into the film, Hank was gone. How does he explain to Jessie that this cannot be entertainment for him ever again? He has lost the ability to disassociate. For everyone else this kind of violence is imaginary; not for him. He thinks they will probably be spending a lot of time in Disney movies.

He reaches for the ringing phone, "Hello?"

"Hey, ah…Mr. Kraft? It's Officer Bill Thomas."

"Hey, how are you?"

"Okay. Detective Crane wanted you and Mrs. Kraft to come down to the station this morning. I think we have some news you're gonna like a lot."

Hank sits up in bed, "Really? What?"

"Crane wants to tell you."

"We're on our way." He hangs up. "Alison."

CHAPTER TWENTY-THREE

WAITING AT THE FRONT DOOR for Alison, Hank watches the last few leaves stuck to the oak tree in his front yard fall. They float to their deaths gracefully. It's so out of character for him to make a morbid association like this. Alison looks like a wary rabbit as she skittishly exits the house and darts to the car. Hank has to run to hold the car door for her. He always holds her car door. He brings her coffee in bed on the weekends, and he sends her flowers unexpectedly. They cherish these little romantic gestures. When they're out with other couples for dinner, and Alison rises to leave the table, Hank always rises as well, and rises again to pull out her chair when she returns. It is a chivalrous throwback that makes them feel special to each other. Other couples smile—a few women kick their own husbands under the table.

The drive to police headquarters requires scanning and concentration. There's a lot for Alison to monitor. She peers out of the passenger car window and is thwarted by the heavy winter coats and hats that make identification tricky. Hank and Alison exchange a few forced sentences about the weather and then have little to say to each other. They sit in prickly silence. Hank turns on the radio and sings along without his usual enthusiasm.

They park and walk into the police station. Once in the lobby, Alison places each individual in a grid in her mind. The security screener uses the wand on them both and then waves them through. As they walk down the hall, all of the officers notice her. They exchange looks with each other after she passes. Hank finds this covert attention irritating and when he catches them, he punishes them with a look that would freeze blood, but there is no hiding; she is a known face in law enforcement circles. Somehow, this little woman killed three of the Burne brothers. After the newspapers and talk shows abandoned their attempts to interview her, she remained a topic of discussion among the police, the ATF, and the FBI. After all, it was the Burne brothers. It was an irreconcilable event, a stunningly unlikely result.

A uniformed officer escorts them to Detective Crane's office. Alison sees every person along the way with intensified clarity: the woman with the big knuckles filling a cup at the coffee dispenser, the Latino officer with the overly stocky frame and flashy teeth, the two uniformed cops holding a folder and pretending not to notice her.

Once inside Crane's office, she takes the seat opposite his desk. Her muscles let go and she relaxes. She feels safe here. As they wait, Hank paces. She is at rest. There is comfort in the deliberate order in this room. Crane is a right angle kind of guy: every sheet of paper on his desk is perfectly stacked, on the corner is a jar with eight sharpened pencils, the top of the file cabinet is a printer and a calendar with pictures of his family. Everything appears brand new. Even the items pinned to the bulletin board are in level lines. Alison breathes and feels calm.

Hank says, "This is a little creepy. Like it's a prototype of an office."

"I like it."

And even these few inconsequential words hurt him, make him feel discounted and minimized. The walls are painted a doughy color that resembles a jar of chicken gravy. The floor moldings only go half way around the room. Alison wonders if they ran out of money or interest. She sees little nail holes in different spots on the walls testifying to the parade of detectives who have occupied this room. Witness to the coming and going of people who cared enough to put up pictures of their spouses, their children, their dogs—people who nail their heart to the wall of their office. She prizes the pictures she has of her family and decides to rearrange her photo albums as a project.

Detective Crane is relatively new to the crumby hallway that leads to his office. He was proud to make detective a few months ago. His wife and kids made him a special pork roast family dinner with a congratulations sign and a balloon. He had wanted to be a detective since he'd been a little boy sitting in front of the TV watching show after show where the good guys were funny and clever and always got their man. Reality has made a series of adjustments to that picture, but he is still proud, and he still loves his job. He may be a touch too refined for the grit of this work, but he was first in his class at the academy so he makes up for that with insight. He nods at Officer Simmons as they pass in the hall.

"Hey, Crane," Officer Simmons says, "AK Allie is in your office. Just give a shout if you need backup."

Crane smiles. "Right, thanks." Inside, though, he doesn't particularly like this kind of jocularity at a victim's expense. As he reaches his office door, Officer Thomas joins him. They enter together.

"Hello, Mr. Kraft, Mrs. Kraft." Crane shakes their hands and Thomas does the same. Alison doesn't move from her chair. She narrows her eyes and studies them. One of the most alarming realizations about this ordeal for her has been how perfectly average the Burne boys looked. She thinks if there is a god, and he was intent on creating monsters, the least he could do was make monsters look like monsters.

Thomas says, "You're a legend around here, Mrs. Kraft."

"I'd like my fifteen minutes to be over."

"Understandable." Crane smiles.

Hank walks behind Alison's chair and puts both his hands on her shoulders protectively. He levels his eyes at these men with a communication that says, "take care." Crane gets it. Thomas is not that sensitive. He's a guy who needs to be told things—sometimes more than once if he thinks you're full of shit or dead ass wrong.

Thomas adds, "We got cops here, me included, who made a career trying to nail any one of the Burne boys and you dusted three in twelve hours."

"You know how good we women are at dusting."

Thomas laughs aloud and then seeing the look on Crane's face, shuts up.

Crane takes the lead, "Mrs. Kraft, may we get you some coffee or tea?"

"No."

Crane speaks gently, "I'm very glad to give you some really wonderful news."

"Oh?"

"Ma'am, Ben Burne was positively identified in Port Arthur, Ontario. He has family there, an Uncle Rafael. The Canadians moved in to arrest him yesterday morning at his uncle's cabin."

"They have him?" Her heart leaps.

Thomas jumps in excitedly, "Burne put up a fight. The gunfire set off some explosives and the whole place went up. He was trapped inside like the rat he was."

Reflexively, Hank gasps happily. "Thank god. Oh, good, great." Alison does not react. He reaches for his wife. He shakes her, "Alison, it's over."

Crane smiles, he understands, "Now, I know some folks prefer a long trial and an opportunity to face him."

Thomas breaks in, "I prefer him charbroiled and six fuckin' feet under. Oh...ah...excuse me." Crane rolls his eyes. Thomas adds, "And also, personally, I wish I could've been the one to light that torch."

"Thank you, Officer Thomas." Crane silences him.

Alison has been sitting and waiting for the rush of relief. Nothing. No rush. No relief.

Hank says, "Thank you. This really helps us a lot. Doesn't it, Alison?"

They all look at Alison for her reaction.

She is staring at her feet. Raising her eyes to Crane, "It doesn't feel right."

Crane speaks with kindness. He directs his words to Alison but he is clearly sending a message to Hank as well.

"Mrs. Kraft, I have trained officers who've been through less violent experiences who take leave to mend and recover."

"I still feel him. He's still around or I wouldn't feel him."

"It's the trauma that's still around—that is what you're feeling. It's like your body is caught in it. I've seen this so many times. Exercise can help. Relaxation techniques. Perhaps you should consider a vacation?"

"I'm not over my last vacation."

Thomas laughs spontaneously. Alison can't help but smile at Thomas. She likes that he is such an open book.

"Sorry." Thomas shrugs.

Crane continues. "Right. What we would recommend is for you to go home. Raise your great son. Get back to your life as soon as possible. Routine is the best medicine."

"Yes." Hank is euphoric. "That's exactly what we're going to do." Now, they will mend; their lives will come back into harmony as they recover the melody line lost in the madness. He will have his wife back. He will revel in an ordinary day: a good bye honey—have a good day at work—what's for dinner—how was school—love you—good night kind of day. He will never underestimate the solace of normal again.

Hank grabs her hand as they walk out of the police station. He squeezes it three times, which meant I love you when they were dating. She looks up at him as the squeeze goes directly to the memories her heart holds dear. They remind her of a time before all of this, when she was young and in love, and the book of their lives was blank. They share a soft smile as he holds open her car door. Now, it will all stop. Her thin body falls heavily into the passenger seat. Now, the terrorizing visions of disembodied eyes, the unendurable dark and sleepless nights, the muscle tremors, the dirty muddy feeling of her skin, the constant flood of primitive hormones, all gone. She sinks into the leather upholstery and lapses into sleep in the time it takes Hank to walk around the car and get in. He turns on the motor. He looks over at her and sees she's asleep and his relief is palpable. He slips off his suede jacket and lays it across her, leaving his hand lightly on her chest for just a moment; he feels her breathing in and out and it is nourishing. A gush of relief, like a cleansing, washes over him and his emotions are so raw his whole body feels swollen and pulpy. He is obscured sitting in the front seat behind the windshield of the car and so he allows himself the luxury of resting his forehead on the steering wheel, closing his eyes, and letting go for a bit, a little deserved relief—a shudder and a few tears of gratitude.

Walking toward his police car Officer Thomas glances over. He sees Alison Kraft crashed-out, head back, mouth slightly open and he thinks she looks child-like. Hank, too, seems to be asleep hunched over the steering wheel. Thomas doesn't like things to get too complicated. Help the good guys. Kill the bad guys. Follow the law. Simple logic and a definitive direction works for him. He likes the lines that society draws clearly. It is when the victims enter his world that his hands feel too big and his mind clumsy. He feels all stuffy and dense, like his brain is soaked and packed with insulation. Victims make it all so messy. You cannot afford to feel for them because that will cloud your judgment. He is thankful that it worked out for these two. He never can figure out what makes one couple survive and go on to live their lives and another wind up chopped into pieces and scattered around in trash bins. There is no way to guess in advance which of the ones in that little fishing group on the island were going to leave, and which of them would end there. Years of police work has taught him there is no rationale for what happens, no predictive tool. He has found it is just as well not to wonder about the why of it all because it is no different from wondering about God, or about what makes a joke funny. Hank looks up suddenly sensing someone watching him. He sees Thomas a few feet away through the windshield. Their eyes meet. Thomas nods. Hank nods. It is the period at the end of their sentence. Thomas moves on. Hank starts the car.

Jimmy and Hank tiptoe around Alison for the next few days as she sleeps nearly continuously. Deep in a flooded slumber, she dreams she is on a down-filled raft in a blue swimming pool of warm water, gently floating with the hot fingers of the sun kneading the tight muscles on her back, and the backs of her legs, and with a gentle cool breeze skimming her face. She is unaware that several times her little boy has sneaked in, his bare feet padding silently on the gold carpet, and he has knelt by the side of her bed when no one was watching and just stared at her face, the face of his mom that finally looks normal again. The two sharp strain lines between her eyebrows have softened and the tightness around her mouth has let go.

Jimmy Kraft knows things about life that no nine year old should know: evil is alive. He knows this because it physically grabbed him by the shoulder and dragged him outside the lodge. Evil is a corporal presence with actual blood and bones and muscles to pull you, cut you, tear off your skin. It is not an imaginary spirit or fallen angel or apparition. It is not an ideology like they teach him in social studies class. It is not an empire, or a religion. It is human. It lives. It breathes. It spoke to him. And while that is terrifying to know, it also makes him feel like he can get it, reach it, hurt it, maybe kill it, and this is where the core of his healing comes from. Evil isn't invincible if it has a shape, a head and a spine. He likes knowing that, likes thinking if he's strong enough, and smart enough, he can defeat it, likes thinking that he can get his hands around the neck of evil and suffocate the life out of it when he grows up. When the police arrived on the island, Jimmy took some good hard looks at the dead Burne brothers. Others tried to shield him from the view, but they didn't understand how badly he needed to see Kent with a hole in his chest the size of a basketball, Theo with his skull in two neat pieces, and Gravel stabbed, shot, completely pale and drained of blood. Jimmy has sublimated the visceral horror of that night and he has done a good job fitting himself back into the before time. A few of the games they play on the schoolyard seem dumb to him now, and all the injuries, the simple bumps and bruises that bring tears to the eyes of his schoolmates seem silly. Doctor Cartwell has warned Hank that there may be residual evidence of trauma as Jimmy grows. It could come in a lot of different forms. They would need to be alert and ready to help. Nevertheless, the doctor felt the prognosis was very good based on Jimmy's ability to do his schoolwork and interact with his friends. They would need to wait to see what comes up.

On the fourth day, Alison wakes to voices downstairs. She looks over at the clock. It's six-thirty, dinnertime. The fog in her brain clears. Music? Music is playing and there are clearly a lot of people downstairs. She picks up her cellphone by the bed and dials the house phone. It rings and Hank picks up, "Hello?"

"Could you come upstairs?"

A few moments later, he comes into the bedroom.

"Great. You're up. Are you hungry?"

"What's going on?" she asks.

"It's Sunday. Family dinner night."

"What? No."

"Yes."

"I'm not ready."

"You don't have to do a thing."

"I can't."

"Everyone brought something and the older cousins are going to clean up."

"Oh, Hank, your family? No."

He closes the bedroom door, walks over, and sits down on the side of the bed.

"You shouldn't have invited them, Hank."

"They wanted to come. They want to see you, to see us. They're our family, Alison. They may be nuts and chews, but they're our nuts and chews."

"I can't deal with it. And I feel responsible for their safety and it doesn't feel safe having them all here near me."

"It's perfectly safe. I promise you."

"There is no such promise."

Hank feels a flash of anger because he knows this is true. He sends his true feelings into his gut and speaks with the kindness he knows she needs.

"Everyone in our lives has been affected by this. Try and think about how you would feel if something like this had happened to your dad?" This is exactly the right thing to say to her. She knows how she would feel. Yes, it helps her understand that others in the family have been injured in some minor way, certainly Carolyn who had a son and grandson to think about. Yes, it makes sense.

"Okay, I'm going to stay up here. I'm not ready for company."

"Not company. Family. And everyone is hoping you'll come downstairs. They want to see you, Alison." He leans over kissing her, "Throw on some jeans and come on down. Aunt Beth just told Jill she's adopted."

"Jill's adopted?"

"No." He grins. She smiles, too. He turns, proceeds to the door and swings it open. He says over his shoulder as he steps into the hallway, "Please come down." He walks out but does not go down the stairs. He stops and leans up against the wall to the right of the doorway in the hall by the edge of the stairs and listens. Did she get up? He waits to hear the bedspread rustle hoping to hear her foot hit the floor. He wills her out of bed with every ounce of energy he has. Get up, Alison, he thinks. Darling, get up. He carefully peeks around the doorway to find her staring directly at him with a little smile.

"I know you're standing right there the stair didn't creak," she says.

"How do you know I didn't fix that floorboard?"

"Did hell freeze over while I was napping?"

"I wouldn't call three days napping, Rumpelstiltskin. Now, get your cute ass out of bed and help me deal with my relatives. Just fifteen or sixteen crushing hugs and the worst will be over."

Downstairs, in the family room, Hank exchanges a hopeful look with his mother and mouths "maybe." Everyone has fallen into their usual patterns of needling and teasing.

Emily complains to Jill, "I can't believe you brought beans."

"I was happy to," Jill answers.

"But I was supposed to bring the baked beans," says Emily testily.

"Yes, but last time you brought them from a can for god's sake, Emily. So, I cooked some homemade."

"Oh is that so? Well Jill, here, try these—they're homemade. Muffins I brought to go with the beans." Jill leans over and takes a bite of the muffin Emily holds for her.

"Mmm, actually Emily, these are really good." She reaches for the rest of the muffin.

Emily levels her eyes at her sister, "And so good for you since I made them with my breast milk." Jill's eyes widen, her mouth full of muffin.

"No you didn't?" Alison says from behind with a smile in her voice. Emily spins around. And even though Hank had methodically explained to each one of his relatives a seemingly infinite number of times how the best response would be for people to just act normally, well, that wasn't in their natures. Emily throws her arms around Alison and the rest of the family swarms her like an agitated hive: sisters, cousins, aunt, uncles.

"Oh, shit." Hank races over and tries to pull away his relatives. "Family please back off. Let her breathe." And they separate.

"Relax, Hank, we're just happy to see her," his mom says.

He takes Alison's hand, "My family—the inspiration for Velcro. Sorry, honey."

Alison talks to herself, smile, maintain, fight the rising panic attack.

"I'm happy to see everyone, too."

Hank's mother says, "C'mon, Alison, let's get a glass of wine away from the crazies."

"We are *your* flesh and blood, Mother," Emily yells after her.

"Every one of you takes after The Father."

Alison's breathing evens out as Carolyn leads her from the kitchen.

The Father was long gone when Alison joined the Kraft family. Over time, she has puzzled together pieces of him based on side comments and a few choice unrepeatable adjectives thrown around to describe the man who had walked out on the family. Hank told her once the entire extended family calls him The Father instead of your father or our father because they don't really want to claim him. It was no small feat that Carolyn managed to raise her three kids on her own. The injury of being left shaped Hank. It is why he is committed to being such a good father, such a good son, husband, and brother, it made him a family man because little in life mattered more to him than not being like The Father.

Carolyn takes Alison's hand and leads her out of the kitchen and into the quieter family room where they take seats on the sofa. Alison's foot begins to shimmy with nervous energy. Her eyes skirt the room. She does not want to be here, or to fake this, or be expected to talk about it. Their curiosity is the problem. Their curiosity, understandable as it is, makes her feel conspicuous and dirty.

"Carolyn, I think I'll go back upstairs."

"No you won't. I have questions," Carolyn begins and Alison immediately turns away.

"Don't ask me, Carolyn. I really don't…"

Her mother-in-law interrupts forcefully, "What I want to know is did you see that Jimmy got an A on his report on ants?" Alison hears this and it feels like a slap across her face even though it wasn't meant that way. Did Jimmy tell her this? Did she miss something? Something important to Jimmy? She clenches her teeth, angry with herself. Even her little boy has found his way back to life. She wrenches her nerves into submission.

"Did he?"

"And I have to tell you it was hilarious."

"It was?"

"He needed to present his report orally to the class. So to remember, he gave each of the different kinds of ants names. Like he called the carpenter ant Mr. Hammer. It was very cute. And then, he made a poster board with drawings, and stapled samples of their preferred food all over the board, and the next morning the classroom was full of, guess what, ants." Carolyn laughs aloud and Alison giggles.

As Carolyn jabbers on about Jimmy's report on ants and Alison listens, she becomes aware that her hearing has changed. She hears everything that Carolyn is saying but she also hears whispering all around her. Her eyes catch the furtive glances of the family, all consciously pretending not to stare at her—she is the accident by the side of the road. Her senses are oddly heightened. How is it that she can discern what's being said in the other room? Even though Jill is at least ten feet away and surrounded by rowdy kids, Alison hears her every word clearly, when she leans over toward Aunt Ruth and whispers, "Well, she looks okay, kind of." Everyone is faking it. The whispering gets louder. Will I always be that woman she wonders? Will people always see the whole horror when they look at me? Do I need to move somewhere completely new to be free of it, to not see it reflected in the faces of those who look at me, to silence the whispering which sounds like a running faucet? She puts her hand on her chest and realizes she is trying to hide the bloodstain that is not there. She forces herself to focus on Carolyn's animated face, but something is off deep in the core of her. An alarm is ringing. It was far away at first like a distant church bell carried on a furtive wind, but it has changed in character, changed in strength. She realizes it is not that everyone else is busy faking it— pretending that all is well—they believe all is well, all is healing, all is over. She is the one faking it because all is not well. It is not over. Is it? Why do I feel like I'm waiting? Waiting for what? Waiting for a dead man. I missed Jimmy's A. I missed the goddamn ants and I cannot get that back.

Monday morning, Alison opens her eyes, pops out of bed, dresses for work and walks into the kitchen.

"How are my men?"

They look up from their cereal bowls, surprised. Hank has classical guitar music playing and seeing his wife there in the doorway accompanied by the soft honeyed chords is overwhelmingly beautiful to him. Music, Alison, Jimmy, he needs nothing else in the entire world.

"Mom, are you coming to school?"

"Thought it was time I went back to work. Daddy shouldn't have to do everything around here."

"Sweet." Jimmy turns back to his Cheerios.

"Yes." Hank agrees.

Alison walks back into Harbor Hills Elementary School and heads for the teachers' lounge to get a cup of coffee. This was her customary practice. Stepping inside the three-story building, she is acutely aware of the sights and sounds around her. Primitive systems in her brain that she never needed before have been activated: she scans rather than sees; she listens rather than hears, and the scents typically in the air hit her in the face: the smells of grass on the sneakers in the long grey locker as she passes, as well as the funky stench of the gym socks crammed inside of them. Her world is visually crisp, loud, and pungent. She has a new exacting attentiveness to every detail. The ceiling feels lower than she remembers. Although, she thinks, maybe I haven't ever really noticed the ceiling before. Walking briskly down the hallway toward the lounge she makes a game of stepping on only the black floor tiles, which makes her feel a little like a child inside the child's world and that feels good. Passing the open staircase to the next floor, she turns the hallway corner and enters the teacher's lounge. She breathes in. Someone has dripped coffee onto the pad under the pot and it has burned there. She smells that, too. The bulletin board is crammed with reminders. She notices the semicircular ghost streaks left behind from the washcloth that wiped off the little red table hours ago. She has walked into this room a hundred times and never noticed those things. She decides to research the brain to learn what activated all of these detail systems. Must be in the brain stem, she speculates. It is a little fascinating to be in this new place, to see and hear the world in such detail. She grabs the coffee pot and a mug from the shelf. Denise and Gary enter behind her.

Denise cries delighted, "Alison!"

Alison spins around dropping the mug that shatters into large porcelain chunks when it hits the floor. Aggressively, she holds the hot glass of the coffee pot in both of her hands unaware of the burning in her palms. Denise and Gary are both startled by her reaction. A tense instant, and then Alison's expression relaxes.

Denise says, "Alison, I'm so sorry."

"Oh." Alison puts down the hot pot and looks at her palms. Red but thankfully not burned.

"We shouldn't have come up behind you like that."

Fighting to regain her calm, "Completely my fault; seems I startle easily these days."

Gary reaches down and picks up the pieces of the broken mug. "Are your hands okay?"

"Yeah, it's nothing." She thinks, really nothing. Pain is relative. It is true there are thresholds. She knows what her body can't take. A little burn like that? Nothing.

Denise puts her arms around Alison, "We are so glad to have you back. It wasn't the same around here." Denise does this partially to hide her surprised expression at how different Alison looks. There are a few little scars on her face from where she was whipped and cut by tree branches and her complexion is sallow. That shimmer of light that used to come from her eyes is gone. She feels oddly stiff in Denise's hug, because physically she hasn't let go of it all, yet.

"Your class will be thrilled to see you," Denise says and then pulls back and looks into her eyes. "You know, Alison, we've been friends a long time. I can't imagine what you've been through, but I'm here if you need to unload on someone."

"Thank you, Denise." Alison is touched by the genuine affection. There is a poignant pause that they both feel emotionally stuck in: so much to say and nothing really useful. And then, Gary, is Gary...

"Personally, I'm just hoping to not piss you off." He makes them both giggle and the fleeting softness that lights Alison's eyes is like a sweet reminiscence from another time.

What is so therapeutic for Alison is the speed with which the kids in her class move on. They gather around to say hello and immediately complain about the series of gnarly substitutes who attempted to take her place.

After school, Alison stays late in her classroom hoping to enhance her newfound peace by a little needed organization. Different substitutes left behind folders of half-graded tests. Returned homework is strewn around the tables. Chaos has ruled the classroom. Alison stacks homework pages by date as she reviews the day in her mind. How did she do? Okay. Not great. I can't believe I didn't remember Jamie Hopper's name. Ridiculous. I know that kid inside out. I suppose that's just a remnant of the exhaustion. It will take time. At least, everyone keeps telling me so. I'll feel better when this classroom is back in order. I think I need to look at the day like a series of little sips instead of trying to gulp it down. I can rest inside the little achievements that way: breakfast: check, driving to work: check, morning classes, etcetera. Alison gives up on the stack of homework in front of her and walks over to the windowsill where a pile of medieval history projects are stacked. She moves the top project on castles aside and reveals a poster board with three models of medieval weapons taped to it, one of which is a knife made out of aluminum foil. She touches it with one of her fingers. It feels sticky. Sticky on the blade. Yes, blood sticky. Blood is sticky. Wait, is this sticky or am I imagining it is sticky? She leans in compelled by the shape and the gleam. She perceives a blurry image on the shiny silver blade. She squints. The indistinguishable image pops into terrifying clarity: Gravel's face. She is back in the shed and she feels his body tissues give way as she twists the knife in his back and his hot blood runs hot down her arm. His rage passed into her body like bacteria—it lives inside of her. Someone is behind her. She spins. Kent stands there with his dead bugged-out eyes and a gaping hole in his chest. He walks toward her. Denise does not recognize this woman looking at her. It is not Alison. Her eyes are wild. Her entire face is contorted. Denise steps back defensively and gasps, "Alison?" Alison's expression clears. She squints. She sees Denise—it is Denise. She tries to pull it together but her throat closes. She can't. She is surging with violent energy. Run. She needs to run. Unglued, she pushes past Denise and out of the room. In a manic frenzy, Alison runs past a few students who jump quickly out of her way. She looks down at her feet and mud—there is mud everywhere. Where? Out? She darts for the back, fire stairwell. Run. Somewhere inside she knows she is home, and then, also that she is not—not home—not—not safe. She bursts into the stairwell. Takes two steps, then another two, then slows one, one, one, then she stops. She stands gathering her wits. She looks around. I'm in school. I'm in the school. She breathes in forcefully attempting to even out her breathing. Muscles in her limbs are shimmying from rolling spasms. She gradually sinks down onto the stair and sits. She rubs her eyes and a few tears fill them. I am going mad. Or am I already mad? Is Hank right? Her head is heavy and her limbs feel weighted. How long can I exist on the edge like this? She puts her forehead down on her knees, her arms fall limply to either side, and she is perfectly still. Recover. Breathe. She tries to suck air deep into her lungs and then out slowly, calming. I need help. I must face that. But these therapists, what they want I don't. I don't want to think about it, talk about it, scrutinize it, or dissect it. I want to forget it. Maybe that's the fallacy, that I want what is not possible. Maybe I can't do this on my own. A noise. From the landing two floors below, an odd noise, slow, like someone is creeping. Her head snaps up. Yes. I heard that. No, no I didn't. It's nothing. Someone is creeping up the stairs. I can't pretend I didn't hear that. There it is again. She rises and presses her back up against the wall. She tries to see down through the opening for the hand railings. Another cautious footfall below her. Someone is slowly climbing the stairs. Too slowly. She slips out of her heels and tiptoes in her stocking feet toward the railing to look over. Yes, she sees something. Something on the railing below, is it a shadow, no a hand. A man's hand. Ben's hand. Twirling around, she rushes back up the stairs out through the fire door stumbling into the third floor corridor. She sees no one. A few teachers are in the hall speaking with the assistant principal and they watch flabbergasted as Alison blasts passed them in her stocking feet carrying her shoes. At the other end of the hall, where there is an open staircase, she leaps down the steps two at a time for three flights, and then bursts through the front door of the school. Shredding her stockings on the asphalt, she races to her car. In a wild panic, she reaches for her purse. No purse. In the classroom. Her purse is in the classroom and her keys are in her purse. Oh, her mind whines loudly, no keys, no keys. She looks frantically around the parking lot. A number of parents stare wide-eyed and mouths open at Alison shoeless, coatless, and trembling. Parents exchange worried glances. What should they do? Alison spins to face the school building. No. I cannot go back. I can't go in there. He's in there. I can't go back in there. I know. At least that I know. She takes a step back, another step. She turns her back to the school and runs away leaving her purse and her jacket back in the classroom racing down the frigid street.

Alison looks up. She is on her back porch stoop breathing heavily. How did I get home? Wait. She doesn't remember. I ran? Did I run all the way home? She looks down at her feet. They're filthy and bleeding from numerous cuts and stubs. Her toes are numb and white from the cold. Oh, god. What's happening to me? She raps on the back kitchen door. Jimmy opens the door and looks warily at his mom.

"Mom?"

She forces normal, "Hi, honey."

"What are you doing?"

"Left my keys by accident."

"You don't have any shoes on?"

"Oh, ah, yeah, stubbed my toe and I just…my shoe didn't. Enough questions young man." She pushes past him and goes upstairs.

In the bathroom, she turns on the hot water faucet for her sink. As it fills with steaming water she closes the connecting pocket door that leads to Jimmy's bedroom, leaving the door to her room opened so she can hear. Pulling off her shredded stockings she tosses them in the little bathroom trash pail. She pulls a bottle of hydrogen peroxide from the vanity cabinet and pours a bit into the hot water. Sliding up onto the bathroom counter she plunges her feet into the sink to soak. I know what

I saw. The hot water hits her toes and they feel like she is walking on fire. She scrunches up her face, vigorously shakes her feet and leaves them to soak. She knows this happens when one is close to frostbite. I know what I saw. She massages the toes encouraging circulation. God, did I look like a crazy woman running barefoot down Hilldale? Who saw me? She drops her forehead to rest on her bent knees and allows the hot water to do its job, to coax life back to her damaged and frozen toes. I know what I saw. The hydrogen peroxide will be an adequate disinfectant because the street was so cold it is unlikely any kind of infection can result from these cuts. I know. Over and over in her head like a line from a song she cannot let go of: I know what I saw. It repeats without her thinking it. It repeats in time with her heartbeat.

Jimmy watches his mom all through dinner with trepidation. His conversation stutters around in aimless fits and he feels no subject is the right one. Clearly, school did not go so well for his mom, but she is resistant to discuss it. He thinks it could be because her car broke down, but he doesn't believe that is what it is. It feels like more of that other stuff, when she's here but she's not here, he thinks. He keeps looking at her and hoping he will see her like she was this morning. He desperately wants to see his mom again.

Jimmy answers his dad, "No I went home with Alan because we had a project. Mom stayed after for work."

"Oh." Hank senses her slipping away just like Jimmy does.

"So…" Jimmy shrugs, "I guess I'll go do my homework."

"Okay, son, always a good plan."

Jimmy carries his plate to the sink and goes to do his homework.

"So you walked home then?" Hank asks her as casually as he can manage.

"Yes."

"Why didn't you call Triple A?"

"I just didn't."

"Did the engine turn over?"

"Sort of."

"Sort of? Alison, did it seem like the battery or something else? I can go over and take a look tonight at the school. Give me your keys."

"No, I'll figure it out tomorrow."

"Honey, I'm happy to go and—"

"I've got it." she snaps at him. She can't tell Hank what happened. This is an impossible situation for them, they are too close to hide things from each other, but she knows she must stay quiet. She realizes some people think she's becoming unbalanced. And I suppose, she thinks, I'm not altogether certain they aren't right. I suppose there is a scintilla of doubt there. How can I not have doubts when what I see and hear is inconsistent with what everyone around me thinks and says? How do I rectify these contradictions? She holds her husband's eyes and Hank sees the confusion, he recognizes the distant look, and they both know she is lying. Hank had believed they were making progress and so he swallows the disappointment and he looks away. He wants to be patient, but he is beginning to feel like Alison isn't fighting to come back to them. His impatience is becoming unwieldy and he wants their life back. He can't persist in ignoring the consequences of her continued detachment on their son. It perpetuates Jimmy's injury and lengthens his recovery time. The impenetrable mask that seemed gone for good this morning is still there. It separates his son from the mother he urgently needs and the threads of Hank's compassion are fraying as he saw unequivocally the loss on Jimmy's face at dinner. Alison picks up the dinner plates and carries them to the sink. She peers out the kitchen window into the pitch black of the backyard. Get spotlights, she thinks. She scrapes the leftovers into the disposal. Hank wipes the counters. As he passes the controls, he switches on the music system and Ray Charles enters the room. Hank sings along "Georgia..." At least there is solace in the music. Alison lifts her head from the sink. She walks over and switches off the music.

"No Ray Charles? Feel like someone else?"

"No music."

Hank looks at her as if she is speaking gibberish. "What do you mean?'

"No more music. We can't have music."

"All night?"

"No music for a while."

"Why not?" He's been patching the family back together by himself, trying to be everything for both her and Jimmy, but now the nightmare is over. He does not have any more energy left for this. His music is not negotiable. It is his identity. He feels his temper rise up and his face turns red. She knows me, he thinks. She knows about music and me. She knows this if she knows anything.

"This is a little like telling me to stop breathing."

"It's too loud," she says.

"So I'll turn it down."

"No. We can't hear."

"Can't hear what?"

"Anything."

Hank raises his voice as he eggs her on, "Like what?" He whips down the kitchen towel and turns to her taking it on. The vein on his forehead is pulsing. She stops scraping the dish, carefully puts it down, and turns to face him.

"We need to hear if someone is around."

"Someone who?"

She grits her teeth, "We can't get sloppy."

The scab is ripped off between them.

"He's dead, Alison."

"On the contrary, he is loving this. The squirming, the fear, the game of us wondering."

"We're not wondering."

"Yes."

"Alison, for god's sake, wake up. This isn't a game it's our lives. You've got to pull it together. I'll do whatever I can to help, but you've got to try."

Jimmy innocently opens the swinging kitchen door.

"Hey, Dad, I need robot batteries."

"End table in the foyer."

"Okay." Jimmy turns and exits.

Alison remembers that is where she keeps the handgun. She goes after him. "No. Wait. I'll get…"

Hank grabs her arm. "It's not in there."

"What?"

"The gun isn't in there."

Angrily, "Where is it?"

"I got rid of it."

Furious, she yells, "Have you lost your mind?"

For a sour moment, they stand like that: Hank with his fingers harshly gripping her arm and Alison half-turned toward the door. The words she just spoke bang around the room. She knows what he is thinking. He thinks she has lost her mind. That is what he thinks. That is what everyone thinks. Too bad, I know what I know. I know it's not over. I can feel he's around.

"Hank, something strange happened out there between us."

"No, we're still the same."

"Not you and me—me and him."

"You and him. Now there's a you and him? There is no you and him."

"Something…some kind of animal thing passed between us and I'm trying to protect us."

"You want to protect us? To protect our family? Give me back my wife. Give Jimmy back his mother." They are squeezed in a fist of conflict. It is all so wrong. They know it is wrong, and they both want it to end, but they cannot see through the fog of the storm between them. They are both certain they are right and being so certain makes compromise untenable.

"I wish you understood." She pulls her arm away. "But I can't pretend it is not happening." She walks toward the swinging door.

"Alison." She stops never having heard that tone from her husband.

There is danger in it; it feels like a tipping point. "It is not happening." She does not feel quite as defiant as she looks when she spins around and pushes through the swinging door. Hank pushes his way out the back kitchen door. He shoves his hands into his pockets and walks around the frozen backyard in circles crunching the rigid blades of grass under fuming feet.

CHAPTER TWENTY-FOUR

THE FOLLOWING MORNING THE PACING continues unabated inside Doctor Cartwell's office. Hank walks around with such concentrated power he has created an oblong-shaped discernible path in the freshly vacuumed carpet. Inside the office, with its cushy armchairs and dark linen drapes, Hank feels it is allowable to let go. A candle burns on the shelf of the bookcase soothingly scenting the air with lavender heightening the sensation of being in a meditative space, a place where it is okay to lift the burden from his shoulders and stash it by the door until he can pick it up on the way out. Hank oscillates between anxiety and wrenching sadness, but his most pressing emotion is his mounting anger, an anger that has begun to bleed through the reinforced borders of his façade His goodness is leaking.

Doctor Cartwell says, "I want to talk about you, Hank. What you're feeling."

"What I'm feeling? Okay. Sure. Let's see. I feel infuriated beyond reason. The blood in my veins is angry, the hairs on my head are angry, my skin is cracked and itching because the anger has dried me out." His voice grows louder as he rants. "I'm mad at the streetlights, at the clock on the stove. I'm mad at the food on my plate. I'm mad at a god I don't even believe in. I feel like shaking someone to death. Yes, to death, that's it. That's how I feel like I want to shake and shake until I shake the life out of something and after all that shaking I know I will still be the same joke of a man I was before all the shaking."

"You think you're a joke?"

"The whole time, from the first moment at the camp, I've been worthless as a father, as a husband, as a man. I couldn't protect my son. I couldn't help my wife. I can't control anything. I can't fix anything. I'm useless."

"You were tied up."

"I'm not tied up now. She's losing it and I still can't help. I thought after a little time things would return to normal. The guy is dead. We have proof he's dead. I thought she would feel safe again, safe with me, but the truth is she isn't safe with me and now she knows that—she knows that for sure." He is shattered. "And that really hurts, you know, for the woman you love to see you in that way. Isn't there some kind of tacit social contract, or maybe it's a basic instinct thing that the female is protected by the male? We've upset some kind of natural order."

"I don't think she'd feel safe with anyone right now. This is really not a reflection on you, Hank."

"I wanted to save my family. I still want to save my family. Maybe another husband, another man, could've done something dramatic, or heroic, or at least mildly effective."

"You're confusing real life for any number of fictional Bruce Willis characters. If you would have been the one left out in the cold that night at the camp you would have done as much or more than Alison."

"I don't know that. You didn't see what she did." Hank stops pacing and leans against the large desk. His voice becomes distant. Doctor Cartwell listens with great focus and lets Hank's thoughts wander aloud. "Even though we are aware on some practical level from hearing the news every day that there is no such thing as "fair" we still function as though there is. I guess we have to. We live in this pathetic illusion that if we are good people then life will be fair. Maybe that's the only thing that keeps us civilized. The bottom line for us all is the belief that being good will lead to some kind of cosmic fairness, maybe we all believe in that kind of karma. Maybe that's why religions invented an afterlife: how else could you explain the unfairness except to believe there had to be more, that there must be a payoff later? And even when people say all the time, well you know life isn't fair, of course you know that," Hank throws up his hands, "we all *know* that, but we still live every day as though it is fair, and we still act surprised when it isn't. When Mike hit the floor dead at my feet, I knew that fair thing was over for me. Life is random. Death is random. Goodness is a choice with no predictive value. Any one of us good or bad can die face down in the gutter tonight. I remember reading about this woman who had been a foster mother to like fifty kids, and who was a revered and loved woman in this poor neighborhood, and she was murdered one day on her front lawn for the four dollars in her purse. There is no balance. The lady holding the scales of justice isn't blind so she can be fair, she's blind so it is random, she's blind because the facts don't matter, the circumstances don't matter, she's blind because it's a game to her, she's like a little kid with her hands over her eyes playing fucking hide 'n seek with all of our lives. And, you know what, Doctor, knowing all of this is not particularly comforting."

Cartwell waits before he speaks as a show of respect. Hank's words have been heartfelt and revealing. Then, he says gently, "Perhaps goodness is its own payoff."

"Resorting to platitudes, Doctor? What if people start to actually believe, believe every day the real truth, the truth that life isn't fair, does civilized society fall apart?"

"I don't know. But it is not that life isn't fair all the time, it is that sometimes it's not fair."

"Fair is an all or nothing thing. How do I explain that to a regular guy sitting here in his expensive office playing by the rules and watching the days go by with seeming predictability, and believing that people are civilized, believing you are in control of your life, and that there's some rationale behind things. How do I explain how helpless you actually are, how everything you've learned in one moment can mean nothing the next, how the person you are is completely irrelevant? You look at your life and you see you've been kind and lived considerately and you think that matters, and then some guy points a gun at your little boy's face and your little boy looks to you for help and all you can do is screech like a rodent in a glue trap. I can't explain to you what it is to be that kind of powerless. Turns out you are not a man like everyone has told you. You are worthless. This is a world full of monsters and predators and without the biggest weapon, you are just so much meat. And when you understand that then the screaming starts inside of you and it doesn't stop. I don't know who I am supposed to be right now. I surely don't know who Alison is. There is no reason on earth why she should remain mentally stuck back at that camp. Maybe the screaming inside of her is too loud to get over. Maybe that's why I can't reach her because she can't hear me over all the fucking screaming?"

Doctor Cartwell is silenced by the naked despair finally flowing from Hank. He waits. A long silence rolls out between them because there are no words, because there is no answer. Hank walks to the window and looks out to the parking lot. He calms himself by looking at the parking spaces, all of those symmetrical white lines on the blacktop. There is a comforting orderliness to them, all perfectly angled, in their place, exactly the same distance apart, lines being lines, simply, plainly, not trying to be anything else, neatly placed next to each other. He begins to count them.

After a minute Doctor Cartwell says, "Hank, I am duty-bound to tell you that there are genuine risks to not getting Alison some professional help."

"She won't go."

"I'm not sure she should be making that decision for herself right now."

"What does that mean?"

"It means when people need real help they are not always the ones who see that clearly. Sometimes they need to rely on the people around them, those who love them, to step in and assist."

"You are not suggesting I commit her?"

"A residential facility may be the perfect place for her to feel safe, get rest, and get the help she needs."

"Is that what they call it now? A residential facility? Is that the euphemism?"

"They aren't the horror places that folklore suggests."

"I don't believe in taking away her rights to herself."

"If she hurts someone that won't be your decision any longer."

"She won't."

"I know you aren't sure of that."

"She would be helpless and alone in the hands of who knows who. Forget it."

"Just think it over. If she is dangerous, or suicidal, it's a temporary treatment to save her life."

"There has got to be a way to prove to her that she is safe now, that it's time to move on."

"If she's having breaks with reality, if she's seeing things that aren't there, she requires professional help and medication. There may be some tough choices ahead for you. I just want you to prepare yourself for that."

Hank sits down in the chair and buries his face in his hands. He sits there immobile for the rest of the hour. He thinks about all of the blameless people in history who in one inconsequential moment made a simple choice: who stepped off the curb one second too soon, who sprinted to catch that doomed train, who took one wrong turn in the wilderness, who ran out for that bottle of milk they needed for the morning they never saw, and a guy who said simply to his son "wanna go fishing for your birthday."

That night they are both up, Alison at her sentry position staring out of the bedroom window to the street, and Hank watching the clock waiting for morning. As soon as Jimmy gets picked up for school, he tells Alison to get dressed. She knows he is furious and hurt and so she doesn't ask any questions she simply throws on her jeans and follows him.

Hank drives. Alison is antsy in the passenger seat, shifting her weight around, putting one leg under her and then the other trying to find the right configuration but always looking out and around: looking for him. She realizes after a few turns that Hank is driving her back to the police station. Maybe he's going to have me arrested she thinks. Would he? Would he do that? That's crazy. Well, not crazy. I don't mean that is actually crazy. I just…and her mind shuts off so she can concentrate on the car behind them. The stress between them is like a pinball banging back and forth. She feels it physically and expects to have black and blue marks later. They don't chance talking to each other. Hank plays his iPod through the car radio and he pretends to listen, he taps his hand to the beat on the steering wheel, but a careful observer would notice he's just a beat off. Alison stares out the passenger window and scans the cars that pass them studying each driver.

Once they are inside Crane's office the tension persists and the words unspoken between Hank and Alison form a messy glob of thick air in the room. Crane feels an ache of sympathy for these folks. He has witnessed years of indiscriminate violence perpetrated on good people like these. He has seen their marriages collapse and their lives ruined. He would like that not to be the case with these two, but really, he has little hope of that. Alison Kraft definitely needs help, but she is evidently resistant. Hank seems like a really good guy, devoted and caring. Maybe they'll make it.

"Whatever we can do to help," Crane reassures them.

Hank says, "Maybe actually seeing him dead will make the difference for her. Maybe that is what she needs."

"Yes," she agrees. This is a good idea and she tries to smile at her husband. That may be exactly what she needs. "I need to see it."

Officer Thomas enters while she is talking and adds "Gotta admit ain't nothin' prettier than a dead Burne boy." Crane rolls his eyes at the indecorous comment. Thomas couldn't care less.

He holds a large envelope full of 8 x 10 photographs of the scene.

Crane turns to Alison and speaks gently, "Mrs. Kraft, just a warning: it's pretty gruesome."

She looks at him plainly, "I hope so."

Thomas smiles to himself. He likes her. He can't help it. There is something so bluntly honest about her. She's no Pollyanna, like her husband, or political pencil pusher like Crane. She gets it. She's tough. She's smart. She just needs to see it. He absolutely understands that. He needed to see it for himself, too. People who have no connection with Ben Burne just can't appreciate how sticky pure evil is—it's real hard to get it off of you. Thomas narrates as he flips through the pictures one at a time. "This is a picture of Burne entering the cabin." Alison lays her eyes on the figure walking up the brick stoop toward the front door of a small log cabin. It is a densely wooded area similar to the fishing camp. Woods will never be pretty to her. She will not be one of the tourists running to watch the colors change in the fall. It crosses her mind just then that perhaps they should move somewhere there are no woods at all. Perhaps a total change of environment is what they need. What about California for the ocean or New Mexico for the desert? Studying the photo, Ben's body is purposely turned toward the shade. He is conscious of being watched, she can tell that by his body language. She can also see quite clearly that it is Ben. It is definitely him and in Canada. Thomas lays down another photo. "This is the cabin minutes later at the explosion. And here's one seconds after the explosion."

Okay, Alison thinks. I see it. Destruction.

Thomas continues, "And inside. This was the living room. And there," Thomas' voice has fallen to a quiet tone. He and Alison share these images as though they are alone. They concentrate. Thomas continues, "See, on the floor by the window, that's him." Hank leans over, looks, and quickly turns his eyes away from the gooey charred skeleton with the hanging eyeball. Alison reaches for the picture. She holds it in her hands. She brings is close to her face and she studies the details. They all wait for her sigh of relief because that man is dead, dead before her very eyes.

She asks, "Did you match dental records?"

"Aren't any," Crane answers.

"How do you know this is him?"

Detective Crane explains patiently, "We had a stake out. We have all these photographs of him entering the cabin. Then the shootout, the explosion and fire directly after."

She studies the picture again. "But this could be anyone."

All three men look at her.

"Mrs. Kraft, we are confident, the Canadian police are confident, the FBI, and the ATF are confident that it is Benjamin Burne."

She looks him straight in the eye. "But there's no proof."

Hank starts to boil, "That's him. Walking in. Right there in the picture. Can't you see that?"

"Yes. I see a body there but how do we know who that is?" She points to the gelatinous glop of bones and burnt skin and blackened eyeballs.

"Alison, they are telling you they saw him inside." The stress between them spills out into the room.

She points to the first picture. "But look. Look there, at how he's walking. He knows they're watching him."

"So that doesn't change this." Hank points to the dead mess of a man.

She looks at Crane, "How about DNA testing?"

"The lab has a huge backlog and since there is no pressing issue here as we are all confident of the identity, the test has been shelved."

Alison asks, "Please, do the testing. If it costs money, I'll pay it. Whatever it takes."

Crane shuffles his feet a little, "Let me see what I can do."

"How long does the DNA take to do?" Hank asks.

"Once you start, five to seven days."

Unconsciously, her foot shimmies back-and-forth vigorously, "That's too long."

Hank speaks over her "That would be fine."

Crane equivocates, "Frankly, resources are tight and I can't guarantee..."

Thomas blurts, "Hey, I think Mrs. Kraft here did society a pretty big favor and she should be able to jump the line." She looks at Thomas and almost smiles. He may be the only person who understands her. Thomas trails off annoyed, "I mean seriously here. She wasted three of the four Burne boys."

"But we have ongoing court cases that require evidence and..." Crane looks at her. He looks at Thomas who throws his palms out in a disbelieving gesture. Crane says, "I'll see what I can manage."

Hank and Alison exit the station and walk over to their car. It did not work out the way Hank had planned. He feels like he has only created more doubt for her. Or maybe she is creating her own doubt for some reason. Maybe some part of her wants him to be alive because it lessens her responsibility for wiping out an entire family. Or maybe it all just happened so quickly, the trip, the chaos, and the death, that she needs this time to slow it all down so she can get a grip on it. Or maybe she's not going to get a grip on it. He opens the door for her. He began doing this on their first date and it is a little ritual that they both like, but today it just feels perfunctory. She slides into the passenger seat. He walks around, gets in, slams his door and starts the engine. She felt more at ease inside that police station than anywhere else so far. Maybe she should ask if she could spend the night in jail to get a good sleep, but no, because that would leave Hank and Jimmy at home and at risk. Maybe Hank would agree for all three of them to sleep a night or two in the jail. She could ask him. Jimmy might think it's cool. Maybe...

Hank blows, "So what is it you want exactly?"

"Excuse me?"

"Finally, the best news, and you can't even accept it!"

"Not sure I believe it."

"Because you're more experienced and smarter than the FBI, ATF, and the police force of two countries?"

"I'm not saying that."

"You're putting your feelings ahead of all their skill and knowledge."

"When he looked at me in the woods and we both knew I'd killed his family and there was my family still okay, this, oh I don't know, there was this thread, or electrical charge, or something that went between us—like a pact. I know it doesn't appear to make any sense. And I know I'm hurting people around me but the alternative is worse."

Hank confronts her derisively, "So let's review: you know it doesn't make any sense, you think you have some kind of deadly pact with a dead mass murderer, and you are aware you're hurting us all."

"I think I would feel it if he were dead."

His words drip with sarcasm, "You'd feel it, so to the above list add you're also psychic now? So what you need his blood on your hands to be sure?"

"What I need is to be sure."

"The police say it's him."

"I just don't see how they can be sure."

"Why won't you let us get back to our lives?"

"I want to."

"I wonder."

"What's that supposed to mean?"

"You weren't the only one on that island, Alison. Your son was there. Remember him? He saw Hobbs and Mike and Bruce shot dead. They had a loaded gun to Jimmy's head. But he's getting better. Working through it, reaching for it. I was there, too. I was there terrified and useless. Do you know what useless feels like?"

"Yes, I know." Her voice has dropped to a whisper.

"No, you don't. You're the hero in this."

"Is that what you think?"

"You killed the bad guys."

"So this is about your ego."

"No!" He slams his fists on the steering wheel. "It's not. It's not that."

And it really isn't that. Hank looks out the driver's window. They are both in so much pain. When he speaks again his voice is breathy and lost.

He says, barely audibly, "It should have been me. I just wish it had been me."

Choking back tears, "So do I."

His expression is twisted with hurt when he turns his whole body toward her in the front seat of their car. The plea comes from the deepest part of his heart and she can feel it all the way through to her bones. "Alison, you have to let it go. He's dead. We have our lives, our little family. We value them more than we ever could have now. Please, pull yourself back from the edge before we're destroyed. Please." He has reached her because beyond all of the paranoia she loves him, still loves him, wishes she could feel that love again, but she has been unable to feel anything. She gets outside of it all and considers what he is saying. He is right. Even if she doesn't think he is right, maybe he is, and maybe she needs to try harder and it will all become all right if she pretends, maybe that is her way home.

"I love you, Hank."

He takes her hands in his, reaches with all of his strength into her soul and pleads, "Come back to us, Alison."

"I will." And she did not know if she could.

They were dainty with each other for the remainder of the day: she turned on his music when they got home and he noticed. He checked the locks on the windows and on the basement door and she noticed. An air of practiced civility smoothed out their conversation at dinner and Jimmy thought they were acting weird. It felt a bit like their first married fight long ago, after which they stepped politely around each other for a solid day exchanging an excessive number of "please's" and "thank you's." That first fight is disturbing because it shatters the new love spell and requires newlyweds to look plainly at one another, realize that bliss is work, and that love is not what they deserve but what they achieve. Hank learned then that love required constant maintenance and sometimes that comes in the regularity of cozy gestures. As the evening ends, Alison wrestles with her anxiety, and standing in front of the vanity in her bathroom she gulps down two sleeping pills while she thinks, really, if I let this destroy my marriage what am I saving? I'm over the edge. It would be dishonest to pretend I didn't know that. She walks out of the bathroom and over to Hank who is hanging up his pants in the closet.

She says, "I know that my daydreams are vivid in a strange way." He can see she has a mind full of things to say and he waits. She continues, "It's like when I was a little girl and I had night terrors. It was right after mom died and went on for a year and I acted on them. I was reacting to things only real inside my mind. I would get out of bed while living inside the nightmare. One time I even left the house. My dad heard the front door open in the middle of the night and he ran after me. I was asleep and crying and walking around in the front yard barefoot. Maybe this is like that—the daytime equivalent of that—day-mares. Maybe I'm having day-terrors. Maybe that explains why it seems so real to me. He... (she finds she cannot say his name) he wasn't in the school stairwell."

"No."

"It's impossible."

"Impossible."

"He is dead in Canada."

"Yes. He is dead in Canada."

"Right." She leans in and kisses him. "I'm going to sleep now."

"That would be good."

She spins around and walks with determination to the feather arms of her bed. She slips in under the sheets. She sinks into the mattress, which feels spongy and cool and glorious, and as the clenched fist that is every muscle in her entire body releases, she makes a tiny sound: half-sigh, half-cry, barely audible, and the most satisfying sound Hank has ever heard.

When Hank wakes, he is lying on his side and she is cuddled into the curve of his body fast asleep, skin to skin, a rush of joy and relief literally shakes him. He lies there feeling her hair soft under his chin and the subtle rise and fall of her breathing against his chest. He waits until the very last possible second before rolling over and switching off the alarm. He sneaks out of bed without disturbing her.

After he made breakfast for Jimmy, they grabbed their coats just as she came down the stairs in her bathrobe and fluffy slippers. She slept so hard that when she wakes the entire side of her face is imprinted with lines from the sheets. It was hard to get out of bed. The sleeping pills made her feel groggy.

"Hey." She stopped them at the front door. "How are my men?"

Her smile is radiant. Hank walks over and kisses her on the mouth.

"Okay that's gross," Jimmy said, "really, I just ate."

She smiles with light sarcasm, "Really, darling, he just ate."

Hank takes her chin in his hand, her hair is clumpy and her eyes are raccoon-like with her smudged mascara, but she has never looked more beautiful to him. It all feels good. She will manhandle her thoughts. She will take back control. She will cut off all malevolent meandering, dig out a specific trail for her imagination and she will not deviate.

"Remember," Hank tells her lovingly, "today is only about relaxing: take a bath, read a book, nap. All good stuff, yeah?"

"Definitely my plan."

"Tomorrow back to work."

"Deal."

"See you later,"

"Bye Mom."

She kisses Jimmy on the head. As they close the front door, she feels blissfully normal. Part of it she can attribute to a full night's sleep and honestly she could go right back to bed and probably sleep for a month but, she is hungry, actually really hungry. She spins around light in her fluffy slippers and goes to the kitchen. I can do this. I can let go and do this.

Alison opens the refrigerator to get the milk for her coffee and sees two leftover casseroles. It gives her a pang the way casseroles always do. Enough, she tells herself, no more of these. She removes them from the refrigerator and puts them in the sink. She opens the cabinet and takes out her favorite cereal bowl. Isn't it funny, she thinks, that people have favorite bowls and cups. Her dad had a cup she had made for him at a ceramic workshop. She went there for a birthday party when she was eight years old and made this ridiculous coffee cup. He used it every morning, insisted on it. I know I saved that cup, she thinks.... Why is the basement door unlocked? She stops and stares. I saw Hank lock it last night. He never goes into the basement, neither does Jimmy. No. Stop. Do not go there. Think about dinner. She will cook dinner tonight. Yes. She will make Jimmy's favorite meal of spaghetti with butter and -- a noise from the basement -- with spaghetti with butter and cheese and a noise from the basement...la la la la la la...cooking really is the perfect synergy of creativity and utilitarianism. I have always liked to... another noise...always cooking liked...footsteps coming up. Damn it. She is not imagining it. Her expression darkens. Her heart pounds. The air in the room turns sour. He is in her house. She slides open the drawer in the butcher's block and removes the carving knife. She darts to the side of the basement door. He's so much bigger than I am. She breathes in rapid short gulps. Oh, god, oh, god; can I do this? The basement door opens slowly. This is it. End it. End it now. Her hand closes tightly around the knife in her fist. She raises the thick meat cleaver above her head. Don't hold back—every ounce. The door gently pushes open. She leaps out. Now. Polly screams in terror! She throws the laundry basket she is holding at Alison. Polly runs out of the room. Disoriented, Alison freezes. She lowers the cleaver. Wait. What? Polly. It was Polly. Alison hears the front door slam as Polly runs for her life. Alison shuffles over to the kitchen chair and sits confused. She reworks what just happened in her mind. "Oh, shit." But wait. I'm not imagining things. Someone really was down there. What I heard was real. "It was real...it was...Polly, but real." Alison runs her left hand through her hair. I'm not hearing and seeing things. It is real. It is all real. I knew it was real and it is. She rubs her eyes and rests her elbows on her knees. Laundered underpants and socks are spewed all over the kitchen floor. Her eyes drop to the carving knife in her right hand. She considers it. She picks it up and turns it around in her hand. "But this is bullshit. This won't do." She tosses the knife on the tabletop, proceeds out of the kitchen and up the stairs to get dressed.

* * *

The room rocks at Pump Up The Volume. Hank sits in the front of the store and enjoys the harmony of Nickelback as he constructs a playlist on his computer for the weekend events. He was so excited when he got to work this morning because he could tell the guys that Alison was on the road to health, that he felt the shift last night, that he woke up with her in his arms again. The glass in the storefront window vibrates discernibly and Hank bops his body in rhythm with the music. This vibration that comes from the beat is what contentment feels like to him. It is what he feels in every cell of his body when the music is raging. The walls of the store are covered with framed posters from every era and genre of music: Joni Mitchell is next to Jethro Tull is next to Jay Z is next to Garth Brooks. Hank is pounding away at the computer keys, immersed in the music, and reveling in his thoughts. I haven't felt this good since before. Maybe I've never felt this good. What if everything in life is felt only in proportion to its opposite? What if I've only been living on the surface and skimming emotions? What if since I'd never known fear and blood and anguish, I couldn't access this kind of relief or joy? What if this is actually the best I've ever felt in my life because I never appreciated things the way I do now. Maybe that's the positive that I can take away from all of this shit he tells himself. Maybe you can learn something from a trip to hell if you survive with your world intact. I didn't feel how great my life was every day like I should have. I complained about piddlely little shit. He hits a few quick strokes on his iPod and Louis Armstrong's voice crackles into the room singing "What a Wonderful World." He smiles at the craggily voice, the sound of a life well lived. Hank sits back on the chair and lets his eyes survey the room.

I will never take my life for granted again. I promise that to myself. I will never take a normal day for granted again. In fact, I vow to remember that every single ordinary day is a gift. He remembers the softness on Alison's face when he left that morning, and he sees Jimmy's wave as he slammed the car door and raced off to school. He feels so deeply grateful that he looks around quickly, embarrassed that the emotion is so obvious on his face, but the store is empty and Newt and Scottie are in the back stacking equipment.

Scott yells to Hank from the back storage room, "Are you working on the Silverstein bar mitzvah?"

"Haroldson wedding."

"Okay, so, the Silversteins have requests, forty of them."

"Why didn't they just make their own playlist?'

"Don't know how to work an iPod."

"Oh," Hank smiles and glances up to see Polly at the front door to the store. She stands ashen and wobbly looking in through the glass. Hank leaps out of his chair and rushes over opening the door and taking her by the arm. His jaw drops as he feels her trembling. He guides her in and flips off the music. The look on her face scares him.

"Polly? What?"

"She tried to stab me!"

Hank grabs her hands. "What do you mean?"

Scott and Newt come in from the back.

"Tell me what happened."

"She almost killed me."

"She couldn't."

"If I hadn't had the laundry basket in front of me I'd be bleeding on your kitchen floor."

Trying to convince her, not wanting to believe what she is telling him Hank insists, "She was better this morning. Good. She was good."

"I wanted to tell you in person. I'm not going back."

"This week?"

She pulls away her hand. "At all. I'm not going back at all, Hank."

"Polly, please, we need you. I need you. Just a little longer. She's so much better. When we left this morning she was so normal, really completely—"

"Look, Hank. I'm very fond of you, well, of all of you, but she needs serious help and I'm not going back. I'm sorry." She steps toward the door. She turns, "And Hank, I'd keep her away from Jimmy if I were you." The seriousness in her tone is like ice on his neck. "Please keep her away from Jimmy." She leaves and closes the door. Hank whirls around as the accumulation of frustrated fury explodes. He grabs the printer from the desk and hurls it across the room and into the wall where it shatters.

"Holy shit." Newt says.

"Hank?" Scottie grabs his shoulders before he picks up something else. "Buddy, chill."

Hank stands shaking with rage. "I want my life back." Scott indicates for Newt to lock the front door and he does.

"Buddy, buddy, calm down." Scott encourages him, "You know she's better. You said so."

Newt adds, "That's right. Today when you came in."

"She pulled a knife on our housekeeper."

Newt says, "Maybe it was like a butter knife."

"Really, Newt?" Scott glares at him.

"But it matters, like maybe it wasn't a real knife, but just a kind of knife that couldn't really do any harm, that would matter, right? Like maybe she was actually buttering something, and she got startled and spun around, and it was a butter knife and Polly overreacted."

Scott tries to shut up Newt. "I do not think the kind of knife matters, Newt."

Hank looks up at them, "What am I supposed to do?"

"Man," Newt says sympathetically. "I cannot imagine"

"How do I make her better?"

"You will," Scott's voice doesn't sound as sure as Hank would like.

"And what if Polly's right? What about Jimmy?"

Scottie rests his hand on Hank's shoulder, "She just needs more time, that's all. I mean, come on, Hank, the woman is so delicate she gets faint passing the meat case at the supermarket. Then she kills three men…cut her some slack."

"Didn't the therapist want to put her on some kind of meds? Maybe that would help," Newt says. "Meds always help me."

"She refuses to take anything because she needs to stay alert. The therapist said she was paranoid. Alison says no one who wasn't there can understand and that's true. All I want in the world is to put it behind us and take our lives back and she just keeps bringing it up, reliving it, looking for boogey men, keeping it all alive."

Newt says, "Go home, man."

"Really, Hank, we've got you covered here," Scottie assures him. "Go on home."

Hank thinks about it and then admits to his friends the sad truth, "It's not good to show up unexpectedly." And Hank faces what he has known: Alison is dangerous, dangerous to him, to Jimmy, to herself. He has to make the right choice here. He needs to think it calmly through and do the right thing for everyone. This must be the moment Doctor Cartwell was preparing him for. Yes, this is it. He must think very clearly, very carefully.

CHAPTER TWENTY-FIVE

ALISON CRANKS THE STEERING WHEEL and maneuvers in between two cars in the strip mall parking lot. It hosts all the usual little businesses: Dunkin' Donuts, McDonalds, Starbucks, Super Cuts and then "Merriweather's Guns, Hundreds of Weapons: Military Surplus, User Friendly." She scans the area meticulously before she eases herself out of the car. She looks over her shoulder and then locks the car doors. She strides to the front. The shop has a security door. The forty-year-old storeowner, Derreck, sees Alison through the glass and buzzes her in. The door shuts and locks automatically behind her. She likes that. She liked the sound of the locks sliding into place. She used to like the sound of the swallows nesting in the eaves, now she likes the metal clank of a world-class lock.

Dust doesn't exist in this spit-shined shop. The merchandise is polished to an eye-blinding gleam. The glass countertops are spotless. Alison feels predatory as she stands in the middle of the shop crammed from floor to ceiling with weapons: handguns, rifles, shotguns, knives, even bows and arrows. The metallic smell is so strong she can taste it. For the second time recently, she is at ease. She walks over to the counter.

"Can I help you?" Derreck asks.

"I need a gun."

"For sport or defense?"

"What sport?" she looks at him confused.

"Hunting birds, game? Target practice?"

"Oh, defense." She scans the handguns in the case.

"Ever handled a gun before?"

Her mind stumbles back. She shoots Gravel point blank into the stomach, over and over, his stunned look, followed by his dead eyes. She thinks dead eyes don't really even look like eyes, they look like marbles: hard and glassy. It is the just-before-dying eyes that stick with you: Theo as he fell to certain death; Kent still alive and harpooned to the shed wall, but no eyes—dead or alive—had the icy everlasting imprint of Ben's.

"Ma'am?"

"Yes?" Confused, she looks around. Oh, yes, the gun shop. I'm in the gun shop. I need a gun.

"I said, have you handled a gun before?"

"Yes."

"Okay. 'Cause you know weapons can be tricky. If you don't know what you're doing it could be a risk."

"Not as risky as not having a weapon."

"True." He smiles. "So, a little lady like you might appreciate this." He holds up the small revolver. "It'll fit nicely in your hand and it's light to carry."

"If I want a toy I'll go to Walmart. What about that one?" She points to the menacing Ruger 357 magnum.

"That's a really good weapon. I could hook you up with a box of Wolf hollow point ammo and you'd be set for anything. But it all kinda depends on what you want."

"I want him dead." She says this fast without thinking. It comes directly from her subconscious. She tries to add a smile after it to lessen the weird pause that settles between them.

Derreck's eyes narrow, "Ah...not something you want to be saying in a gun store, lady."

"What I mean," she softens, smiles, exposes her most vulnerable face, "I want something that if I ever have to shoot, I hope not, but if I do, I only have to shoot once. I may only be capable of once." Gravel's eyes are fierce: bang, bang, bang, bang; he is on top of her and his midsection spasms up with each shot as she empties the gun into his stomach.

Derreck's just not sure about this woman. There is something peculiar about her, but he is in the business of selling guns and really, nothing comes before business. "I'll need to see some ID and then we'll fill out the permit info and you can pick it up next week."

"Next week?"

"There's a seven day waiting period."

"Oh. That won't work."

"It won't?"

"What in here doesn't have a waiting period?"

He looks at her long and hard. He probably should not sell this woman a weapon. Still, it's definitely not his job to police this woman or anyone actually. He's a salesperson, not a detective. The shop could use the income.

"You don't want a waiting period?"

"I'm here now and I don't want to have to drive all the way back again."

"Uh, huh. Any of those rifles or shotguns are cash and carry."

"So which is reliable?"

"Personally, I like the Mossberg 8 Shot, 20 inch barrel, with the pistol grip. Load her up and then just cock and shoot." He lays the weapon on the countertop.

She runs her hand along it. She lifts it up. Not too heavy. She looks the weapon up and down. It looks powerful, intimidating. She rests it carefully back down on the counter. "I'll take two."

"Two?'

Forty minutes later, Alison stands in her foyer holding the two rifles and thinking strategically. Where are the best places? Obviously, one upstairs and one down. Yes, that will work best. She takes one, loads it like the gun shop owner showed her, and carries it down to the basement.

Alison likes to collect up things and box them so she can drive them to Goodwill twice a year. She's never been able to throw anything useful away. There are too many people who need things and her heart won't allow it. Consequently, the basement resembles a thrift shop with hanging racks and old furniture. She walks past the washer and dryer sees the job half done with a washer tub full of water and soaking sheets. She feels a pang of regret about Polly. She climbs over an old set of folding chairs to get to the chest of drawers against the wall. This is where she keeps all of Jimmy's baby clothes. There is no reason for anyone to go into these drawers. She pulls open the second drawer and is sidetracked by the sight of the one-piece green and black Batman pajama. She remembers the two-year-old who loved that footsie, oh, that sunny grubby pot-bellied little boy. She misses him with such an intense pang she feels it like a little bursting in all the cells of her body. She misses hearing him stumble around with his words, and she misses the way he would hold her hand extra tight whenever they were in a crowd. Why is motherhood all about saying good-bye? She pulls out the pajama and holds it up seeing that more than half of the cartoon Batman has flaked away. Jimmy insisted on wearing it to bed every night. He loved it. He felt safe in it. It will take more than Batman pajamas for him to feel safe now, she thinks. The fabric is limp and soft from so many washings. The colors have faded and there's a hole in the knee, and when she sees that she feels his little hand on her heart. She rubs the pajama against her cheek. It still smells like baby after all these years. Why does that feel like a lifetime ago? She carefully lays the rifle down in the drawer. It fits perfectly. She replaces the pajama on top and tucks in around the sides, six pairs of baby socks with the rubber no-slip strips on the bottom. She closes the drawer. She takes a step back and stares at the chest: life and death—all in the drawer of her basement.

She takes the second Mossberg upstairs to the bedroom. Not a lot of options. It is too long for her chest of drawers, or her little desk. She drops to her knees and shoves the weapon under her side of the bed. She admonishes, that won't do at all, but it's okay while I search for another spot. The novel she was reading had slipped behind the bed board and is jammed into the corner. She reaches for the book and pulls it out. She isn't reading anymore. Why is that? She sits down cross-legged on the carpet and looks at the book. Reading was her joy, her escape. She used to say that to friends. I love to escape into a book. From what, she now wondered. What was she escaping from? Her nice job, her beautiful family, her healthy body, her life, which she thought was stressful? What an unappreciative woman I was. Unconscious. Stupid. When this is over, I will ask for different things from life. I will ask for mornings so quiet I can hear my husband shave and evenings loud with laughter and love and music.

* * *

At Pump Up The Volume, Hank sits staring into space. He has not moved since Polly left. Newt and Scottie tried to get him to eat some lunch, but he couldn't. He is frozen and thoughtless. He just feels completely blank as he waits for the clock to hit two-thirty, so he can go pick up Jimmy, and then drive home to deal with whatever he finds there and confront Alison about Polly. Maybe, he thinks, it wasn't as bad as Polly said. Crazy as Newt can be with the whole butter knife concept, maybe he has it right and it was a misunderstanding. Polly could have overreacted because she knows how Alison has been.

Scottie yells, "Hank, phone."

Hank picks up the call in the front. "Hello, this is Hank."

"Hi, Hank, it's Denise at school."

"Hey, Denise," he hears the fake cheer in his tone and hopes she doesn't.

"Um…Hank," she pauses.

"Yeah?"

"I know what you're going through, and I hate to give you more bad news, but I thought you could use some warning."

His stomach cramps. Not something else, please, not something else. "Okay, what's up?"

"The School Board voted to lay off Alison."

"No. It is the only positive thing. Working will help her."

"I know, but she's acting really strange. She's scaring people."

"Oh."

"A lot of the parents are complaining."

Crestfallen, "Complaining?" He jumps to defend her, "They should be giving her a medal. Don't they know what she has done? I think the police department really is thinking about giving her a medal." This is not true but he likes the sound of it.

"I'm really sorry, Hank. Listen if I can do anything..." she trails off.

"I know. I know. You've been great." He stands and starts pacing in really small circles as anxiety floods him. "And thanks for everything, Denise. My other line is ringing. I'll talk to you later."

"Okay, tell Alison I love her."

"Will do." Hank is almost yelling as he picks up the second line. "Pump Up the Volume."

"Is Mr. Kraft available?"

"Speaking."

"Hello, this is the fraud department from Citibank regarding some charges on your credit card."

"I'm too busy now. I need..."

"Yes, sir, but there are charges today that are out of the ordinary and so for your protection—"

"What is it? What charge?"

"A charge to Merriweather Guns and Military Surplus on Bloom Street."

Hank slams down the receiver. "That's it." Hank grabs his keys. "Scottie?"

Scott looks in, "What?"

"Pick up Jimmy for me now at school so I can get home first."

"You got it."

And Hank is gone.

He breaks every speed limit driving home. I can't believe she did this. His mind reels. This is a complete break of our trust. This is truly crazy, scary paranoid. How could she do this? How could she? Damn it. He screeches into the driveway. He throws open the front door to his home and yells, "Alison!" She is catapulted by the sound of his angry voice. She rushes in from the living room where she was trying to read. By the time she gets into the foyer, Hank is already wrenching open every drawer. Then, he moves into the living room where he begins a serious search under the sofa cushions.

"Hank?"

"Where?"

"Hank?"

"Where is it, Alison?"

"What? Where's what?"

"Where's the gun?" Surprised, she doesn't answer. He throws the books off the bookcase. "Tell me now. Where's the gun?"

"Are you following me?"

"No. Although I guess I should. The credit card company called. They thought it was kind of odd your expensive purchase at Merriweather's Military Surplus." He moves toward the stairs. She follows him. "Where is the gun, Alison?"

"In a safe place."

"Give it to me right now."

They stand face-to-face in conflict. She answers with her eyes firm but her voice shaking, "No."

"Alison," he turns on her with force, "Give it to me or I'll tear this house apart." She has never seen this kind of fury from him. It is so out of character and she is unnerved and frantic.

"I need it, Hank. I have to have it."

He takes the stairs three at a time and blasts into their bedroom. She follows and stops at the doorway. He starts in the far corner of the room, opens her little desk and empties the contents on the rug. He moves to the next drawer and then the next, throwing everything onto the floor.

"Okay," she says. "Stop."

He slows and turns to her. "Where?"

"Under my side of the bed."

Hank walks over, bends down and pulls out the rifle. "Oh my god, it's huge."

"There was a waiting period for a smaller one."

He turns away disgusted, "Is it loaded?"

"Of course it's loaded. Not much use if it's not loaded."

The door slams downstairs.

"Mom? Dad?"

Alison answers with a forced calm, "Upstairs, honey."

Hank shoves the gun in the hidden area behind the opened door to the bedroom as Jimmy appears in the doorway. He looks at them. Clearly, something is up.

"Um…hi?" Jimmy says leery.

"Hi, how was school?" Alison asks. Her voice sounds high-pitched and strained.

"Kinda normal. Why did Scottie pick me up?"

Hank turns away from Alison and speaks to his son with a bare-knuckle calm because now he is finally absolutely certain of what he must do. "Jimmy, please go into your room and pack a suitcase."

"What?" Alison whips her head to him.

"Why?" Jimmy asks worried.

"Hank, we need to talk."

Ignoring her, Hank continues speaking directly to Jimmy, "Make sure you have clothes for school, a toothbrush, and all your books."

"But, Dad, I don't want to go anywhere."

"Hank." Alison tries not to further upset Jimmy but it is no use. Her son's brow is furrowed and his eyes alarmed.

Hank says, "Bring a couple of video games, too. Now go."

Troubled, Jimmy backs out of the volatile room. "But where are we going?"

"We're driving to Grandma's"

Jimmy asks tenuously, "All of us?"

Hanks replies, "Just you and me. Your mom has some things she needs to do."

Jimmy stands for a moment. He looks at his mom. She holds her words but the quivering of her face is undeniable. His dad nods his head at him and Jimmy crosses the little hallway and enters his bedroom. Alison turns urgently to Hank and speaks in a nearly hysterical whisper.

"You can't do this."

"I can."

"No."

"I have to." Hank walks to the closest and takes out a suitcase. He packs aggressively throwing clothing into the suitcase while Alison pleads.

"Hank, please, don't do this."

"You need help, Alison."

"I need a bazooka."

"Your judgment has gone to shit."

"I have good judgment." She feels panic rising—alarm soaks her.

"You're seeing things, you're hearing things, and you refuse to help yourself."

"I am helping myself. I'm helping us all."

"You won't take your medication."

"It makes me feel sick and groggy."

"You refuse to go to therapy."

"I don't need to talk about it. I need to be prepared."

"You're going to shoot me or Jimmy on our way to the bathroom some night."

"No. I won't. I wouldn't make that mistake. Never."

"You pulled a knife on Polly."

"She was sneaking up from the basement."

"Sneaking?"

"Okay, maybe not sneaking. But I didn't imagine it. I really heard something. She was in the basement."

"Doing our laundry."

"So maybe I overreacted."

"Maybe? Maybe you overreacted by pulling a knife on our sixty-year-old housekeeper?"

"Please stop packing."

"It's no wonder they are laying you off work."

"They're laying me off?" Alison feels like she's been physically struck.

"Yes, what did you think? You think you can run around fleeing from ghosts and acting crazy and no one will care that you're around their children?" He slams shut the suitcase. "I can't trust you."

She begins to cry protesting, "You can."

"You're buying weapons behind my back. You've turned away from everyone in your life who has tried to help you. But this is where I draw the line. Jimmy comes first. I know that now. I need to protect my son."

"Our son. And how can you protect him when you won't even face that there's a threat?"

"Oh," he levels his eyes at her deadly serious, "I know there's a threat."

"It's not me, Hank."

"We will be at my mother's. We'll come back after you return the gun, when you have gone back to therapy, when you are on the medications that have been prescribed, and when it is safe to bring Jimmy back into his home." Hank spins around with his small suitcase and meets Jimmy in the hallway.

"Let's go, son," he says.

"What about Mom?"

"Mom has some stuff she needs to do first."

Alison cannot tolerate the worry on her little boy's face. It pains her to see the distraught look in his eyes. This reaches right through the wall of her fears and into the very heart of who she is as a mother. She knows at this moment that she cannot stop Hank. She has to help Jimmy. She must do what she can to lessen this blow, to make it okay for him. She clears her face, manages a half-grin, bends down and hugs him tightly.

"Hey, my little man, it's okay. Just temporary. It's better if you go on with your dad. I actually do have a few things to take care of and then I'll come over. Don't let Dad drive Grandma nuts with his music all the time, okay?"

"Okay." Jimmy looks down at his shoes trying to mentally organize his feelings.

And even through the betrayal and all the fury, Hank loves her for this. He knows how this must feel to her. Somewhere inside, beyond all the paranoia at the core of her, she is still the selfless caring woman he fell in love with. Hank and Jimmy load into the car in the driveway. Jimmy looks back at his mother standing in the doorway. His anxiety reaches her and feeling it, she quickly smiles to reassure him. She watches them back out. She has no idea how to stop them, whether to stop them. She has doubts. Of course, she has doubts. Standing in the front doorway, she attempts to bring some semblance of order to her deteriorating world. What is best? She does not know. She waves weakly to Jimmy who sits next to his dad in the front seat. Jimmy places his opened hand on the window as they drive away. He cranes his neck and watches until he can no longer see his mom. He feels somehow that he is letting her down.

She says quietly, "Love you."

And they are gone around the corner. Gone. She has killed to save her family and now they've left her because she's a killer, because she thinks like a killer, and acts like a killer, and because she buys weapons like a killer. She did pull a knife on Polly. I did that, she thinks. I did do that, but, no, no buts...I did that. What if I am confused? What if the fear I'm feeling isn't about the return of Ben Burne at all, maybe it's transference, and what I'm afraid of is who I've become. Maybe I'm running from myself, running from looking at what this all says about me. Am I keeping the fear of a dead man alive so I don't have to confront the truth? What if the trouble is that it is too hard to accept that the line between me and a mass murderer is so thin that it can be crossed in one night? If what you've done in life is the true gauge of who you are as a person, what does that make me? I guess as long as I'm still running, still fighting, I don't have time to examine my own behavior, or to face the blood on my hands. I don't need to think about what happened, because for me it is still happening, and so there is no time to think. Perhaps the ghost I'm running from is the apparition of me: of the me that died that night, the me who was kind and incapable of harm. So, then, am I running from the old me or the new me?

Once Jimmy can't see his mom any longer, he starts to fidget in his seat. He tries to keep his mouth shut because he can see the conflict and pain on his father's face. But he can't keep his mouth shut. It's his mom.

"Dad, we can't leave mom alone."

"Right now we have to. It may be the only way we can shock her into helping herself."

"We have to go back, Dad."

"Jimmy, you need to trust me here."

"But we're letting her down."

"It's only for tonight. I'm going to bring the doctor over tomorrow and we will get her the help she needs no matter what it takes."

Jimmy is straining, working hard to hold his emotions in like a man. Hank can see this. It only adds more emotion, which he is already barely controlling.

"I don't want to leave her, Dad."

"Me either, buddy, me either."

Jimmy slumps down in his seat. Hank looks over sadly. They have tried so hard to keep Jimmy on the outside of what's happening to his mother, but of course, he sees it all. He knows this is a big step. Hank runs a series of well-known platitudes through his brain searching for something to say that will ease Jimmy's mind. Nothing. There doesn't seem to be anything that can make this easier. He rests his hand for a moment on Jimmy's hand lying on the seat next to him. He squeezes. Jimmy squeezes back. Exactly the way Alison would and Hank aches for her.

CHAPTER TWENTY-SIX

G RANDMA CAROLYN WAS SURPRISED TO see her son and grandson pull into her driveway. Usually they call first. The fake grin on her son's face told her that things were very far from okay and that the horror of the unimaginable events of these last many weeks was continuing to tear up the family.

"What a super surprise." Carolyn kisses them both. "If I'd known you were coming I would have made Jimmy's favorite chicken pasta."

"It's okay, Grandma, I'm not hungry," he says deflated. Carolyn and Hank exchange a quick message with a glance.

"So, we'll eat later." She sees the suitcases and asks leerily, "Are you staying?"

"Just for a little," Hank says.

Forlorn, Jimmy pushes past them, "I'm gonna watch TV."

"Okay, son, go ahead."

Jimmy heads off to the TV room. They watch him. From behind, it is evident that the spark has gone from this child. He shuffles off, scuffing his heels, with his chin dropped down and his hands shoved completely into his pockets. Hank follows his mother into the kitchen where she closes the door.

Carolyn is a formidable woman, worldly, and matronly in her bulky flowered caftan. She seems out of place in her own kitchen, which has been decorated with a surfeit of delicate items: porcelain teacups, champagne flutes, little picture frames, all of which only serve to make her loom larger in comparison. But she loves all of these sweet things. She turns to her son with trepidation.

"What's going on?" she asks.

"Mom, we just need to give Alison a little space."

"Space? A little space? What is this, high school? What's that supposed to mean?"

"It's between us."

"It isn't between you. Please don't make the mistake of thinking it is between you. It's between you and Alison and Jimmy and you'd better not think it's between you two alone."

"I know."

"There's nothing you two could do that won't affect that little boy."

"Mom, I know."

"So, what are you doing in my kitchen holding a suitcase, Henry?"

Hank plops down in the kitchen stool and rests his elbows on the Formica countertop. How much can he really tell his mother? He must be cautious. He must not say anything that could turn his mother against Alison. He can forgive Alison anything, but can his mother forgive Alison for putting her grandson at risk? No. She will protect her grandson with ferocity. He must choose his words with care. He must say enough for support, but not enough to damage Alison in his mother's eyes. Jeopardizing their relationship is a risk he cannot take. He is having a tough enough time trying to hold his little family together. They are strung too tight to add any other stresses to the cord that binds them. Besides, he couldn't stand it if his mother thought badly about Alison even for one second.

"Mom, look, I know you don't understand what's been going on. But Alison is my wife and I can't tell you some things. It would probably be best if you just let it be."

"Let it be?"

"If you can't do that, then Jimmy and I can go to a hotel…"

"Now, stop that. You can stay here as long as you like. You know that."

"Then, no questions."

"For a time."

"For a time," he agrees.

"And you understand that boy is distraught."

"Oh, I understand, believe me. I'm thinking of only him. You have to trust that." He looks into the face of his mother and wishes he could explain everything to her. He would love to sit down and tell her about the hallucinations, the paranoia, the craziness, and the weapons. If he does, his mom will throw her arms around him and he will enjoy the solace of a connection that he craves right now. He genuinely needs someone to say they understand, to confirm he's done the right thing. But he can't. He knows he cannot. This is a burden he must carry in silence, or risk being the source of more destruction. He must protect Alison and so he cannot tell his mother any of it.

Carolyn asks, "Then just tell me—is she all right?"

"If she were all right I wouldn't be here."

Carolyn nods. She walks over to the sink, turns on the faucet, reaches for her little copper teakettle and fills it. She puts the kettle on the stove. These rote gestures give her a moment to consider. This is not an easy position he has put her in. She is frantic inside to hear what's going on. She turns the gas on under the kettle as she reviews what she should say. Her son loves his family. He is asking her to trust him, to trust his judgment. She turns back to face him.

"Then, I'll get dinner going."

"Thanks."

* * *

Several hours later, Alison sits with her forehead planted on the kitchen table. An untouched cup of chamomile tea beside her went cold hours ago. She lifts her head three inches from the table and then just lets it flop back down with a thud. She can't do this any longer. She knows Hank as well as she knows herself. The only reason Hank would have left her side is if she really were crazy. I have to face it. I've cracked. I mean, maybe, maybe I've cracked. I see things. I hear things. Oh god, how do I end this when it all feels real? Is this what all crazy people say? My husband has left me. My husband who I know loves me has left. What does that tell me? She picks her forehead up again and lets it drop into her hands. I have no one. No one understands. Everyone around here has already decided about me. I have no one. She picks up her phone and dials 411.

The operator asks, "City and State, please?"

In Hobbs' cabin, Curtis reaches for the ringing phone. "Sport Fishing."

"You really did get a regular landline up there." She tries to make her voice sound normal.

"Alison?"

"Not indoor plumbing too I hope."

"And ruin the ambiance? No way. Evidently, you city folk like a good crap in the woods. How's civilization?"

Her voice cracks, "A lot harder than I remember."

"True that. Reality sucks. People are animals."

"Yes. That's been a hard lesson."

"But useful."

"Maybe. Maybe we're better off not knowing that. Maybe we're better off living in a dream world."

"We're surely better off that way," he says almost wistfully, "but once you wake up…well, you're up, ya know?"

"Yes." She sighs.

"Why don't you come for a visit? Be my guest."

"Not a chance."

"This time you could really go fishing."

"I hyperventilate when I see fish sticks."

There is an unnatural pause. Curtis waits for her to continue. He knows she called for a reason.

She says, "So he's dead, you know, the last one."

"Yeah, I saw that on the AP. You must be relieved."

"Uh…not actually."

"Why not?"

"Can't shake him."

"Oh."

"It's like he put some kind of invisible cage around me. Or more like he's actually inside in my brain. Sitting there pulling strings."

"That doesn't sound too healthy."

"Actually I may be seeing things…you know, things that aren't there."

"Uh, oh." Now, Curtis realizes the seriousness. She was such a fragile thing when she burst into his cabin that night. He remembers thinking she looked like a half-drown kitten in his doorway: wet, freezing, terrified. No one was more surprised than he was when she survived. But that kind of violence has a cost. She has images in her mind that must shake her sanity.

"How serious is it?" he asks.

"Hank left me. He took Jimmy."

"Oh, that sucks, Alison."

"I got laid off."

"Ouch."

"Truth is I'm not completely sure what's real anymore. A few minutes ago I was wondering if you were real."

"I feel real."

"But maybe you're not. Maybe I didn't actually call you right now and I'm not really talking on the phone. Maybe I'm sitting in an asylum at this very moment staring out randomly and being spoon-fed succotash."

"I can't confirm anything else except you are definitely talking to me and no one has said succotash since 1950."

"Everyone around here thinks I'm crazy."

"You gotta right to be crazy for a bit, but then you need to get your act together, get your job back, and start doing mom things again. If you don't, then, it doesn't matter whether Burne's dead or alive; he still owns your ass."

"Yeah. I guess that's right."

"You know it."

"What about you? You know we have a guest room. It's yours when you're ready."

"Thanks, but I hear you're crazy."

She smiles. She hears him chuckle.

"Take care, Curtis."

"Bye, Alison."

Night slipped into the kitchen as she sat there immobile. She had adjusted to the darkening room and hadn't noticed. When she finally rises from the kitchen chair and grabs the teacup, she has to turn on the lights to put the cup into the sink. Her right leg, which was bent underneath her, had fallen asleep and she shakes it as she walks toward the stairs. She and Hank have never voluntarily slept apart. By tomorrow, surely Hank will be back. He will talk to me. I will go to therapy. I will do whatever it takes to bring them home. She turns off all the lights downstairs. She walks over to switch on the alarm system. She reaches for the touch pad, but yanks back as though she has been shocked. No. This is part of it, she thinks. The alarm, the weapons, the night watch, they are all symptoms. This fear is like an infection that has spread out and devoured my life. Enough. She turns her back on the alarm panel and she feels empowered by this simple move. She starts up the stairs to the second floor. The aggressive adrenaline that has been fueling her muscles for a month turns off like a spigot, and as she lifts her feet from one step to the next, she feels crushingly weary. Her legs are dead as stumps, and her arms hang useless and heavy by her side. She feels as if all the blood has been drained from her body. She drags herself up the last few steps to the little landing that separates her and Hank's bedroom from Jimmy's. She stops and peeks into Jimmy's room. The paradox hits her: stuffed with so many things and yet utterly empty. She hates that his bed is perfectly made and it reminds her that Polly had been there that morning. Yes, how could she forget that? Poor Polly. She will call her tomorrow, call and apologize. How does that conversation go? Gee, hi, sorry I tried to stab you with the butcher knife, could you finish the laundry now? Damn. How could I have been that confused? I must have scared her to death.

Leaning against Jimmy's doorway, Alison would prefer it if his room were a complete mess, the kind of childhood jungle that only a nine-year-old could create, the kind of mess that would indicate without question that her little boy was home. I want him. Her chest aches. She looks around at all of his toys; they are waiting, too. His noisy prized robot is silent in the corner. His school books are gone from the desk and when she sees that she feels a sickening free fall inside. She is all alone in her own home at night. When has that ever happened? Not since before Jimmy was born. She turns toward her bedroom. Even with all the furniture, the family photos, the drapes, the bookcases, and silk flowers, her house feels hollow. She feels hollow. She thinks, if I open my mouth right now there would be nothing but a long hollow echo because the inside of me is dark and empty. She enters her bedroom and walks over to the window blinds where she has stood diligently night after night since their return, scanning the street for a dead man. She couldn't even count the number of hours she has wasted staring into the bleak nothingness of the night, instead of making love to her husband, instead of curling up skin-to-skin in his arms where she belongs. She grabs the cord, and she takes a slow long breath, and then, she shuts the blinds. She steps back and stares at the blocked window. Her home has finally closed its eyes. The relentless vigilance has ended. Alison turns her back on the window blinds and she proceeds into the bathroom. She feels compelled in an almost ritualistic way to wash thoroughly and finally. She forces herself to close the bathroom door and she does not lock it on purpose.

She pulls down a big fluffy towel and twists the shower faucet to hot. She strips down and catches sight of herself in the mirror. It stuns her. Turning fully front, she tilts her head, and blinks her eyes. The image in the mirror slaps her face. Naked, she studies herself honestly shocked: her chest looks corrugated as the bones that make up her ribcage are prominent, and the space on either side of her collarbone looks like a trough. How much weight have I lost? Her skin is loose and sallow. At the hairline, she sees the beginning of grey roots. Her shoulders appear hunched and the whites of her eyes are bloodshot. So, this is what crazy looks like, she thinks bitterly, not a pretty picture. Bereft, she turns away from her reflection and steps into the shower. This time, however, she forces herself to completely close the shower door and not leave it part way open so she can hear. Instead, she turns the water on full force, gets under it, and stands with her head submerged in the downpour. She prepares for the panic. Here it comes: heart rate up, puffy breathing, jumpy muscles. Now, she will mount a different kind of fight. She will not give in to the panic. She must master her negative thoughts and pull herself back from the lip of destruction. The enemy is no longer outside of her. In the gush of the shower water, she can finally understand this and even as she does, her primitive instincts taunt her screaming: Open your eyes. Open the door. Open the blinds. Listen. Watch. She clenches her fingers and her toes. "Stop." Do you want your life back? Your husband? Your son? Your job? Feel the water hot on your head, good and hot on your back; feel it, you're fine. See, you are fine. I am done being a hostage. Tomorrow I will go to the therapist. Tomorrow I will start the meds. Tonight will be my one and only lonely night. She scrubs her hair and scalp vigorously. She soaps every inch of her body twice. She tips her head up and allows the free flowing water to flush her face, hoping it will flow through her eyes and ears and pores and wash her brain clean.

Fifteen minutes, later she steps out of the shower. The bathroom is steamed up; the mirror is fogged to a solid white. She slips her puckered skin into her favorite pair of flannel pajamas and they feel glorious. She takes the few steps to the bathroom door. She reaches for the doorknob and hesitates. What if…what if right behind this door…it's not as though she could have heard anything in the shower like that. He could be… No. Stop. The problem is inside me. She closes her hand around the knob. Blood rushes to her face. Adrenaline swamps her limbs: pump, pump, pump. Do it. Do it. She swings open the bathroom door and sees…no one. This is the tiny reinforcement she needs. She breathes out a long slow stream through pursed lips, calms, almost smiles. She has turned the corner. She climbs into bed and grabs the novel on her nightstand. This is a transitional night. Tomorrow she will start the real journey home from the island.

CHAPTER TWENTY-SEVEN

H ANK'S OLD ROOM SMELLS OF familiarity. There is a distinctive scent in his mother's house: a blend of cinnamon, which she uses every morning in her coffee, and Charlie perfume, which she sprays liberally on her clothes. It is an odd mixture but that is what makes it so uniquely his home. The scent reminds him of innocent times when all he cared about was music videos, winning at tetherball, and grapes. He smiles nostalgically and tries to fix the time when he started wanting so much more. What he wanted and needed when he was young felt so immediate, so much more visceral than the things he wants now. He remembers, in middle school, wanting to kiss Heather Roseman that day she came to school in her little sky blue shorts. And he did kiss her when she leaned over the water fountain. He got a detention for that, which seemed grossly unfair since everyone wanted to kiss her, and he was just the only kid who had the courage to do it. He thought he deserved a medal. He also remembers vividly when all he wanted in the world was to punch Mr. Caughey right between his beady eyes.

"Henry Kraft, your homework was not in the pile yesterday."

"Yes, it was, Mr. Caughey," Hank responded surprised.

"No. It wasn't. I went over all the papers last night and yours was missing."

"I put it there with the rest."

"Are you calling me a liar, Henry?"

"Um…no? But I did the homework and I put it right there." Hank's cheeks were blooming red and fiery as the attention of the entire class was on him.

"You get a zero."

"No. That's not fair."

"You should get graded on homework you didn't turn in? Is that fair to the students who worked hard?"

Every cell in little Hank's body was outraged. He had put the homework there, just like he always did. Mr. Caughey was so mean, he teased kids and called it humor, he was petty and self-important; and then he became solicitous and sickly sweet in front of the parents. Hank's feeling of powerlessness was eating away at his insides. He could feel it chewing up his stomach. He had put his homework on the table with the others. Why wasn't he believed? The zero would ruin all the good grades he had struggled for all year long. He slammed his fist on the desk.

"I did it and I put it there."

"See me after class."

After school, Hank waited outside Mr. Caughey's classroom and turned wide-eyed when he saw his dad striding down the school hallway.

"Dad, what are you doing here?"

"I thought I should ask you that. Mr. Caughey called my office."

"I did my homework, Dad."

Once inside the classroom, Mr. Caughey turned into an alien being from planet Suck Up. There was a sympathetic lilt to the tone of his voice that Hank had not heard in six months of daily class. Hank's eyes narrowed as his teacher spoke to Hank's dad as though they were colleagues and they both understood how trying middle school boys could be. Hank sat there as the teacher explained to his dad about Hank's outburst in the classroom, his disrespect, and his lying about his homework. Hank's fists were clenched beneath the desk and his desires were simple, direct, and all consuming. He waited for his dad to defend him. Mr. Kraft said, "I see" a few times and then apologized for Hank's behavior and Hank thought his head would blow off. That was a moment of pure want, one item want, one thing wanted—to punch out Mr. Caughey. No rage in life is more passionate than the rage of the disrespected and defenseless. He couldn't believe his dad was even listening. Why didn't his dad believe him? Why was he unbelievable just because he was a kid? Why are all of the parents around always demanding respect but never showing any? Where was justice? He wanted to hit Mr. Caughey full-fisted right in the jaw. He wanted to do it so badly he jumped up out of his seat and ran from the classroom. Mr. Caughey shrugged his shoulders in complicity with Mr. Kraft who apologized again and went after his son.

Hank rolls over big in his childhood bed trying to get comfortable but not wake Jimmy. Some teachers are like his wife, a gift to every child in her classroom, and some are petty bullies who humiliate with impunity and are fetid with arrogance. Since it can be hard for the parent to determine which teacher is which, that day Hank made a decision that he carries with him every single time he steps onto school property. Hank promised that he would always believe his own child, at the cost of being wrong, at the cost of alienating the teacher, at the cost of taking down the entire School Board, he would always side with his child, and he has always done so.

What he wanted back then: to kiss Heather, to punch out Mr. Caughey, to be believed, all contributed drops to the groundwater of his character. Tonight, reminded of his basic self, he feels stripped of the trivial desires that grew up untamed like ivy on the inside of him. What made him want so many things? Was it the television? His friends? Did it invade like a virus from the outside, or were all these wants something that grew naturally within. He rolls onto his back and stares at the ceiling. The moon is bright and throws its pasty gaze in through the window. Lying here, he realizes how much he truly does not want and he lists them: he does not want a bigger house, or a new car, or a 55" flat screen TV. He wants his wife, his son, and everyone healthy. Everything else is profoundly inconsequential. Everything else is negotiable.

For five hours, Hank lies in bed and lets his mind wander like this. He tries to find relief in happy memories but nothing has been able to distract him. The discomfort in his mind has become physical. The mattress is lumpy, the sheets are scratchy, and the room feels excessively hot. The digital minute hand flips and the clock now reads 3:16 a.m. He turns over and looks at his son deep in sleep beside him. Do all parents think their children are beautiful, or is Jimmy really as beautiful as he seems? Hank feels envious of the peaceful sleep of children, the sleep that comes when nothing is your responsibility. He reviews the steps that led him back to his childhood home and he is suddenly certain that running out like that was wrong. It was just wrong. I know some of this is my inability to deal with the situation. She needs me. It's Alison. It is my Allie. What if leaving sent her over the edge? What if she's crying, or hysterical? What if she hurts herself? They have each been forever changed, and they need to adjust to this new world. He and Jimmy have been face-to-face with evil. It was an experience they shared on the floor that night, but it must have been easier to be together, to at least have had each other. Neither of them really knows what it was like to be Alison, to stand alone, to understand that it is kill or watch your family die, to stand in abject terror in the icy rain feeling the responsibility for all those lives, and to know you are their only hope of survival. How many other people would have been paralyzed? How many would have just hid behind a rock in the dark woods and wept? Is there some relief in being the helpless ones? What does it do to a peaceful spirit like hers to plunge a knife into the flesh and organs of another human being? Of course, she is stuck in that horror. How could she not be? He has not tried hard enough to save her. He has only wanted it all to go away, but there's no blood on his hands. By her side is where he belongs. Those were the vows they took and she is his partner for life. No matter how hard. Bile in his stomach backs up and burns his throat as disgust overwhelms him, how could he have left her that way? Cautiously, he slips out of bed, careful not to wake Jimmy. He pulls on his worn jeans and Zeppelin sweatshirt. He grabs his socks and sneakers and silently leaves the room. He tiptoes across the hall to his mother's room and enters.

"Mom?" He speaks in a loud whisper.

She rolls toward him, "Henry?"

"Jimmy's asleep. I'm going home. I shouldn't have left her."

"Good. You two go work it out. I'll take care of Jimmy."

Hank sits down on the floor near the front door to put on his shoes and socks. His fatigue dissipates. Energy surges through him. He is certain where he needs to be. Jesus, I should not have left her. He pulls on his sneakers without untying them, grabs his car keys, and bolts out the front door. It only takes a few minutes of driving through the deserted suburban streets to hit the highway ramp. He considers calling Alison, but decides that she may have taken sleeping pills and have fallen asleep. He will be quiet so as not to wake her when he gets home just in case. And if she is asleep, he thinks, I will crawl in next to her and hold her safe until morning, and then I will get her the help she needs, and I will never desert her again.

In her bedroom, Alison is soaked clean and velvety and warm in the arms of her feather comforter. The scalding shower reached into her soft tissues and unwound her knotted tendons and muscles leaving her deliciously limp. She had taken the time needed to do everything: cream rinse in her hair, shave her legs. The skin on her calves is smooth and slick and so her legs are slippery inside the threads of the fresh flannel pajamas. She turned off the bedside lamp not long after she began reading and promised herself tomorrow she would read more. She rolled over onto her side, pulled her legs up toward her chest, burrowed in like a furry rabbit and then without the help of pills and deep in a down-filled palm of comfort she drifted to sleep. Inside her mind, she is aware that she is sleeping and it feels glorious. She is finally on the path. In her dream, she is half-floating, half-skating over a glass-smooth frozen pond. She is wearing chiffon and it billows out behind her in gentle waves. She glides free of gravity and spinning with her arms up over her head in praise of the movement and the beauty of the pond all around her. She hops onto one foot and raises her back leg in an arabesque. Balanced, she leans her face forward into the cool breeze created by her own movement. And then she takes off on a spin so slow and so graceful that she feels it...clink...her eyelids spring open. What was that? The clink of the metal tongue of the front door knob as it opens. Someone has opened the front door. Or not. Or maybe not. Or maybe it was only part of my dream. The clink of the metal blade of the ice skates. Of course. It is only part of my dream. I will not be tormented by my imagination any longer. Only crazy people let crazy thoughts ruin their homes, steal their families. I am more resilient than that. I am smarter than that. I have too much to lose to allow this disintegration into madness. It has been remarkably easy to give in to the lunacy. How many times have I passed disheveled people on a public street, seen them talking to themselves, and never realized how thin the line is between them and me? I am ready now to take back control of my life. Damn it I am safe in my bed in the home I love. I will rise above this. No one is in my house. She smiles to herself and sinks her face into the soft forgiving cotton of her pillow. No one is in my house. She can feel there has been some kind of turning point and she is grateful. Her thoughts drift to Hank as she tumbles back toward sleep. How hard this must have been for my dear husband. How over the edge I must have been for that man who has loved me all of my adult life to walk out like that. I can't imagine it now that my feet are back on solid ground. And look, miraculously, instinctively, my sweet husband did exactly what I needed. It was the proverbial slap across the face and it worked. I feel the dread that has been lying like dead weight on my chest has lifted. I can take a full breath of air without that constricted sensation. I needed another shock. I needed a serious shock like when they shock someone's heart and it comes back to life. That is what happened to me when Hank and Jimmy walked out that door. Tomorrow will be a special day. And her thoughts are interrupted by the smallest sound, the tiniest nearly imperceptible creak from the loose floorboard, the floorboard in the foyer immediately to the left of the thin-legged side table. She knows exactly which board. She has wanted to have that fixed, wanted to get it nailed back down. She knows the sound of a foot on that board. She has heard that sound a thousand times. She knows it well, too well to pretend she did not hear it. With slow intensity, she rises up to sitting in her bed. Her ears are trained because she knows precisely where the next floorboard will sound. She waits for it. Nothing. Perhaps it is the house settling, one of the various innocent noises made by homes every day, like when the windows make a snapping sound as the bright sunlight hits them. Houses make noises: wood and glass expand and contract. This is fundamentally true. She knows this is fundamentally...creak—there it is. Her eyes narrow in on the bedroom doorway. Yes, she is sure. She is completely awake. She waited for a particular sound and that was it. Someone is slithering up the stairs taking care to be very quiet. Her heartbeat pulses in her throat. The dread hits her chest like a baseball bat knocking the wind out of her. He waited. Of course, he watched and he waited until she was alone. She slides her legs silently out from underneath the bed covers and she slips her body down onto the carpet. He is here. Where can she hide? Should she hide? He will find her. He will smell her like a beast. She reaches under the bed for the rifle. Where is it? She throws both her arms under the bed and sweeps them around frantically. Where? Panic clutches her and she begins to tremble. She remembers. The rifle is leaning up against the wall near the door to the hallway where Hank stashed it as Jimmy came up the stairs. She looks. Yes, she can just make out the shape of its outline in the dark. On her hands and knees, she scurries over to it while he takes the stairs one-by-one to the second floor cautious not to wake her. Fear strips away her pretense of sanity. She is an animal again. Her skin becomes damp as her heart races. Her breathing puffs staccato. Her eyes dart back and forth calculating her options. The comforter on the bed looks bunched up. That's good because it looks like someone is sleeping there. That will give her an added second or two. In a quick blast of motion, she crawls over to the opened door to the Jack-n-Jill bathroom, which links her bedroom with Jimmy's. She positions herself crouching to the side of the door. She lifts the rifle aiming exactly chest-high at the open doorway to her bedroom. She rests her elbows on her thighs and takes a secure and steady position. Ready. She's going to blow him away. Time slows and the waiting feels endless even though she knows it takes only seconds to climb the stairs to the second floor. There! The dark silhouette of a man appears in the doorway. The figure takes a step toward the bed. The body is exposed. It is a clear shot. She's got him. She begins to pull back on the trigger. Stop. She freezes. Disoriented. Wait. Is this real? Is it her husband? Inside, she screams at herself, don't shoot! It's Hank! Oh my god, and a split second before firing, in horror she puts the rifle down on the carpet.

"Oh, god." She shoves the rifle out of reach with her feet. "Oh god. Hank? You came back."

He turns toward her. He sees her crouching in the bathroom doorway. "Of course I came back," Ben says with a smile. "You knew I would. We have unfinished business."

What's real? Wait. Is she still in a dream? He's dead. Ben's dead. It's Hank. I need to see that it is Hank. Ben raises his handgun aiming at her head and she reacts reflexively. Using power from both her legs, she launches herself backward into the bathroom as he fires! The sound of the gunshot thunders out piercing the serenity of the neighborhood and then she knows. I am not dreaming. I am not imagining. I am not crazy. I have been right all along. She scuttles across the bathroom tile, which feels hard on her knees. The bathroom still smells of the lavender soap and citrus shampoo she lathered on in sweet luxury earlier. I'm glad I'm clean, she thinks in a passing second. I'd hate to be found dead and dirty, too, a last humiliation. I've been dirty, I've been soaked in mud and covered in blood and I really do want to die clean. Does this explain why we clean a body before we bury it? She feels oddly peaceful about that even as she realizes it is such a strange thing to be pleased about. And no matter how this ends, at least it will end and that is something to be thankful for she tells herself. She scrambles into Jimmy's room.

Ben walks after her following with the ease since he is the greater more powerful predator. He will do this deliberately. He has a right to enjoy this. She killed Theo. He steps into the bathroom and glances into the shower stall—empty. She killed Kent. He steps toward the other bathroom door, which leads to Jimmy's room. She killed Gravel. Bitch. He wants her suffocating in fear. He is excited by her terror and thrilled to see her crawl. He has been patient for this moment. Now, he owns her and all the waiting is worth it.

Alison rolled to the left as she scurried into Jimmy's room and so now she is trapped. She must get across to the doorway that leads to the hall and the stairs. Moonlight streams in white through Jimmy's bedroom window. She wedges up against the side of his dresser trying to calculate her chances of making it to the door. She is only partially hidden. She has seconds—only seconds to decide but time stretches as her brain works at peak efficiency. To get out and into the hallway she must cross the bathroom door opening. Stupid, stupid, she scolds. I should have gone the other way. Crossing the door now will expose her to him as he walks through the bathroom. It would put her directly in his line of fire. What? What to do? Too late. Ben emerges from the bathroom into Jimmy's room. He turns toward her. He has her. There is nowhere to go. She reaches for the remote on Jimmy's dresser and presses it. Bells! Whistles! Lights! Ben twists around startled as Jimmy's robot bursts to life nearby and walks toward him. "What the fuck?" He fires at it. He's never seen anything like it. Alison uses the one instant of his distraction to cross behind and at a dead run she escapes the bedroom. With big strides nearly flying she heads for the stairs. The Mossberg, she thinks. I need the Mossberg in the basement.

Ben smiles at his reaction and surprise. She tricked him, very funny. She is so inherently competent. He takes off after her with huge powerful strides and complete confidence.

He will not expect another weapon. If I can just get to the basement. Her legs know these stairs. Her body has learned the curve of them and the width of them. It is ingrained into her muscle memory from going up and down them thousands of times. The darkness is no impediment. She easily springs down three stairs at a time landing with exacting surety and sure-footed. At the halfway point, where the staircase opens up to the first floor, she throws her legs over the banister and vaults to the foyer floor below easily clearing the little foyer table she knows is there. She feels a twinge in her right knee when she lands. She ignores it.

Ben giggles at himself for being startled by the toy robot as he takes the stairs. He is really having such a good time now. He pursues her with agility and speed. He vaults over the banister too, but lands on top of the foyer table smashing it to pieces and getting thrown off his feet. Knowing every inch of this house intimately is her advantage. This is her home, her ground. She scrambles into the kitchen. He is only seconds behind her. She knows there is not enough time to get safely across the kitchen to the basement door. It would allow for at least one clear shot. One clear shot is all it would take to bring her down. Immediately as she enters the kitchen and darts by her microwave she presses the preset timer button. She could do this in her sleep. It starts automatically at 15 seconds. She dives down behind the far side of the center island's butcher's block and freezes. It is the only solid thing between them as Ben enters the dark kitchen. The timer: thirteen…twelve… There is only five feet between them and she tries with brutal desperation to control the sound of her panting but she must take in air—her body demands oxygen. She needs a few seconds more.

"Come out, come out, wherever you are." Confidently, Ben flips on the kitchen lights, which really panics her—she likes the dark—she needs the dark—it is her friend and she knows that. It's so bright. God, so bright. The timer: nine… eight… He easily figures out where she must be. He starts slowly to circle the butcher's block.

"I'm looking forward to seeing your son again when we're done here. Such a cute boy reminded me of Kent when he was little."

Alison slides open the drawer and pulls out the very long two-pronged barbecue fork. The timer: three…two… He's at the corner of the island.

He smiles, "Peek-a-boo." He looks over. She's right below him.

The microwave buzzer goes off. He spins involuntarily toward the unexpected sound from directly behind him. Alison rises up and jams the barbecue fork into the flesh of his side. He lurches forward and releases a wail of angry pain. It is the scream of an enraged and injured beast. She uses the moment to bolt for the basement doorway thankfully open. Alison dashes down the stairs while Ben has to pull the fork from the soft tissues of his body and from where one of the tongs has punctured his right kidney. Game over. He is injured. He is in a fury of hate. No matter what happens, even if he has to go with her, he's not leaving until she is dying painfully at his feet. He stuffs a kitchen towel under his shirt to quell the bleeding. He turns and moves to the basement, and then, he stops abruptly. He has underestimated her all along. He will not do that again. She's a survivor, a fighter. He knows there is a chance someone has heard the gunshots. He will need to move it along. His eyes slowly take in the scene and he considers his options. The basement must be a trap. Why else would she run there instead of out the back door of the house? It's not logical. And she has proven to be logical. Ben walks over to the kitchen sink and opens the cabinet door underneath. He reviews the products available to him. He pulls out the can of oven cleaner. He opens the drawer where she got the barbecue fork and removes the long sticks of matches. "What a predicable little homemaker." He ignores the pain in his side and with only the ghost of a limp, he walks to the basement door where he strikes the match, points the can and sprays into the flame creating a blowtorch. He moves the torch meticulously around the door molding setting the paint and wood trim on fire. He grabs the newspaper from the kitchen table and tosses it on the floor; the pages catch quickly and begin to burn throwing off plumes of black smoke.

Downstairs, Alison scrambles over all the obstacles and wrenches open the dresser drawer. She throws Jimmy's Batman pajama to the floor and unearths the Mossberg rifle. Gratefully, she grabs it and lifts it out. She spins quickly around expecting him to be right there. Where is he? Why hasn't he followed her? What's keeping him? Then, she smells it.

Smoke. She moves quickly back to the stairs. Her eyes widen as she sees the flames at the top. Oh, no.

Ben revels in the colors of the flames. Exquisite, he thinks. Even while he was watching Uncle Rafe burn to death tied up inside his Canadian cabin, Ben had to note how brilliant and attractive the flames were as they licked their way up the walls. Fire is truly captivating. Something about the energy, the waving shapes, and bright yellow and blue, makes him want to stick his hand in it. He did that once as a kid and he remembers it as being thrilling although he still carries the scars. With the flames eating up the kitchen wall and steadily on its way, he proceeds out the back door. Once outside, he turns the corner of the little home, passes the barbecue, and stops in front of the two wooden trap doors a few feet from the ground that lead down to the basement. The two doors are partially covered with ivy. He noticed them a few days ago when he was casing the house. It had been so easy to find the Kraft home thanks to all the news coverage. It was as if they were pointing him the way. News teams—really such a helpful bunch, he thinks, it would have taken him a long time to track her down without them. He would have, of course, but it would have been inconvenient. He positions himself outside the trap doors. He is slightly favoring his injured side, but playing in pain has always been easy for him. He sees pain as a challenge. He knows he will have to get that side stitched up somehow after he leaves here.

He watches the trap doors to the basement. She will come right to him. She will have to. He shifts from foot to foot as he becomes excited. He has always loved the hunt and especially trapping, luring them in, where they walk themselves right into his arms because they have no choice. He prefers that to stalking because stalking just seems like the weasel's way of winning. He favors inducing the victim to walk to him. Such a yummy sensation of power as they hand over their lives. It simply confirms the superiority of his mind. When he thinks about what this bitch has done to his family his blood heats and surges inside his veins and he swelters. He takes a nice long breath in—this is going to be luscious.

Smoke billows into the basement and Alison feels it sinking down into her lungs. She looks over at the steps up to the trap doors that lead to the backyard. It is bolted on the inside. She knows he's out there waiting—certain death. Do what he doesn't expect. How do I get through those flames? The smoke alarms sound in the house. Move! She yells at herself. She runs to the washing machine. The smoke thickens. She opens the top of the machine. A set of Jimmy's sheets are sopping wet inside, left halfway through their cycle this morning by Polly. Yes, Polly stopped in the middle of doing the laundry. She reaches in and yanks out the wet sheet. She runs to the bottom of the basement stairs. The top steps of the staircase are beginning to burn. She has no time to think this through. She throws the wet sheet over her head and knows speed is her friend. It will be like when you run your finger through a candle flame, she tells herself, if you go fast enough it doesn't hurt. With every ounce of energy, ramped up, she barrels up the stairs in her bare feet while covered in the wet sheets and carrying the Mossberg. At the third step from the top, she flings herself through the flaming doorway and onto the kitchen floor. She pulls off the smoldering sheet and looks around. The kitchen is engulfed in flames. It's hot! Her skin is beginning to burn. Too hot all around her. Out—out now! Out the backdoor or burn alive. She blasts out the back door into the yard choking on the smoke. She takes a number of quick breaths. She knows there are some burns on the bottom of her feet and they are just beginning to sting. She coughs and looks around.

Above the noise from the cracking and popping of the fire as it consumes the kitchen side of the house, Ben hears her coughing. What, he thinks? She went up those stairs? How? Goddamn it. He runs back toward the kitchen door.

Exposed in the open yard she whips her head all around. The overhanging branches of the large trees surround her. They reach out their many limbs toward her. Her throat tightens and she struggles for clean breaths of the cold night air. She turns for the garage, opens the door, and stumbles inside. She just needs to hold on now. Help is coming. Help must be coming. The smoke alarms are blaring. The fire rages. She looks for a safe nest, a place to wait, but as soon as she stands still in the two-car garage, she realizes this was a grave mistake. Bad choice. There is only one way in or out of this garage. A very bad choice. And he is coming. The two-car wide rectangular space is just as crammed with a wide range of miscellany as the basement of her house. One small window, high up on the far wall, allows in the flickering red and gold light from the flames consuming her home and making the garage look ghoulish with large undulating shadows. She could never reach that window with all of the boxes and lawn equipment stacked in front of it. It will not serve as an escape route. The hairs stand on her neck and icy fingers run down her spine as she senses him walking toward the garage now. She knows he is coming. The garage feels like Hobbs' shed; it even smells like the shed with the scent of gasoline, paint, and rusting metal from the gardening tools. She imagines Kent and sees him nailed to the side of the garage wall. No, she reprimands, no, think straight. Then, Gravel is there in the doorway. No, not here. You are not real. Stop, she pleads with herself. Focus. It is Ben. Ben is real. Ben is here. This is happening, right now, isn't it? Or have I gone mad? Have I set the house on fire? Have I gone mad and set my home on fire? No. She jumps over the lawn mower and ducks under the three bicycles suspended from the ceiling by ropes. The skin on her bare burned feet stings as she shuffles around the snowboarding boots. She begins to breathe through her mouth to keep up with her pounding heart and to expel some of the inhaled smoke that tastes dirty on her tongue. She burrows in toward the back wall of the room behind the old broken-down Ford, which hasn't moved in two years. She shrinks down into the corner with the Mossberg sleek and heavy in her hands. And this is when it all becomes clear. This is the exact instant when she finally realizes that it is not about her life. It is an epiphany: this has never been about her life. It was a fluke that she survived. It was not meant to be. Everyone knows that, and that is the reason why people look at her strangely, and why they do not understand her. It created an imbalance. It was one enormous cosmic mistake. Yes. And that is what has prolonged this nightmare, and that is why she has been in a half-alive condition all of this time; because she was self-concerned, because she was not focusing on what was really her task, her function, her responsibility. It was her destiny to trade herself for Jimmy and Hank. It was supposed to be her life for their lives. She has thwarted fate and so she has been stuck in this altered state of delusion and hallucination, suspended in a half-living, half-dead form all this time because she was unwilling to commit her own self, unwilling to make the needed sacrifice. She looks back over the course of the last month and realizes she was not meant to survive the island. If she would have stood out in the open at that one moment in front of the lodge, and if she would have taken the clear shot at Ben that was offered to her in that moment, then that would have ended this when it was meant to end and how it was supposed to end with both of them dead. That is why this is not over, that is why this has all felt unfinished, and that is why she and Ben are tied to each other in this cyclical death dance. She wanted more than she was meant for; she wanted it all, to save herself and her family. She wanted too much. She should have been grateful to step out from behind that rock and take out Benjamin Burne no matter how many bullets he sank into her chest while doing it. That is what Hank would have done. That was what was required. She has not really been alive since she left the island that night and this is how she knows that what she is thinking is the truth. She has not lived one single day in a whole state. He is coming, yes, he is supposed to come, and it is time. It is past time. Instantly, she feels lighter. She has all the time in the world and calmly she waits for Ben to step into the garage. Now, she understands what is meant by destiny, by fate, what is truly meant when someone says, "It is written." It has been incomplete because she has been a coward. She has been uncommitted. What was needed was an unconditional commitment to end it. She asks herself, am I ready for that now? Am I strong enough to stand up and take the bullets into my body so I can end this? Do I have the courage to stand there and shoot? Will it hurt? I know I have to die to get him, because that is what he does not expect me to do, and that is the only way to beat him. I know that. I know if I don't end his life he will never stop tracking me, never stop hunting my son, my beautiful son, and my loving husband. There is no other option. He will be back again and again until it is over. I have to do this tonight—now. I have to stand and take that shot regardless. Am I ready? There is nowhere left to run, no more tricks to surprise him, and no place left to hide. There is only what is meant to be. I see this vividly, and I know that he does not see it, and that is my advantage—the only advantage I have left, and the only one I will need. He will not expect me to reveal myself to him and put my life on the line to get the clear shot. He will assume I will hide, run, fight for self-preservation and that has been my flaw. I can see that now. I am at peace with that. My life has been good even if it has been short. I have been truly loved. And I have loved truly and now I will prove that. I will need precisely the right shot so I am certain to kill him, so he cannot be resuscitated, so no form of him survives. When I stand, he will want that moment to gloat -- that will be my moment, the moment for that final surprise. And so, she commits, that as long as she can take him with her, then she will gladly go violently into that good night.

This thought process all happens in a flash for her and it is liberating. She is convinced to a moral certainty that she can do this. This was what she was supposed to do all along. Now, finally, squatting down, burned and hurting on the floor of her garage she understands it all. Her time has come, but she knows, with savage certainty so...has.. his.

Outside the garage, Ben grins realizing she has made a fatal error by dodging into the garage. It is a closed space. There is no way out of there. She is cowering like a scared rodent in there waiting for him to finish her. He struts up to the garage door triumphantly. Before he steps inside, he glances around the yard for his escape. He knows the chaos that he hears forming in the front of the house will be useful. The fire trucks, the neighbors, the distraction, will all supply a cover for him to sneak away unnoticed. She has been an annoying little gnat. Time to squash her.

The siren ends as the massive red fire engine grinds to a stop at the curb in front of the burning Kraft house. Five firefighters jump out. Two police units arrive simultaneously. The flames light up the night sky as they chew up this pretty little home. In their coordinated and well-rehearsed routine, the firefighters unroll the main hose and attach it to the fire hydrant. Two firefighters pull their hot suits out of the truck and begin to step into them preparing to enter the burning home. No one is aware that twenty yards away, in the unattached garage, Alison has made up her mind, Ben stands ready to enter, and the end is in sight.

The neighborhood is wide-awake and every light is on. People spill frantically out of their warm homes and into their frigid yards in their robes and overcoats with boots slipped quickly over their bare feet and with children in their arms. The police herd them across to the other side of the street where they gather side-by-side. The neighbors exchange sad deliberate looks with one another. Families nod to friends, but no one has the heart to speak. They are heavy with grief. They understand they are the audience for this: the last act of a family tragedy and they are silently respectful as it plays out on a stage of fire and sirens. It feels as though it has been inevitable, this final destruction. Everyone knows what has been going on inside the Kraft house. They have been gossiping and worrying ever since Alison returned, and while they feel distraught, not a single person is surprised to see this house go up in flames. Even though in the last few days there have been some concerns voiced for their own individual safety as Alison got noticeably "crazier," still every single neighbor gathered here now on this block feels personally injured watching this scene. A shared sorrow binds them together because this family was so much like their own. It could so easily have been any of them. Alison was a genuine person who cooked noodle soup when a neighbor was sick, who collected toys for foster children, who wrote letters to the military overseas, who put out the big candy bars on Halloween, who carried out hot chocolate in the frigid early morning winter for the snow plough drivers. They have all watched with profound anguish the agonizing ruin of this ordinary family. They have spoken of little else between them this last month. And now shivering in their pajamas in solemn unity every single one of them is thinking about Alison in the past tense and hoping that Hank and Jimmy are not in that house.

Driving only blocks away, Hank sees the night sky lit up by flames. He smells the smoke and although there is no way to know which home it is, he is nevertheless certain it is his. He jams the gas pedal to the floor. He is possessed with anxiety and a sudden blinding remorse. His head throbs and his heart pounds like never before. "No." He breaks out in a sweat. He pushes the car to eighty miles an hour on the residential street, taking the curve on two wheels sliding into a parked car. The blow smashes in the passenger side of the car but he does not care and he does not slow down. "Oh, this is not happening." He cranks the wheel right and careens onto his street. Up ahead smoke climbs in dense gray clouds illuminated by the dazzling yellow arms of fire that gesture out of the windows of his home. "Oh god; oh god." People are everywhere. He slows and searches the faces as he pulls down the street. Alison? Where is she? He looks anxiously from face to face. Where? A police officer leaps out in front of his car forcefully waving his arms. He points a flashlight directly into the driver's area trying to stop Hank from proceeding down the road. Hank yanks the steering wheel left, swings around the police officer, jumps the curb, and crosses the sidewalk. He tears up the grass yards of three of his neighbors before skidding to a stop in the middle of his own front lawn. One of the firefighters comes running toward him. Hank throws open the car door, jettisons himself out and charges toward the front door ignoring the shouts at him to stop. One of the firefighters grabs him from behind before he reaches the stoop.

"Sir?"

"My wife. My wife!"

It takes a great deal of physical strength to hold Hank back. The firefighter tries to connect with Hank. "We're going in. Please stand back. We're equipped. Look." He points to two firefighters ready to enter the house. They are fully covered in protective wear and attached to oxygen tanks. "How many in the house? Sir, how many?"

"Just her. Just my Allie."

The firefighter speaks into his radio, "One woman inside."

"I have to go, too!" He tries to wrench free.

"Please, Sir, you will only get in the way."

"I left." Hank wails wretchedly. "Don't you understand? I left her."

Hank's anguish is palpable and the firefighter feels for him. He drops his voice and looks intently at Hank's pained face. "Please, sir, I understand. Let us do our job. If she's in there we will find her."

"But I can help. I know where she is." Hank can't take his eyes off the flames reaching his bedroom window. "I know the house." And for a second he thinks he sees her there in the window, looking out as she has night after night, but then the apparition is gone. Was that her? Was that the ghost of her? Is she gone? He howls.

The firefighter shakes him and Hank looks. The firefighter connects. "You can only help by staying out of the way so we can focus completely on your wife and not have to think about you." Even in this distraught state, the logic of this reaches him.

The two outfitted firefighters go in through the front door.

"Upstairs." Hank screams after them. "Go upstairs!"

The fire hoses burst on full force and begin to flush the house creating huge white plumes of dense smoke.

"Oh, god," Hank says, "My fault. This is my fault."

"Sir, did you set this fire?"

"No."

"Then, it is not your fault."

"She needed me and I left." He collapses to his knees in agony, sinking into the wet cold ground. "I should never have left. I will never forgive myself."

The neighbors see Hank sink to his knees and several of them turn their faces away in wounded sympathy. Tears come to their eyes. The children ask no questions, they only stare, even the littlest of them can sense the gravity of it all and instinctively they are silent.

When the initial report of a gunshot came over the police scanner Officer Thomas recognized the address. He jumped into his car and drove over with his siren blaring. He pulls up along the curb, sees Hank, and charges onto the lawn.

"Mr. Kraft?" Thomas says.

Hank jumps up. "Thomas."

The firefighter is grateful to have Officer Thomas' help. "Good. He's yours." And the firefighter runs back to the truck and to the business of the fire.

"She's inside." Hank tells Thomas.

Thomas says, "A neighbor reported a gunshot. We were on our way already when fire got the call."

"Oh, no. I left her there. I left her there distraught with a gun." What must have happened dawns on them both.

"Mr. Kraft, I am so sorry. But the fire guys will find her. She may be all right."

"She shot herself." Hank can barely form the words; the thought alone has knocked the wind out of him.

"We don't know that for sure."

"She could be dying on the floor right now!"

"They're already in. They're good guys."

Hanks pleads, "Help me get in there. Thomas, help me get in."

"You could never find her without a hot suit in that smoke. You'd be dead before you hit the stairs. Think about your son."

Hank looks at his home. The whole upstairs is engulfed. "What's taking them so long so find her?"

"They're being careful."

The neighbors are being pushed even farther back away from the heartbreaking scene. One man won't move. He stands and argues and pushes back. He yells and points. It is Hank's next-door neighbor, Jessie Collins. He screams over the noise to get Hank's attention.

"Hey, Hank!" Jessie persists. He tries to break through the barricade but is stopped by the police so he yells again, "Hank."

Hank hears him and turns, "Jessie?"

"I called." He yells, "I'm the one who called. I called the cops."

Thomas and Hank walk toward him. "Yes?" Thomas indicates for the policeman to let Jessie through.

"I heard them say they think Alison may have set the house on fire and then shot herself but I don't think so. It couldn't have happened that way. Not possible."

"Why not?" Thomas asks.

"There were a bunch of gunshots."

Thomas demands, "A bunch? More than one? You're sure?"

"Yeah, like four maybe five, with space in between so unless she's shooting herself over and over—you see, it doesn't make sense."

Hank whirls on Thomas with a fury, "You said he was dead." Hank lashes out at Thomas explosively angry with the police and with himself, "You said he was dead."

"You saw the pictures." Thomas responds as he works this new information through his head.

"DNA?"

"Not finished yet."

"All this time I didn't believe her."

"Jesus." Thomas yells into his radio. "Get everyone out of there. We may have a sniper inside."

"No. Help her!" Hank spins again toward the burning front door and runs. Thomas rushes after him, jumps out, grabs him around the legs and brings him down hard on the doorstep. Hank rolls over and swings closed fisted at Thomas landing a hard punch on his right cheek. Thomas takes the hit hard and then tries to hold Hank without hitting back. Another Officer sees the scuffle and runs toward them when two gunshots ring out from the garage and they freeze.

Inside of the garage, it is just the two of them. Inside their world, it is just the two of them. Ben has his prey cornered and he is feeling relaxed. He sees nothing else, hears nothing else, because he is hunting. He will avenge the deaths of his brothers and then he will disappear into the night as he always does. He slides along the wall near the doorway utilizing a little cover from an old door and window screens that are leaning there. Alison is crouched on the far side of the broken-down car near the front passenger tire. She peeks underneath the car and sees Ben's feet at the other end of the garage. She decides to shoot his ankle. She has a clear shot. It will slow him down. It may give her some time to get into the perfect position. She knows she has no experience with this rifle, with any rifle, and so she must do what she can to be sure she sets herself up for a clear shot. She must have a perfect shot. It will be her last. She cannot leave him wounded. That would not be good enough. She lies down on her stomach onto the cement garage floor and aims the rifle under the car at his feet. Yes, two good bullets into his ankle will serve her purpose. She needs the ground to steady her aim. Her body perks up with a burst of energy and her finger evenly squeezes the trigger. This is it. Ben peers around the door and analyzes where she might be. She shoots twice in rapid succession. Bang! Bang! She misses. The bullets lodge a few inches from his ankle into the door he is using for cover. Now, he knows exactly where she is. Ben springs up onto the trunk of the car like an agile cat and then strides up to the roof and down onto the hood.. He jumps to the garage floor landing only ten feet from her. She barely has time to stand. And then…there they are. Finally. Feet from each other, facing each other, again. Ben with his gun aimed at her forehead. She with the rifle aimed at his chest. Both fingers feeling the triggers. Their eyes fall hard onto each other's face and looking at each other again, they are both certain of only one thing: they will both fire.

"So, here we are again, Alison."

And she is ready. She longs for the end. Her resolve solidifies.

"I'll make a deal with you." Ben says. She is ready to fire. She knows she will fire. This is not a man who makes deals. "If you drop your rifle I'll go ahead and take you, of course, which is fair, but I'll leave your son alive. So, what do you say, my dear?"

"You had better hope there is no god."

His chest pumps with a little laugh, "God taught me everything I know."

"Put down the gun, Burne." Thomas interrupts with his tone strong and steady surprising them both. He has entered the garage and stands just off to the left inside the garage doorway. Alison and Ben were completely wrapped up in each other and they are momentarily confused to find someone else inside their world. Thomas' gun is aimed point blank at Ben's head. It is an easy shot and Thomas will not miss. Ben does not lower his gun. He calculates what his best move is. "Put it down, Burne," Thomas continues forcefully, "or I shoot you in the head. If you pull the trigger, I shoot you in the head. So you only have one option unless you're looking to get shot in the head."

A slow knowing grin crawls across Ben's face. He tilts his gun up and bending down he places his handgun on the cement garage floor. He raises his hands in surrender and says, "Gee, Alison, interrupted again. It's time for me to go along with this nice officer and be rehabilitated."

With Ben's gun down but without taking the aim from Ben's head, Thomas speaks to Alison kindly and carefully. He can see the tense determination in her eyes. "Mrs. Kraft, you can lower your weapon." She does not move. "Alison, it's okay. You can put down your weapon."

Ben and Alison have not looked away from each other. Ben cocks his head and whispers to her with frank honesty, "It's...not...over."

She whispers back, "I know." And then she pulls the trigger over and over blowing Ben Burne over the lawn mower and into the wall! Thomas' mouth drops open. He shifts his weapon to point at Alison. She watches the life drain from Ben's opened eyes. Then, she moves very cautiously laying her rifle on the floor and stepping back from it. She says to Ben, "Now it's over." A dead breath sighs out of Benjamin Burne's mouth.

Two Officers in bulletproof vests and with automatic weapons drawn burst into the garage. They assess the scene. Thomas lowers his gun as he stares at Alison. It was an execution. He knows this. She knows this. He witnessed it. The other officers holster their weapons. Alison's eyes finally leave Ben's dead body and she looks over at Thomas. Resignation is clear in her eyes.

An officer asks, "Thomas, what went down here?"

She knows what she has done. She knows Ben was unarmed when she killed him. She knows what Officer Thomas must do and she is prepared for it. She accepts it.

Without looking away from Alison, Thomas says, "Mrs. Kraft shot in self-defense. I saw it."

She nods. Thomas nods.

The officer speaks into his radio, "We need the M.E. and a paramedic back here."

Hank looks into the garage terrified by what he expects to see. And then, he sees her. She looks at him and really sees him for the first time since the island. A gentle smile graces her as his eyes light up with surprise, with relief, with love and longing. Hank walks over and tenderly takes her in his arms and then they drop to the garage floor together. He begins to rock her softly. They are completely lost in each other.

"Forgive me"

"Yes."

"Say you forgive me."

"I do."

"I didn't know."

"I know."

"I didn't understand."

"I know." And she snuggles into his chest, burying her face in the soft fleece of his sweatshirt. The officers go to move them and Thomas puts up his hand. They back off. Holding on tightly, on the floor of this garage, they sink deeply into each other. Hank notices the burns on her feet and he pulls her even tighter into his body. He wraps his legs around her, enveloping, clutching. Their breathing synchronizes. Their heartbeats synchronize. They rock back and forth on the garage floor and she begins to cry softly.

"Okay," he whispers, "I'm here. I will never leave you again. Okay. Okay, Allie? Never."

"Yes." She whispers back, "It's over."

"It is over."

*   *   *

Later, holding hands with their fingers intertwined, Alison and Hank will sift through the grey insubstantial ashes of their home, and save what they can while knowing with complete certainty that everything of value has already been saved. The number of neighbors and family members offering them solace, housing, and food, will bring them to tears. The entire community will rush in and cushion them with generosity. Alison will find she welcomes the casseroles, finally recognizing them as a physical expression of affection. She will be accepted back into the school, and she will teach with all the talent and care that she always has. Hank will turn up the music and it will blast out all over his world making him smile. And Alison will tell Jimmy over and over how his little crazy robot turned on exactly at the right moment and saved her life.

17196412R00118

Made in the USA
Lexington, KY
30 August 2012